Aloha Rose

Other Books in the Quilts of Love Series

Beyond the Storm
Carolyn Zane
(October 2012)

A Wild Goose Chase Christmas
Jennifer AlLee
(November 2012)

Path of Freedom
Jennifer Hudson Taylor
(January 2013)

For Love of Eli
Loree Lough
(February 2013)

Threads of Hope
Christa Allan
(March 2013)

A Healing Heart
Angela Breidenbach
(April 2013)

A Heartbeat Away
S. Dionne Moore
(May 2013)

Pieces of the Heart
Bonnie S. Calhoun
(June 2013)

Pattern for Romance
Carla Olson Gade
(August 2013)

Raw Edges
Sandra D. Bricker
(September 2013)

The Christmas Quilt
Vannetta Chapman
(October 2013)

Tempest's Course
Lynette Sowell
(December 2013)

Scraps of Evidence
Barbara Cameron
(January 2014)

A Sky Without Stars
Linda S. Clare
(February 2014)

Maybelle in Stitches
Joyce Magnin
(March 2014)

A Promise in Pieces
Emily Wierenga
(April 2014)

A Stitch and a Prayer
Eva Gibson
(May 2014)

Rival Hearts
Tara Randel
(June 2014)

A Grand Design
Tiffany Stockton
(August 2014)

Hidden in the Stars
Robin Caroll
(September 2014)

Quilted by Christmas
Jodie Bailey
(October 2014)

Swept Away
Laura Hilton & Cindy Loven
(November 2014)

Masterpiece Marriage
Gina Wellborn
(December 2014)

A Stitch in Crime
Cathy Elliott
(January 2015)

Aloha Rose

Quilts of Love Series

Lisa Carter

Aloha Rose

ISBN-13: 978-1-4267-5273-5

Published by Abingdon Press, P.O. Box 801, Nashville, TN 37202
www.abingdonpress.com

Published in association with the Steve Laube Agency

Library of Congress Cataloging-in-Publication Data has been requested.

Printed in the United States of America

1 2 3 4 5 6 7 8 9 10 / 18 17 16 15 14 13

. . . [Jesus] said to the man, "Stretch out your hand." So he did, and his hand was made healthy.
—Mark 3:5

Dedication

To my husband, David. Mahalo for Hawai'i and the willingness to explore together life's adventure. And for giving me the wings to fly.

To my dear friend, Lynn, whose own huakai'i—journey—like the Lokelani quilt has come full circle.

And for those who seek what is lost and discover they themselves are found. Blessings upon these Imiloa—who are willing to search for truth no matter how far the journey.

Acknowledgments

Corinne and Kathryn—Both of you are my pot at the end of the rainbow. I pray your journey will always reflect what is of first importance as God stitches together the beautiful quilt of your life. Mahalo for cooking the dinners when I was on deadline. And never forget we live our lives in the power of prayer.

I am so thankful for insight into the pre- and post-adoption process so graciously extended to me by Morgan Doremus, Dr. Gery and Abby Sandling, and Beth and Ted Bartelt. Mahalo for sharing your adoption journey with me. And your heart.

Mahalo to Tom Henderson, owner of Triangle Helicopter, for your expertise and advice. Any resulting errors are my own.

Mahalo, too, for explaining how piloting choppers "isn't so much flying as it is beating the air into submission," a phrase you allowed Laney to borrow.

Mahalo to Dr. Allan Moseley for your shepherding heart and sharing your insights on Mark 3.

Mahalo to Janice Baehr, quiltmaker, designer, author, and co-owner of Pacific Rim Company, for your expert Hawai'ian quilting guidance. www.prqc.com

Mahalo to my Aunt Betsy for sharing your family's struggles and victories in dealing with Alzheimer's.

Mahalo to writer friend Carrie Turansky for brainstorming the aloha spirit with me and reminiscing about your sojourn in America's beautiful 50th state.

Hope Dougherty—Mahalo, friend and critique partner, for your insights into *Aloha Rose*. You made it better.

Tamela Hancock Murray—Mahalo for being my friend and advocate. You've made The Call on that August day and this writing journey so much fun.

Ramona Richards—A true imiloa—you've lived your life with extraordinary courage and heart. I'm blessed to know you.

My Abingdon o'hana—family—Cat Hoort, Teri, Katherine, Mark, and the sales and marketing teams. Mahalo for all you've done to make *Aloha Rose* the best that it can be.

Jeane—Mahalo for taking the time to help a newbie like myself with your excellent advice and guidance.

Readers—It is my hope that *Aloha Rose* will make you laugh. Make you cry. And warm your heart with the greatest love possible in this life, God's.

And most of all to Jesus, the soon and coming King, who like Kamehameha, rolled the stone away . . .

1

Are you sure there's no message waiting for Laney Carrigan?"

Laney leaned over the information desk at the Kailua-Kona Airport. "I was supposed to be met here . . ." She gestured around the rapidly emptying lobby. "By my Auntie Teah. Maybe she's been delayed and she left a note for me with instructions?"

The airport employee, a willowy blond, craned her head around Laney at the line of people queuing behind her. She pointed down the corridor. "You can rent a car over that way." She raised her gaze above Laney's five-foot-three-inch height. "Who's next?"

Laney tightened her lips. Dismissed. Again.

"Maybe an intercom page directing me to meet someone in Baggage Claim or Ground Transportation . . . ?" Laney sighed at the bored face of the woman and stepped aside as a middle-aged man wearing a flamingo pink aloha shirt shouldered past her to the front of the line. Grabbing the handle of her wheeled carry-on bag, she skirted past a group of Asian tourists who'd been greeted by hula girls bearing fragrant yellow leis.

No point in trying to rent a car when she had no idea where she was going. She paused in an out-of-the-way corner and fumbled in a side pocket of her luggage for her cell phone. Pressing the phone to ON, she waited for it to come to life.

Auntie Teah, whom she'd yet to meet, had assured her over the course of several phone calls that she would be here to welcome her long-lost niece to her ancestral home. An ancestral home to which she'd not been given directions or an address.

Hitting the Rodrigues phone number she'd stored in her cell, she tapped her navy blue stiletto-clad foot on the shiny, white airport floor and waited for someone to pick up. And waited. After ringing four times, voice mail—a deep, rumbling man's voice—informed her that no one was currently at home—duh—and instructed callers to leave a callback number at the tone. Laney snorted, not trusting herself to speak, thumbed the phone to OFF and stuffed it into her bag. She stalked down the passageway toward Baggage Claim.

Some welcome.

Laney pushed her shoulders back, trying to ease the tension of her muscles. As her brigadier father never failed to point out, when stressed, she hunched down like Quasimodo. And at her diminutive stature, there was no one Laney wanted to resemble less than that hunchback of literary legend. She scanned the dwindling crowd encircling the baggage carousel.

Where was her Auntie Teah? Her cousin, Elyse, or Elyse's sweet little boy, Daniel? They'd promised to be here. Laney glanced at her black leather sports watch, noted the time in addition to the barometric pressure and altimeter reading. Her own barometric pressure rising, Laney shoved her bag to the ground, threw herself on top and faced the doorway. Nobody had ever dared ignore Brigadier General Thomas Carrigan.

Apparently, his daughter not so much.

She'd told her dad this was a bad idea, but he'd insisted she answer the inquiry in response to the information he'd posted regarding the scant facts they knew of her birth twenty-eight years ago. The website, which specialized in reuniting adoptive children with their biological families, had been silent for months. And Laney was fine with that.

Abso-flipping, positutely fine with that.

Really.

She'd never been curious as to her biological family. She'd always known her real parents, Gisela and Tom Carrigan, adopted her when she was a few months old. They'd chosen her—as her mother had often reminded her. Loved, cherished, protected her. But Gisela succumbed to a lingering, painful death to cancer three years ago.

Then her dad—administrative guru to the five stars at the Pentagon, able to cut through bureaucratic red tape and leap over snafus in a single bound—had the bright idea to post a picture of the quilt in which she'd come wrapped on their apartment doorstep.

And voilá, a hit less than twenty-four hours later.

He did some checking—to make sure none of them were serial killers—and declared it would be good for Laney to plan a visit to their home on the Big Island. Good to connect with people who knew something about her family background. Good to fulfill her adopted mother's last wish that she one day reunite with her biological family.

Laney swallowed a sob. She'd believed she'd already found her forever family. She glanced around the claim area. Her lower lip trembled at the sight of a suitcase going round and round the carousel.

Unclaimed. Alone. Like her.

She squared her shoulders. Who needed these people? The ones who'd abandoned her, deserted her. Left her behind.

Laney closed her eyes on the hateful, treacherous tears that threatened to spill out from beneath her lashes and wondered how soon she could book a return flight to D.C.

This had been a very bad idea.

"I don't get why I have to be the one to go get this woman, Mama Teah. Why can't Elyse—?" Kai held the phone a few inches away from his ear.

When the roar on the other end subsided, he cradled it once again between his head and his neck as he negotiated a curve around the lava-strewn rubble dotting the mountain side of the highway leading toward the airport, a now dormant volcano's last little hiccup some two hundred years ago. He gripped the wheel of his truck and glanced to his right at the cerulean hues of the Pacific.

"Okay, okay. I get that Elyse was called into work and Ben's on Daniel duty, but I just stepped off the helipad and I didn't get your message until a few minutes ago." Kai frowned. "I'm on my way." He peered at the clock on the dashboard. "ETA in ten. But what aren't you telling me, Teah? Has something happened to you?" His voice caught. "Or to Tutu Mily?"

A pause on the other end.

"Teah? Where are you? You're scaring—" Kai banged his hand on the steering wheel. "I knew something like this was going to happen. I told you this was a bad idea to bring in an outsider at a time like this. I—"

"Kai Alexander Barnes." Teah's voice trumpeted in the truck cab.

Never a good sign when your foster mother used your full legal name.

Kai winced as Teah told him in no uncertain terms what she thought of his thoughts on her ideas. "But surely, there's another way, Teah. We take care of our own. We don't need some overprivileged East Coast socialite barging into our business. Family takes care of family. Like you and Daddy Pete took care of me." His chin wobbled.

A sigh on Teah's end. "You're family in every way that counts, Kai." Her tone toughened. "Laney Carrigan is family, too."

Kai made a right turn into the airport parking lot, willing himself not to relent. This woman—and you'd better believe he'd Googled her—was as elusive as an ice cube in a lava flow. Even with his connections, he'd not been able to blast through the security firewalls her prominent army dad raised for her protection over the years. Not a single photograph to his knowledge existed of the mysterious Ms. Carrigan.

He snorted. "Anyone can post a picture of a quilt. We don't know if that quilt is really hers or how it came into her possession. We don't know if that quilt is the quilt Tutu Mily made years ago for her unborn grandbaby before Mily's daughter ran off to—"

"Bring her to the house as soon as you can," Teah interjected. "I've prayed about this, Kai. Didn't know what to do to solve our dilemma and more importantly, with Tutu's condition worsening, I'm hoping this will bring Mily some peace. I'm still praying. But I believe God's going to work this out."

Kai heard the smile in her voice over the wireless.

Teah continued. "How else do you explain after all these years of wondering when Elyse met a tourist at the resort who mentioned how he'd found his biological parents through that website and then just one day later when Elyse logged into the site, Tutu's quilt appeared?"

He ground his teeth. "I'm parking now, Teah. I promise to deliver Ms. Carrigan safe and sound to your doorstep ASAP."

"You be sure you do that, son." Teah clicked off.

Kai stared at the phone in his hand. The dial tone echoed in the truck cab. Nabbing an empty space, he pulled to a stop and put the F150 in Park. Killing the engine, the door dinged as he thrust it open, swinging his boot-clad feet to the pavement.

She'd made up her mind. And when Teah Rodrigues got something in the bit of her teeth, she was worse than any stallion on the ranch. Unstoppable. Unquenchable. Unswerving.

A force of nature. A regular Typhoon Teah. And like a silent, offshore earthquake, the aftershocks of this unknown family prodigal—Laney Carrigan—returning to the fold might prove to be their undoing.

His face hardened. Just let her try.

No way, no how, he'd let some *haole* bimbo take advantage of his family. Not on his watch.

Feeling the whoosh of air over her closed eyelids and the sound of the glass doors of the terminal sliding open, Laney opened her eyes. A Caucasian man stepped through and stopped, his polarized sunglasses obscuring his eyes. As the doors swished shut behind him, Laney took in his appearance—the khaki cargo pants, the ocean blue polo shirt that stretched taut across broad shoulders, the rugged jawline in need of a shave. He searched the room for someone.

Lest he catch her staring, she dropped her eyes to the floor and noticed his scuffed boots.

Tall, dark, and cowboy.

Definitely not Auntie Teah or Elyse. Whoever he was looking for, it wouldn't be her. He wasn't here for her.

Guys like him never were.

Cowboy pushed his glasses onto the crown of his close-cropped dark hair revealing eyes as tropical blue as the waters off the Seychelles, her last assignment. His head rotated from side to side, scrutinizing the remaining occupants of the baggage claim area. His eyes eventually came round to her. With the intensity of an electric blue flash.

Resisting the urge to fan herself—was it just her or had the temps risen another notch?—she pushed her glasses farther up the bridge of her nose and sat prim atop her carry-on case. His eyes traveled over her from the top of her head to her best-interview pointy-toed shoes. Self-conscious, she tucked her feet under her body, smoothing the edges of her pleated navy skirt over her ankles. Cowboy's eyes narrowed before flicking away at the sound of a voice down the corridor, dismissing her as she knew he would.

"Kai! Wait up!"

Laney turned her head as did Cowboy when a leggy redhead strode across the room, latching onto his coiled muscular arm. His nose crinkled. Then a practiced lazy smile flitted across his handsome features. Those baby blue lagoon eyes of his dropped to half-mast. A whirring of the air around Laney fluffed her shoulder-length hair as another figure rushed forward.

The willowy blond from Information seized Cowboy Kai by his other arm. He inclined his head as the I-Can't-Be-Bothered airport employee whispered something for his ears only. Too far away for their conversation to register—and who cared?—she did catch Cowboy's deep-throated chuckle in response to whatever witticism Blondie had murmured.

Typical. She'd seen his macho, arrogant type many times following her father around the globe in the rolling stone life of Uncle Sam's army. Laney folded her hands in her lap. His kind loved the fluffy kittens of the world like Blondie and the redhead. He probably wasn't a real cowboy, either. Probably didn't know one end of a horse from a—

A mountainous shadow inserted itself between Laney and the fluorescent lighting of the terminal. She jerked at the sight of Cowboy looming over her.

"Ms. Carrigan, I presume?" A mocking smile flickered at the corners of his lips.

Laney's hackles rose, and she hunched her shoulders as she struggled to rise from her awkward position on the floor. The heel of her shoe caught on the handle of her bag and she fell—make that *sprawled*—into his arms.

Wishing she could sink into the floor, she felt the blush matching and mounting from beneath the collar of her pink shirtwaist blouse.

Great, elegant as always.

But she'd give him full kudos for quick reflexes.

In a full face plant against the blue fabric of his shirt, Laney noted—in the half-second before Cowboy pulled his own nose out of her hair—an enticing blend of smells on the man, a spicy aftershave like her father wore, cocoa butter, and something indefinable that belonged to him alone. Awkward . . . this was long past getting out of hand.

Laney took herself in hand and cleared her throat.

Cowboy, his hands wrapped around her upper arms, set her aright upon her two left feet. His black-fringed eyes—eyelashes the envy of any girl—blinked. Not that there was anything remotely girlish about him.

His fingers lingered. Stepping back, Laney almost fell again over her suitcase. His hand shot out restoring her balance. He nudged her bag out of the way with the pointed toe of his boot.

Was it her imagination or did a rosy flush darken his sculpted cheekbones? "Carrigan, right?"

She shook free of his grip. "And you would know that how?" Settling her hands on her hips, she looked past him to where two fluffy kittens glared mayhem in her direction. "Who are you?"

He jammed his hands into the front pockets of his pants. "Kai Barnes. I'm here to perform a SAR for Auntie Teah. A search—"

"I know what a SAR is, Mr. Barnes. Search and rescue."

The full beam of his oceanic orbs lasered her. She extended her neck upward, refusing to let his six-foot height intimidate her.

"Sure." A derisive smirk crossed his too-handsome-to-live features. "I forgot about your military background."

"I take it you're military, too?" Should've seen it sooner, but the boots had thrown her off. She could spot 'em, all right. That distinct swagger, that I'm licensed to kill attitude, that . . .

"Army pilot." His eyes shuttered again. "Former. Flew SAR in medevacs." He removed his hands from his pockets and crossed his arms over his chest. His mouth flatlined. "Search and rescue seems to be what I do best." His gaze raked her over. "I'll take you to Teah who's waiting for us at the ranch. My—"

"I'm not going anywhere with you." Laney's chest puffed out. "I was told to wait for my Aunt Teah or Elyse. I don't know you from Adam. You could be some psycho cowboy serial killer for all I know." She crossed her arms, mirroring his stance.

Kai raised his eyes toward the ceiling, his jaw working. An exasperated sigh rose from the depths of his being, rolling through the airwaves like a rumbling volcanic eruption. "Teah's not your real aunt." He stabbed Laney with a fierce look. "If you are who you claim to be . . ."

Laney fixed him with a matching glare.

"She and your mother were first cousins, which makes Elyse, Teah's daughter, a more distant cousin. Auntie is a term of respect for elders in our Hawai'ian culture."

"Hawai'ian? Our?" She let her eyes roam up and down his muscular form in a deliberate repetition of his scathing perusal of her earlier. Kai flushed again. This time though—and she could tell the difference—with anger.

Muttering something under his breath, with a sudden move, Kai whipped a brown leather wallet from one of the ubiquitous pockets lining his pants. He extracted a driver's license and held it to her face. "Kai Barnes. My address—Franklin Ranch. Near Waimea. There's been a slight emergency with Tutu Mily so they sent—"

"Tutu? Mily?" Laney's arms dropped to her sides. "Do you mean Miliana Franklin, my grandmother? What's happened?"

"Your understanding of our culture underwhelms me. Tutu means grandmother. And yes, I refer to Miliana Kanakele Franklin, although whether she's actually your grandmother or not remains to be seen."

Laney stiffened.

"Teah said she'd explain when we reached the ranch. Until then, if you want to meet your Hawai'ian relatives, then I suggest . . ." His arm swept the room and pointed at the glass doors.

"Fine. Have it your way." Laney bent to retrieve her bag but found Kai to be quicker, his hand grasping the handle. She tugged.

He held on.

Laney let go.

So, he was a gentleman, too.

"This puny thing it?" He heaved it to his shoulder.

"I learned a long time ago to travel light."

Laney sashayed past him toward the double doors and the parking lot, pretending as always she knew exactly where she was headed. And if things got too uncomfortable with these virtual strangers . . . She fingered her escape hatch in the pocket of her skirt, her return ticket via Jakarta.

She'd give them three weeks. Three weeks before she winged out to her next assignment. She eyeballed her teeth-clenched companion.

Maybe sooner. They didn't know it yet, but the moment Cowboy showed up, her clock started ticking.

A disconcerted feeling settled over her at the truth of that statement.

Ticking in more ways than one.

2

Kai received the shock of his life when after a futile attempt to locate the gold-digging haole Carrigan woman in the lobby, Della Reynolds had pointed him to the petite figure—like a tiny Polynesian bird—perched on top of a suitcase. This was turning out to be a worse disaster than he'd feared.

The jury was still out on whether the sharp-tongued Ms. Carrigan was a gold digger or not, but she definitely was not a haole. Like the trained operative he was, he'd taken note of the doe-eyed woman with the large, owl-like pink spectacles who was plunked down in the middle of the terminal. Her creamy complexion. The dark hair that framed a heart-shaped face. The flashing pain of a vulnerability that tugged at his heart.

His mouth tightened as he jammed her case behind the seat of his truck, but that tug on his heart dissipated like the cool morning mists over the Upcountry as soon as she opened her mouth. 'Cause what Ms. Carrigan lacked in size, she more than made up for with mouth. A big mouth, albeit it lovely he acknowledged, as he offered a helping hand to the Carrigan woman. Which she studiously ignored, clambering on her own steam into the cab.

He painted a smile on his face as he closed the door. It was all good. He'd been rewarded, despite her obvious attempt to slight him, with a brief glimpse of sturdy, well-formed calves. And after a lifetime of helping Daddy Pete run Tutu Mily's ranch, he knew quite a bit about calves.

Those ridiculous shoes should have sealed the search for him. Where did she think she'd arrived? Manhattan? The fiftieth state, his home state of Hawai'i, defined casual with flip-flops and t-shirts as a lifestyle choice.

Still . . . Kai made his way around to his side, removed his cell phone from a pocket and slid in. He chucked his phone on the seat between them. Her pale pink blouse, tucked at the waist in all the right places he couldn't help but notice, hinted of an alluring feminine side underneath the prickly pineapple exterior.

He yanked the door shut and thrust the key into the ignition, further irritated by the conflicting thought of the sweet fruit that lurked underneath the pineapple's spiny husk.

"What exactly is your problem with me, Mr. Barnes? I don't, to the best of my recollection, believe we've ever met before. Or is this how you greet island visitors? So much for that famous aloha spirit I've heard so much about." She sniffed and gazed out the window.

Kai gritted his teeth, reached his arm across the seat to reverse out of the parking space, his fingers brushing bare skin below her scallop-shaped sleeve. She jumped and edged away. He withdrew his hand as if Pele herself had singed his flesh.

"Aloha means different things, Ms. Carrigan." He dragged out the Miz to let her know—in the off-chance she hadn't picked up on it already—that she irritated him like sand rubbed at the more delicate parts of the anatomy. "My *'ohana* means everything to me and I won't allow you to swindle them, much less hurt them."

Those almond-shaped Kona coffee eyes widened. "Swindle? Is that what you think I—?"

His cell phone beeped with an incoming message. He pulled onto Highway 19 and headed toward Waimea, ignoring the steady blip.

"Aren't you going to answer that?"

He kept his face straight ahead.

"It could be important. Why on earth would you think I've come to swindle anyone?"

He set his jaw but picked up the phone, scanning the messages.

"And what does *o*—whatever you said—mean?"

Kai exhaled a long sigh to let her know she tried all the patience in the world. "'Ohana. Means family."

She repeated the word to herself. At his quizzical look, she nodded. "I'm trying to learn about my biological mother's birthplace, Mr. Barnes, despite what you think. Besides," she gave a tiny shrug, "If you want to understand a peoples' heart, listen to their words. I make it a habit to learn the language wherever I go."

Fair enough. Teah and Mily's emergency had put them both in an awkward position. He decided to dial back the hostility for the moment.

"I'm sure you've noticed." He jerked his head in the direction of the stark, jet black lava fields on either side of the highway. "The view is hardly the tropical paradise most visitors expect."

"Result of an 1801 lava flow from the dormant shield volcano, Hualālai."

Kai gave an appreciative whistle. "Good for you. You've done your homework." He found himself pleased beyond reason for the shy, answering smile she turned his way.

He cleared his throat and tightened his grip on the wheel. "*Kona* means leeward. And leeward means—"

"Downwind because the trade winds blow east to west, right?"

The corners of his mouth twitched. "The Kona side gets more sun and has the calmer, clearer water and the best beaches, hence . . ." He gestured at the resort signs dotting the entrance to five-star tropical fantasies. "But the Hilo side's greener. More rain and—"

"Waterfalls?"

Kai shifted in his seat, stealing a look at her rapt expression. "You like waterfalls, huh?"

She sighed. "My father spent the greater part of my childhood in the Desert Southwest. Yes, Mr. Barnes, I'd like to see waterfalls."

An unfamiliar swirl of anticipation swelled in his chest. "I think we could arrange that."

The phone beeped again. He ignored it as the usual afternoon rain shower kicked in. "No worries." Kai switched on the wipers. "These things never last long." The rain beat against the truck, isolating and cutting them off from outside contact.

Her eyebrows rose. "You sound like a tour guide now. I thought you said you were SAR."

Kai broke eye contact, fixing his gaze to the asphalt. "I said former. I am a tour guide of sorts. I fly helicopter tours over Kilauea when I'm not working the ranch."

She shivered. "Over an erupting volcano."

He let his shoulders rise and fall. "It's glorious. Beautiful. New parts of the island formed every day. Like being present to watch God create the earth all over again."

Kai's face heated. What had made him go philosophical on her? She probably thought he was some sort of . . .

"It's dangerous." Her soft tone was thoughtful, not mocking, however.

His eye caught the flicker, a blur, of movement ahead beyond the high-end luxury rental car in front of them on the highway. "What's life without a little risk? I figured you, of all people, would totally embrace that concept."

"Because I've flown halfway around the world?"

The rental braked. Over the pouring rain, Kai detected the sound of a thud. He tapped his brakes, slowing.

Her voice wobbled. "To meet a woman, my biological mother, who abandoned—"

Kai wrenched his head in her direction. "Is that what Teah told you? That you'd—?"

"Stop!" She screamed, grabbing hold of the dashboard to brace herself.

Kai slammed on the brakes, skidding and sliding the last few feet. "What? What's wrong?" He glanced in the rearview mirror, relieved to see no one behind them. He released the breath he hadn't realized he'd been holding, willed his heart to beat again.

She pointed. "That car hit an animal and now it's driven off."

Red taillights disappeared around the bend ahead. "You almost got us killed over some animal?"

She made a grab for the door handle and with a click released the seat belt buckle. Kai put a restraining hand on her arm. She shook him off. "Unlike my birth mother, I don't abandon people or animals. I don't leave anyone behind like discarded trash." She flung open the door.

"Laney, wait." He tried to inch over, but the seat belt held him fast. "You don't understand. It's not that simple. Teah should have explained the situation. I thought you knew."

But she didn't stop to hear him. Jumping from the club cab, she landed with a splash in an expanding puddle of water. She shoved the door behind her. Those crazy stiletto heels caught in the uneven gravel and Kai was sure she'd go down on her face, but in a feat worthy of a fire-dancing Tahitian, Laney managed to right herself and plunged out of his sight into the ditch bank.

Fighting the urge to curse—he wasn't that man anymore—Kai's heart skipped a beat at the sight of headlights emerging from behind. Spotting a service road turnoff a few feet ahead, he maneuvered a quick ninety-degree turn and parked the truck. Feeling shaky—like after that last disastrous mission over Helmand province—Kai laid his head on the steering wheel, his clenched hands white-knuckled.

Laney Carrigan—not the Taliban, not PTSD, not a buddy's suicide—was going to be the death of him. He raised his eyes toward the cab ceiling. "Why me, God?"

Silence, except for the unrelenting monsoon, his only answer.

"Why not me, right?" He flung open the door, preparing himself to get drenched. The door dinged. "Who knew when I got out of bed today it was going to be Let's-Make-Kai-Crazy Day?"

He stuck out one boot, watched the rain change it from a sandy beige to a darker brown. "Too late for crazy. Already there." He hunched his shoulders as the rain rolled down his neck underneath his collar. On the Big Island in April, a warm wet.

Shutting the door, he stalked, slid, and barely avoided tumbling down the slope in search of that nutty *wahine*. And he found her, about the time the rain let up, crouching on her heels, hovering over a lump of motionless fur curled in a ball.

"A cat?" He swiped a stream of water off his brow. A ray of sunshine poked through the cloud cover.

Laney squinted at him, resembling a drowned rat. Rivulets of water coated both sides of her glasses. Rain droplets glistened like tiny rainbows on the edges of her lashes. "He's hurt. We have to do something."

"He?" Kai stepped closer. She was right about the he part. He crossed his arms over his chest, planted his feet even with his hips. "We?"

Laney rose. "We can't leave him here to die."

"He's already dead, Laney." Kai bent and extended his forefinger, touching the cat's chest. The cat, a seal point Siamese by the looks of him, reared his head and hissed. Kai withdrew his hand. "A feral island cat most likely. Best leave it be."

"I told you. I. Don't. Leave. Things."

Great. Just his luck when he was trying everything in his power to get out of the search and rescue business—cause he'd been such a success at that—to meet up with some wacky, bleeding-heart woman with a messiah complex.

"Please, Kai." She laid a hand on his arm. Her featherlight touch sent his heart into a tailspin.

So she wanted to play that card, did she?

"I know the army gave you training in first-aid. He needs your help." She tilted her head toward him.

A gentle breeze blew a strand of her rain-flattened hair in his face. A pleasing scent of jasmine floated past his nostrils, reminding him of the pīkake jasmine that latticed one side of the lanai at his house. The fragrant aroma that intoxicated him at the airport when he'd buried his nose in her hair.

He was a sucker for lost things.

And somehow, she knew it.

"I'll get a cardboard box left over from our last grocery run to Costco out of the truck."

She nodded and moved closer to the cat.

He slogged to the truck, retrieved the carton, and returned to find Laney cradling the injured cat like a baby.

"No blood or broken bones that I could tell," she reported at his raised eyebrows. "Maybe a cat concussion."

"Do cats get concussions?"

"Everything that has a brain would, I imagine." Tiny lines radiated out from the corners of her eyes as she smiled at him, the unspoken implication hanging between them.

He blinked as he realized she was teasing him. Kai thrust the box at her. "Better let me see."

"You don't want to hold him?"

"It doesn't like me."

"He doesn't know you yet. I'm walking in faith, choosing to believe the experience of knowing you improves over time for all of God's creatures."

Kai laughed out loud. The cat stirred. Laney lowered him into the box, stroking and crooning baby talk. Kai frowned. This was getting out of hand. He headed up the incline with Laney right on his heels.

"What shall we name him?"

"We're not naming him anything, Laney. He's going straight to the pound."

"The pound? In his weakened condition, they'll probably euthanize him right away."

Reaching the truck, Kai balanced the crate in one arm and opened the cab door with the other. "This is Hawai'i, Laney. Not Nazi Germany."

Laney paused at the running board of the truck. "Please, Kai?" This time, she waited for him.

He offered her a hand. "Just till he's back on his feet."

Laney high-stepped it into the cab. "All four feet."

"Whatever." Once she was seated and buckled, he handed over the box.

Closing the door, he took a long look at her, the beatific smile on her face and the drowned Pacific Islander look of the rest of her.

This would not do. This would not do at all. Teah would kill him.

Laney adjusted the seat belt as Kai drove past a sign providing info on the distance yet to Waimea. The cat had gone to sleep. Sleep, Laney prayed, not a coma. This little adventure was turning into something like the scene from *Breakfast at Tiffany's*, one of Laney's favorites.

She'd spent the better part of her life wishing to look as elegant and ethereal as the princess of *Roman Holiday*. Instead, she'd assumed, having been found not far from the lands of the Navajo, that she was part Native American. Or—that nasty rumor started by an envious army wife wondering aloud for Laney's German-born adoptive mother's ears especially—if perhaps the Irish-American Carrigan had returned from Okinawa with more than chopsticks.

Laney peered over at Kai, his face settled into its previous grimness. He was a native Hawai'ian, born here, he'd told her a few moments ago as his travelogue continued, versus her being Native Hawai'ian. Who'd have ever guessed that?

Kai made a sharp left turn off the highway between twin pillars with the name Moana Loa inscribed in gold letters.

She shot him a look. This wasn't the way to the Upcountry. Where was he taking her? What did she really know about this self-proclaimed SAR dropout?

A frisson of fear goosebumped her arms. Kai Barnes she'd never heard of and—like an idiot—she'd taken him at his word and hitchhiked a ride to her long-lost relatives in his truck. Maybe he *was* a serial killer . . .

She fought to keep her voice from revealing the panic threatening to engulf her. "Where are we going?"

The grand entrance to the five-star loomed ahead. But he wheeled past several cars around to the back and parked next to a dumpster outside the service entrance. Kai shut off the motor, swiveling to face her. "Elyse works here as the cultural historian. She was called into work. That's why I was sent in her place to pick you up. I can't take you home looking like that."

Laney took stock of herself in the side mirror. She slumped in the seat. With her best clothes worn only on trips to meet her New York editor plastered to her body and her hair a tangled mess, her feeble effort to dress beyond her usual fare of hiking boots and outdoor gear had gone down the drain.

Kai exited the vehicle, stuffing his cell into a pocket. "No worries. Elyse will fix everything." He came around to the passenger side. "The cat's asleep. I think the jolt from the other car just stunned him, knocked the wind out of him. He'll be fine while we're gone."

Her lower lip protruding, Laney gave him a doubtful look but relinquished the box on the seat beside her. Kai punched in some numbers and in a terse voice informed Elyse that they were out back. Moments later, the service door flew open and a graceful woman emerged. Laney recognized Elyse from photos Auntie Teah sent via the internet.

"Howzit, *brudda*?"At the sight of the pair of them, Elyse teetered to a stop and punched Kai none too gently in the arm. "What did you do, Kai Barnes?"

Kai took a step back, hands in the air. "Nothing. It wasn't my fault."

Elyse, not as tall as Kai but taller than Laney, scowled. "You always say that. Mama's going to kill you when she sees what you did to Laney."

Kai's mouth formed an *O*, opening and closing like a guppy. "What *I* did to *her*?" He raked a hand through his own plastered-to-his-head hair.

"She's going to give you the stink eye for a week. Speaking of stink . . ." Her nose wrinkled. "Both of you smell like a wet dog."

"Wet cat." Kai threw up his hands. "You've got to help me."

Elyse raised one eyebrow. "And I should help your sorry butt, why?"

"For Laney's sake." He darted a wide, blue-eyed look of complete innocence in Laney's direction.

Kai Barnes could sure work the ladies, Laney would give him that. A niggling feeling of disquiet settled into her belly at the easy camaraderie between Kai and Elyse. Everybody had a sweetheart but her.

Her destiny in life. Always the outsider looking in.

Elyse fluffed her hair behind her shoulder. "And you'll take Daniel body surfing next week like you promised?"

"Cross my heart and hope to die. Stick a needle—"

Elyse trundled him aside, but affection sugared her words. "We Hawai'ians have been known since ancient times to do that and more to you island-invading haole no-accounts." She stepped forward to Laney, her hand outstretched. "I feel like we've already been introduced through our emails, Laney, but let me be," she cast a sardonic look Kai's way, "the first one to welcome you to the Big Island and our 'ohana."

Laney allowed the tension in her shoulders to ease. "Family, right?"

Elyse nodded and put an arm around Laney, shepherding her toward the building.

Kai relaxed his stance, grinning. "I'll get Laney's suitcase."

Laney followed Elyse into an employee break room with an adjoining bathroom. "Sometimes the housekeeping staff are on call all night and with today's exorbitant island cost of living, a lot of us locals, like Kai, work more than one job. It's the only way most can afford to live and raise children in our own ancestral birthplace. Too many have to go off-island to the mainland. The management here at the Moana is good about providing us a place to catch a few winks and take a quick shower. Not everyone lives in town like I do." She gave Laney a quick hug. "I can't tell you how excited Mama and Tutu Mily are about meeting you."

Laney hugged her back. In the smiling, open features of her cousin, for the first time she embraced the welcome she'd longed to receive in her heart. "I didn't realize you and Kai lived in town. I hope him taking me to the ranch and then having to turn around back to your house won't be a problem for you and your son, Daniel."

Elyse straightened, confusion crossing her face. "Kai doesn't live in town. He's got the old plantation manager's house down the road from the main ranch house. Why would you think . . . ? Oh." Her eyes rounded. "You didn't think Kai was my husband, did you?" Her lips quivered.

"Here's the suitcase." Kai's shoulders brushed the sides of the doorway. His gaze ping-ponged between them. "What? Did I miss something?"

Elyse fell into a multi-cushioned chair, her sides heaving. She pointed at Laney. "She thought you and I . . ." She put a hand over her mouth to smother the laughter.

Laney wished she was in Jakarta.

"You and I what?"

"She thought you and I were married." Elyse collapsed prostrate over the arm of the chair.

"Ewww!" Kai's face scrunched into a semblance of movie horror. "Not hardly."

Elyse regained control and kicked him in the shin. "Ewww on my part."

Laney moistened her lips. Although currently without a boyfriend, this wasn't the way romantic relationships usually worked where she came from.

Elyse squeezed Laney's arm. "We're brother and sister."

Laney recalled Elyse's earlier *brudda* remark. Duh, brother. Still, she took a long look at the Caucasian, a true haole to use the local lingo, and the chic Hawai'ian beauty standing before her.

"I'm the foster kid Mama Teah and Daddy Pete took in," Kai explained, tracing the diamond pattern on the linoleum with the toe of his boot.

"You'll find most Hawai'ians to be a rainbow mix of ethnicities." Elyse fluttered a hand. "The real natives like Teah and Mily. Portuguese like my daddy Peter Rodrigues and those pesky haoles like Kai and your grandfather Franklin." She smiled. "It's one of the things I love most about our corner of paradise. Not perfect but better than most places about accepting people for who they are. And not forgetting to add my adorable Chinese-American husband, Ben Ching, into the mix, either."

"Let me clean your glasses while you change," Kai offered, taking a surreptitious look at his wristwatch. Laney handed them over and took the suitcase from him.

"Oh, and before I forget," Elyse opened a half-size refrigerator and removed a purple lei, with an intoxicating fragrance that filled Laney's nostrils before Elyse had a chance to place it around her neck.

"Plumeria. But we call it frangipani." Elyse fussed with an errant bloom. Laney inhaled, closing her eyes as Elyse allowed the wreath to drape over her body.

"Aloha, dear cousin." Elyse took her hand. "Welcome home at last."

3

My house is down that road." Kai gestured as he pointed the nose of the Ford toward home. The terrain had changed as they wound their way up the greener slopes past Waimea to gentle, rolling hills and verdant pastureland bounded by the wire fencing of fellow rancher neighbors. Cattle grazed in the bucolic countryside. Mountains loomed in the distance.

Kai threw up his hand, waving at the Stetson-clad neighbor passing by in his monster truck.

Laney typed something into her tablet. "I didn't realize Hawai'i had its own cowboy culture."

"We call them *paniolos* here." He drew his brows together for the second time in as many minutes as Laney whispered the word into the handheld recording device she'd retrieved from her luggage.

"Say again, please." She thrust the device into his face.

Kai reared back. "What are you—?"

"Pan . . . ?" she prompted.

Persistent as a bloodsucking mosquito.

"Pah-nee-OH-low. The Hawai'ian language has only twelve letters. Seven consonants and five vowels."

Laney cocked an amused eye at him. "And you pronounce every one of them."

He grinned. "You'll also notice a predilection for words that begin with K."

"Like Mily's maiden name, Kanakele."

He nodded. "The 'a' is pronounced like ah. The 'e' like day. The 'i' as in bee. The 'o' like your nose." She jabbed the receiver in his direction. "The 'u' just like few. And I'm not going to get into the diphthongs."

"Okay, but there's always tomorrow." Laney went back to amusing the cat, languid but alert, with a shoelace she'd found discarded on the floorboard.

He sneaked a look in her direction, admiring the plain white t-shirt and fuchsia above-the-knee eyelet skirt she'd donned at the Moana. The soft, curly waves of her hair tumbled around her shoulders. When he'd cleaned her eyeglasses, he'd discovered clear glass in the frames. She'd forgotten to ask for them when they returned to the truck though she'd spent the better portion of the drive typing into her tablet.

Which left Kai with three questions: Why did she sport glasses she didn't need? And, an inevitable conclusion: Why did she choose to hide behind the glasses? What else was Laney Carrigan hiding?

Feeling his gaze on her, she looked up. Flushing, Kai turned his attention to the road. The truck passed under a large arched entrance sign, rattling over a iron cattle guard.

He pointed. "Franklin Ranch."

Laney craned her neck. "How big?"

He bit the inside of his cheek, distrust churning in his gut. "One hundred acres. The tract of land King Kamehameha the Great bestowed on the original Franklin, son of one of those early New England missionaries, was much larger. But over time?" He shrugged. "Most of it sold to pay the taxes and keep a roof over our heads."

She typed in a flurry of keystrokes.

Kai decided it was time for the mysterious Ms. Carrigan to answer a few questions. "Why are you doing that?"

Laney paused in mid-stroke. "I'm a writer. I thought I'd freelance a few articles about Hawai'i while I'm here. Help pay the bills when I get home."

At the word *home*, his skin prickled. Or, was it the thought of Laney going off-island?

"Where is home, Laney?"

Her shoulders tensed. She returned to her typing. "Wherever I happen to be at the time."

She related to him the painful story of how her mother died.

Kai glanced at her. "I'm sorry, Laney. What about your dad?"

Her mouth dovetailed. "He has his own life, a new wife, and a brand-new stepson." Laney twisted her face away.

"Sounds lonely for you, always on the move, I mean."

Laney threw him a sharp look. "There's all kinds of lonely out there. Roots don't work for me. Not the way I was raised. And now that Dad's retired and settled down . . . I've found I prefer wings." She reached for the glasses on the console, slipping them on. "I'd think a pilot like you would understand wings."

Oh, he understood, all right. He'd longed for the sky from his earliest memories, to escape his violent childhood existence, to touch the Someone he'd known all along had to be there. The Someone that Pastor Kahanamoku had introduced him to after he'd returned home from Afghanistan, broken and despairing.

He also knew all about lonely.

The smartphone on the console chirped.

"Aren't you ever going to check your messages?"

Kai licked his lips, smiled. "You're a nag, did you know that, Laney Carrigan? Some of us don't feel the need to stay on the grid 24/7. This is paradise. Relax."

"Best I remember from Sunday school, paradise had its serpents."

"No snakes in Hawai'i." He picked up his phone to get her off his back. "Nothing earth-shattering. A reminder of a special tour I'm flying midweek. I usually fly on weekends." Flicking his eyes between the road ruts as they bounced closer to the house, Kai scrolled through the rest of his text messages. "And an email notification of a blog I follow."

Laney perked in the seat. "You read? What kind of blog?"

Kai rolled his eyes at her and laid down the phone. "Yeah, I'm the total package. Handsome and literate."

She rolled her eyes back at him. "And modest, too."

This girl . . . Kai pressed his lips together in an effort to keep the smile off his face. She was funny, he'd give her that. "Maybe you've heard of him, you being a writer, too. The blog's called Chasing Rainbows. We Hawai'ians know a thing or two about rainbows and the writer is—"

"A. Hoffmann."

Kai rolled to a stop under the forty-foot fiery red African tulip tree. "You know him?"

"You could say that." Laney bit her lip. "What do you think of Hoffmann's writing?"

"Love it. First came across his series of articles when I was still stationed in Afghanistan. He embedded with a platoon of guys, one an old Fort Rucker pal of mine. Hoffmann told the real story of the war from real guys' perspectives. He followed with another series on what their families endured on the home front during their deployment."

"And then one last article about what happened when the soldiers returned home," Laney whispered.

Kai's eyes widened. "You read them, too?"

Her mouth drooped. "The PTSD some, not all, suffered. The adjustments. The suicide of one who didn't get the right help in time."

Kai clenched his fists in his lap. "That was my friend—who I should have been there to help. I should've recognized how bad the depression had hold of him." He snorted. "Should have seen the signs, since I've been there myself. Should've done something."

Laney touched his forearm. "Kai—"

"You hoo! Kai! Laney!"

Kai jerked away as Auntie Teah bounded out onto the porch in the bright orange muumuu she wore for tourists at the quilt shop. Laney waved at the rotund, sixtyish lady who'd rescued Kai from a life of abuse and disease.

His new life and faith. Home. His earlier suspicions returned.

Just where did the never-a-dull-moment Laney fit in with his beloved 'ohana?

That frightened look of vulnerability he'd noted at the airport creased Laney's face. And despite his doubts, Kai found himself hoping, praying, that Laney found a forever place to belong, too.

With Auntie Teah talking a mile a minute asking about Laney's trip, her dad's health, the ride into the hill country, Laney found herself hugged within an inch of her life, caught and enfolded within the voluminous fabric of Auntie Teah's embrace. Following Kai's example at the front door, she slipped off her white sandals and allowed Teah to usher her into the high-ceilinged, sprawling Franklin ranch house that nestled among the lemon and lime trees.

It was hard to maintain her customary shoulder tenseness, Laney decided, with Teah's arms draped across them.

Like her pictures, Teah's personality was as upbeat as Laney had discerned from phone conversations over the last month. Her brown eyes sparkled, her more gray than black hair pulled into a tidy bun at the base of her neck. But stubborn tendrils refused to stay in place. Their thick, wiry texture, Laney's breath hitched, identical to her own.

Teah paused in the koa-floored foyer, took Laney's face between her hands, and placed a gentle kiss on Laney's forehead. "Aloha, my beautiful cousin. You're going to be the joy of Mily's life. Yeah?"

Kai, hovering with the boxed cat in his arms, vanished into one of the rooms that lined the hall on either side.

"How is Tutu Mily, Auntie Teah? Kai said there'd been an emergency. Does Tutu know I've come?"

Teah looped an arm around Laney's waist. "She knows. I told you about her deteriorating condition since the Alzheimer's diagnosis three years ago. A mild to moderate case as of now." She squeezed Laney. "That's why I'm so thankful you were able to come right away once we found each other. Bits and pieces of her memory disappear every day. You're going to bring her a peace she's not known since your mother . . ." Teah's voice choked.

A figure materialized in the doorway through which Kai had disappeared. A slim, fiftyish woman in a long, denim skirt and green blouse. A Hawai'ian woman, her long, salt and pepper hair hung down her back. Granny spectacles perched on the end of her nose.

Feeling the quake of nerves, Laney made a motion forward. "My . . . " She put a hand over her heart. "Is this my birth mother?"

Teah's brow wrinkled. "No, honey. That's Mrs. Kahanamoku, our pastor's wife."

Mrs. Kahanamoku stepped into the light of the setting sun casting its rays through the open door. Her face constricted. "I'm sorry, Ms. Carrigan, Teah. But Mily's asking for you both." She gestured to the room behind her. Her shoulders hunched, she retreated into the shadows.

Kai appeared empty-handed, his face clouded. "Why didn't you tell her, Mama Teah? Before she came all this way?"

Teah released Laney and stepped back near a wall lined with portraits of long-ago haole Franklin ancestors, her hand resting on the exquisitely carved mission-style side table. Her wide shoulders sagged. "Mily needs closure, Kai. I thought I'd have time. I intended to meet Laney at the airport and explain everything on the way home."

She banged her fist on the table, startling Laney and rattling the set of hand-turned wooden bowls. "I didn't know Mily would wander away from the day care program at the church today or that Social Services would get involved." Her eyes blazed. "I will not allow Mily to be removed from the only home she's known since she came here as a young bride."

Kai's jaw clenched. "You have to work. I have to work. Elyse and Ben . . . We can't keep riding herd on Mily every second of every day to prevent her from wandering off." He strode forward, placing a hand on Teah's shoulder. "You haven't had a decent night's sleep in months. You can't go on this way. None of us can. I don't want her placed in a facility any more than you do. But what else can we do?" He raked a hand through his hair, leaving portions of it standing on end.

Teah straightened. “A solution in God’s own time has presented itself. Mrs. K was a former hospice nurse on Oahu before Pastor and she transferred to our little church a few months ago. She’s offered to sit with Mily during the day while we’re at work.”

“What about at night, Teah? And, nursing care is expensive.”

Teah sashayed past him, reaching out to Laney. “Mrs. K has offered her services free of charge. A labor of love, she called it. We’ll do shifts at night. Maybe Laney would be willing to do a rotation.” She smoothed her dress. “Mily only wanders because she’s looking for Rose’s baby.” Teah pushed back her shoulders. “Laney, home at last, brings a wonderful conclusion to that haunting loose end in Mily’s life. Yeah?”

Laney gripped Teah’s hand. “What happened to my birth mother, Teah? She’s dead, isn’t she?”

Teah’s mouth pulled downward. “When Rose came home pregnant from the university on Oahu, your grandfather Franklin . . . ” Teah gulped. “A fierce, proud man, he was enraged. Rose and he were so much alike in that regard. Too much alike.”

“Who was my biological father?”

Teah shrugged. “We never knew his name. Rose wouldn’t say. She told her mother, Mily, that he was stationed at Schofield, that they’d fallen in love. When he transferred to another base on the mainland, he promised to send for her when he got settled.”

“And he didn’t, I’m guessing.”

“Rose came home to share her wedding plans with her family. Her father had big dreams for his only child. Then, Rose realized she was pregnant.” Teah took Laney’s hands in hers. “I wasn’t here for any of this. My mother and Mily grew up on Maui where I lived until Auntie Mily, in her grief over losing a daughter and grandchild, sent for me. Offered Pete, our baby daughter, Elyse, and me a home."

"I wasn't welcome news to anyone, was I?" Laney gave a self-deprecating laugh. The confirmation of all she'd ever suspected—unwanted, unloved, discarded at the first opportunity. Kai made a move toward her, hand outstretched but he hesitated, dropping his arm at his side when Teah reached her first.

"Rose and her mother started that baby quilt for you." Teah's finger raised Laney's chin. Her eyes bored into Laney's. "Jared Franklin had always called his daughter, his Lokelani Rose."

Laney nodded. She'd done some research on the pattern. She walked over to where Kai had left her bag. "Because Mily was from Maui." She removed the dark rose pink and white baby quilt from the main compartment.

Teah's eyes lit up. "And Maui's flower is the Lokelani Rose. Your name Alana means sky and as they sewed the quilt and you grew in your mother's belly, they dreamed of your future."

Laney clenched the edge of the quilt in her fist. "But my biological father never contacted Rose," she whispered.

Teah sighed. "Once he learned about her pregnancy, Rose's father threw an ultimatum in her face, the taunt that she'd been used and abandoned by the haole soldier and that she could either—" Teah's hand covered her mouth.

Laney's knees buckled. Kai rushed forward and seized her arm. Clutching the quilt to her chest, Laney felt the warmth of Kai at her back. "He wanted Rose to get rid of me, didn't he?"

Teah's double chins wobbled. Tears trailed down her cheeks. "Or get out of his house and never return." She shook her ponderous head from side to side. "Oh, what that pride cost him, Mily . . ." Her lips quivered. "And you. Rose took the unfinished quilt and departed out of their lives forever." Teah scrubbed the tears with her work-callused hand. "I thought you might know what happened to your mother afterward, before Rose . . ."

"I know this part of my story from what she told my real mother, Gisela Carrigan, when they met at a GriefShare group at a local church outside the base. When she arrived, Rose discovered her fiancé had been killed in a training accident not long after he'd transferred there."

Teah swallowed, her voice raspy. "We never knew if you were with your father or if you'd . . . like Rose . . ."

Kai's arms tightened around Laney. "All I know is by the time my real mother met Rose I'd been born and Rose was destitute. My mother was recovering from multiple miscarriages. They bonded over grief. She and my father had begun the process to adopt before he deployed overseas. One day, my mother found me wrapped in the finished quilt, alone and hungry on her doorstep. My mother never heard from Rose again."

For a moment, Laney allowed herself to lean into Kai's comforting embrace. The cocoa butter aroma vied against the wet cat smell. A measure of her sadness was slightly alleviated by the humorous memory of their search and rescue of the cat. Kai, whether he wanted to admit it or not, was born to be a rescuer.

But she was tired of playing the role Rose had consigned her—the victim.

That part of her—the part that learned the hard way that sooner or later everyone lets you down—stepped out of the circle of his strength. Best to stand on your own. Weaklings and the faint of heart, the brigadier taught her, didn't fare well in life.

"How do you know she's dead?"

Teah glanced at Kai, then over to Laney. "Two years after she left the Big Island, we received a phone call from a police detective in Las Vegas. He'd recovered a driver's license off the body of a dead, drug-addicted homeless woman."

"Rose . . ." Laney let a slow breath trickle from between her lips.

"I'm sorry, Laney." Kai stuffed his hands into his pockets. "I didn't realize Teah promised—"

Laney held her hand, palm up. "As you say, no worries. She only talked about Tutu. My fault for assuming more."

Teah's face crumpled. "I feared you wouldn't come for a dying grandmother whose painful memories have been addled by dementia. I should've told you. I just didn't know how to begin over the phone."

A little bit of General Carrigan crawled up Laney's spine. "I would've come anyway. Unlike my erstwhile absentee mother, I don't run away when things get tough." She squared her shoulders and folded the quilt over her arm. "But I intend, while there's time, to know my grandmother."

4

In the living room, Laney received a timid smile from Mrs. K seated next to a fragile, elderly woman whose restless fingers plucked at a small rectangular piece of white fabric. She stabbed the cloth with her forefinger, in a frantic motion in and out, up and down.

Using her finger, like a needle?

Faltering, Laney threw an uncertain look over her shoulder at Teah.

"That's when we realized something was wrong." Teah placed an arm across Laney's shoulder. "She'd cut up the red drapes in the study before we took the scissors away. Then she kept pinning rose petals to every dish towel in the house. She's been trying to finish your quilt."

Mily turned her wistful, brown face at the sound of Laney's footfalls on the sisal rug. Her black eyes narrowed, clouded with confusion. The old woman gripped Mrs. K's hand. "Is this my Aloha Rose? Where's your baby, Lokelani?"

Laney came to an abrupt halt. "Rose?" she whispered.

Had her grandmother called Mrs. K, Rose? Teah bit her lip. Mrs. K's eyes watered, sadness mixed with a mute apology written on her features.

Teah edged around them, joining Mrs. K on the sofa. "God's solution, I told you, Kai. Mrs. K found her today on the beach where Rose—Lokelani Rose Franklin—departed."

Kai dropped to his knees, taking the old woman's blue-veined hands in his own. "Mily walked all the way home from town?"

Teah cast Laney an imploring look. "It comforts Mily that she's found her daughter again, her Rose. Please Kai, Mrs. K says it's okay. Laney?"

Laney stood frozen, afraid to breathe.

"It's Rose's daughter, Alana." Teah smoothed a strand of wispy white hair behind the old woman's ear. "Grown up, Mily. Both of them home as you've dreamed all these years."

The old lady's eyes traveled to Laney, inspecting her face, searching. Whatever she detected there satisfied her. She smiled and patted Mrs. K's arm. "I think she looks more like me than she does you, Rose."

Her aunt nodded, relaxing against the tropical hued cushions. "You're right, Mily. I see it, too."

Mily laughed, a sound resembling tinkling bells. "Like me when I was a young hula dancer who caught the eye of Jared Franklin."

Kai rose slow, as if in pain. "I can't fight you both. You know what I think about this whole thing, Teah."

A mistake?

Laney was so tired of being everyone's mistake. She fingered the e-ticket she'd transferred to her skirt.

Mily pointed a birdlike finger at the quilt draped over Laney's arm. "You finished it, Rose." She clapped her hands together. "Alana, let me see. Let me see."

Time—an eternity of heartbeats—hung suspended. Laney sensed everyone in the room holding their breath, waiting for her next move. Teah's lips moved in a silent, pleading prayer.

Laney sank to her knees in front of Mily and handed the quilt to her grandmother. "Tutu," she whispered, a tingle of something unfamiliar but longed for tugging at her heart. The first and only person she'd ever met who actually shared the same bloodline as herself.

Mily's eyes gleamed at Mrs. K. "Beautiful finished work you did, Rose." Her gnarled finger traced the outline of a pink rose petal appliquéd to the white background. Before Laney had time to react, Mily removed the pink glasses from Laney's face, cupping her face between her hands. "Beautiful like my Alana Rose."

Laney hugged the railing on the front verandah, her hands wrapped around the coffee mug for warmth. The mug, from Teah's quilt shop, sported a Hawai'ian appliqué quilt motif. The morning air caressed her skin like Oriental silk, but the warmth Laney sought at this early hour was for the soothing of her fractured emotions.

It had been a long, restless night on the four-poster mahogany bed—draped with mosquito netting for decorative purposes less than utility. The same room, Teah told her with a laugh, that was once occupied by the teenaged Rose Franklin. A king-size blue and white appliqué quilt adorned the mattress. A surreal night during which Laney tossed, pummeled like the relentless waves of the surf, by the myriad of strange new experiences and people.

And thanks to a fierce case of jet lag, Laney rose with the sunrise at the sound of a door slamming in the direction of the stable behind the house. The thought of truck doors, a specific burgundy F150 to be exact, drove her from the twisted sheets. Hiding behind a lace-paneled curtain, Laney's early bird behavior rewarded her with a too brief glimpse of Kai's broad shoulders that tapered to a narrow waist. She exhaled as Kai disappeared on a sturdy coal black quarter horse to dispense with his morning chores. She'd let the lace panel drift into place.

Kai Barnes. Obnoxious to a fault. Arrogant.

But real easy on the eyes.

Dinner had been a tense affair, everyone afraid to speak lest they say the wrong thing. Mily, unconcerned with strained undercurrents, chirped like a little bird, doing her best to put Laney and "Rose" in the know of the activities available on the ranch and around town. Dinner had also involved Spam. And not the junk that cluttered the internet.

Spam burgers. The look on Laney's face, despite her best efforts, betrayed her, for Kai laughed out loud.

"Tutu's favorite meal and Teah's cooking specialty," Kai informed her. And when Teah returned to the kitchen, he offered to split his burger with her, too, if she wanted more.

Following Elyse's lead at the Moana, Laney kicked him under the table.

This morning Laney took another welcome sip of the aromatic Kona coffee. A distant cloud of dust billowed down the lane as a car drew closer to the main house. A distinguished, fiftyish Hawai'ian man drove the Chevy. Mrs. K occupied the passenger seat. Must be her husband, Teah's pastor, Laney concluded.

Exiting the vehicle, Mrs. K shook her head in response to something he said. Laney, not wishing to intrude, hung back into the shadows of the deep-fronted porch. Laney edged toward the door. The man blew his wife a kiss before taking off toward the main road again. At the squeak of the front door, Mrs. K 's head bobbed as she spotted Laney.

Some of the tension left the woman's face, and she smiled as she made her way up the few steps to join Laney. In the bright morning sun, Laney noticed the lifetime of wrinkles radiating from the woman's eyes and bracketing her mouth. Kind eyes, Laney decided. Welcoming, don't-expect-anything-from-you eyes.

"Good morning, Laney."

"Good morning, Mrs. K." Laney sighed. "Or should I get in the habit of calling you Rose?"

"You call me whatever suits you, Laney." The pastor's wife gave her a tentative hug. "Or you don't have to call me anything, if you'd prefer."

"This is one crazy situation." Laney returned her hug. "I don't know how to thank you for making these last days before Mily loses the ability to recognize anyone so happy and safe for her." Laney drew back. "Another fine mess Rose left for others to sort out."

Mrs. K's gaze shifted to her wine-colored toenails. She gestured toward the car disappearing from sight. "My husband is not so comfortable with our charade. I'm not sure I am, either." Putting a hand to her chest, she took a deep breath of flower-scented air and changed the subject. "Where are Teah and Mily this morning?"

Entering the house with Mrs. K on her heels, Laney gestured to the back of the house. "Mily's cooking a special Hawai'ian breakfast and allowing Teah to assist." She winked to let Mrs. K know she was kidding.

Mrs. K took Laney's arm and drew her into the front parlor. "I wanted to show you something that might be of interest to you. Yesterday after we found Mily and brought her home, I decided to help Mily put together a book of remembrance."

At Laney's quizzical look, Mrs. K pulled out a spiral bound scrapbook from the side table beside Mily's favorite chair. "In Oahu, with some of my former Alzheimer's patients, it proved helpful to record major events, people, and memories of the person's life. Helped anchor them and temper the confusion as short-term memories went first and then long-term memories eventually faded away as well."

Laying down her mug, Laney ran her hand over the cover of the book, inset with an oval encased photo of Mily, the young, beautiful hula dancer with a wreath encircling her head and *lauhala* leaves encircling her waist. "When Teah told me about Mily's condition over the phone, I did some research. That's one of the reasons I came so quickly."

She glanced at Mrs. K. "Before she loses the power of speech and the ability to communicate."

"Which doesn't always mean the same thing as losing the power to recognize."

"But this record might help her keep track of the memories longer?"

"It couldn't hurt and it might also help you connect with a family of strangers who've been sprung on you all at once."

Laney nodded, unable to trust herself to speak. She squeezed Mrs. K's arm. A kind woman. It meant the world to Laney that someone else understood.

Mrs. K gathered the quilt, lying across the arm of Mily's chair.

Laney smiled. "She slept with that last night. Teah only pried it away from her this morning because she told Mily she didn't want to run the risk of getting Spam grease on it." She made a face.

Mrs. K laughed. "An acquired taste, my dear. A beloved Hawai'ian food group right there alongside fish. Did you know that Hawai'ians consume more Spam per capita than any other people group on earth?"

Laney gave a tiny shudder.

"Give us a chance, honey." Mrs. K flipped one corner of the quilt, holding the handwritten label up to the light of the bay window. Her finger traced the letters Laney knew by heart.

"Alana, born October 25. Aloha, Rose." Mrs. K's voice read. She gazed at Laney, a sheen of tears in her eyes.

"Lokelani Rose wrote that before she placed me and the quilt on the Carrigans' doorstep." Laney shrugged to show she didn't care. "Left me and walked away."

Dropping her eyes, Mrs. K folded the small quilt into meticulous thirds and placed it upon the chair. "It must have been the saddest day of her life."

Laney tensed and cleared her throat. Time for a topic change. "Do you have children of your own, Mrs. K?"

"Two. Both are grown and one is at college on the mainland."

"Do both of them like Spam?" The front door creaked open in protest.

Mrs. K opened her mouth to comment, but she and Laney pivoted at the sound of boots on the foyer's hardwood floors.

Boots pried off and left on the bootjack inside the door, Kai poked his head around the door frame. Laney fought down the surge of pleasure from seeing his familiar, handsome face.

Catching sight of Laney, his face broke into its customary mocking grin. "Well, well. An early riser. Who would've guessed? I had you figured for a victim of our Polynesian paralysis for sure."

Mrs. K stifled a laugh.

Laney raised her eyebrows. "Polynesian paralysis?'

Kai leaned against the frame, his long blue jean-clad legs extended in front of him. "Yeah, you know. Overcome by a sudden need to lie in a swinging hammock beside a crystal blue lagoon sipping fruity drinks with umbrellas in a coconut shell."

"Is that what it means to be a true Hawai'ian?" A teasing smile lifted Laney's lips.

Teah emerged from the kitchen. "Breakfast is ready. Yeah?" She gave Kai a gentle shove out of the doorway. "Laney tells me she's got to do research for an article she's writing about the Big Island."

Kai loped into the dining room, followed by Laney. He placed a quick kiss on Mily's cheek from where she sat at the head of the table. "Rose" pulled a side chair and scooted close to Mily's elbow, in case she needed assistance.

He rubbed his work-hardened hands together. "Malasadas. Yum."

"Did you wash your hands after feeding those cows, Kai Barnes?" Teah settled her skirt—a riotous pattern of red hibiscus—into the cushioned rattan chair Kai held out for her.

"Yes, ma'am, I did," he mumbled with an audacious wink over her head.

Teah harrumphed. "Some people, because they're over thirty, have a tendency to get too big for their britches. Yeah?"

Laney and Kai reached for the back of Laney's chair at the same time, their fingers brushing on the koa-carved wood. Remembering her e-ticket and her resolve, Laney decided retreat might be the better part of valor. She removed her hand and allowed Kai to hold the chair for her.

"I have a list of must-see places for my articles, and I asked Auntie Teah if I could borrow a ranch vehicle to get to town." She passed a steaming platter of scrambled eggs to Kai as he seated himself across from her. "I can rent a car there, right?"

Teah tsk-tsked. "No need to throw away good money. Try these, Laney. A specialty of my late husband, Pete's family. From his Portuguese ancestors. Yeah?"

Laney speared the rounded ball of fried dough with the serving fork.

"Oh," Kai took the plate and helped himself to three or four or six. "You'll need more of these, I promise you."

"Malasadas . . ." Laney whipped the tape recorder out of her white jean shorts.

"A doughnut hole." Mrs. K cut a piece of fried Spam on Mily's plate. "Rolled in sugar."

Kai clucked his tongue when Laney passed on a helping of Spam. "Only the tourists want them rolled in sugar and in cinnamon. Real Hawai'ians—"

Laney plunked her elbow on the table, her chin in her hand. "And what constitutes a real Hawai'ian, Kai Barnes?" She jabbed the tape recorder in his direction and held it in midair awaiting his response.

Teah's gaze hopscotched between the two of them, a speculative look creasing the folds of her face. "Laney's not a tourist, Kai. She's family." Teah helped herself to several slices of Spam. "A Hawai'ian is anyone who considers Hawai'i home and understands our values." She took a sip of mango juice. "They are devoted to their 'ohana and—"

"And they got to love to body surf." Kai popped a malasada in his mouth. "Broke da mouf good as usual, Mama Teah." He smacked his lips and reached for another.

Teah smacked his hand. "No make big body."

Laney swiveled to Mrs. K. She loved Teah's old-fashioned pidgin English but once in a while, Teah required a translation.

Mily cackled. "Try not to act like you own the place."

Laney laughed. "A Hawai'ian lesson Kai is still learning?"

Kai rolled his eyes and poked his lip out. "It's not fair when you females gang up on a guy."

Teah clapped her hands together. "I have the perfect solution."

Kai groaned. "Here we go again."

Laney felt a niggle of unease at the gleeful look Teah bestowed upon her and Kai. "Laney needs a tour guide. Kai doesn't have anything on his calendar for the rest of the day."

"Now wait a minute, Mama Teah. Nothing 'cept this hundred-acre ranch to run," Kai protested. He balanced a malasada between his thumb and forefinger, his eyes admiring the sugar-coated treat from every angle.

Auntie Teah shook her finger at him. "Ben doesn't report to work at the Moana till late afternoon—he's one of the chefs. I'll go to the shop. Mily will stay here with uh . . ." She gulped. " . . . with Rose. Ben can take care of the ranch long enough for you to take Laney on an outing to the Pu'uhonua Hōnaunau National Park."

"The what?" Laney thrust the microphone in Teah's direction. "Say again?"

"Are you serious?" Kai dropped the malasada onto his plate.

"Oh, Auntie Teah, I don't want to put any of you to any trouble." Laney glanced from Teah's complacent smile to the frown forming like a Pacific thundercloud between Kai's dark brows.

"No trouble, honey." Teah slid back her chair, the feet scudding across the koa-planked floor. "Pu'uhonua is a sacred site in the ancient culture. Royal tomb of chiefs. Much history."

Kai scowled. "No trouble for you."

Laney rounded on him. "Look, I said not to worry about me. I'll be fine. I'm used to taking care of myself."

Teah's eyes narrowed. "How else Laney gonna learn about the 'ohana and how to be a good Hawai'ian? Yeah?"

Kai gave a sigh of resignation. "Okay, but first I have to stop by the house and change into beach wear. No way I'm driving all the way to Hōnaunau in jeans and boots."

Mily nodded. "Kai, show Laney the *honu*, too."

At Laney's questioning look, Kai pushed back his chair and got to his feet. "Green sea turtles. Might as well bring that electronic contraption you keep shoving in my face and get this over with."

Laney stood and crossed her arms. "I'll do that." *You cocky, self-assured* . . .

Teah began clearing the table. "You young people have a wonderful day together. Get to know each other . . ."

"I'm here to do an artic—"

"I thought you said she needed a tour—"

She and Kai glared at each other. Turning as one, they glared at Teah. Teah's smile almost split her face.

"Oh." Realization dawned as to Teah's ulterior motives. Laney hated the rosy flush that began at her collarbone and worked its way up. Kai shuffled his sock feet.

Teah wiped her hands on her apron and waggled her hips. "Have fun. And I'm sure I can count on you, son, to make sure Laney understands our aloha spirit."

5

Laney braced herself as Kai's truck bounced and swayed along the shortcut between his property and the ranch. Waxy, dark green coffee shrubs stretched as far as the eye could see on either side of the gravel road. He fixed his eyes on the rutted lane, avoiding eye contact. She noted the dark smudges under his eyes.

Going to be a long ride to wherever this Poo-oo place was located. They'd seemed to reach a rapprochement last night, but today they'd returned to Kai's unexplained hostility at the airport.

Moody. Probably mental, too.

Well, if Mr. If-You-Don't-Know-If-I'm-Handsome, Just-Ask-Me, And-I'll-Tell-You wanted to play this game, she'd put on her big girl britches and teach him a thing or two about hostility.

"You don't have to do this." Her lips compressed. "Drop me off in town. I work solo anyway. I don't know why Teah felt she had to involve you—"

"I could tell you why Teah thinks she has to involve me . . ."

She darted a look at his clenched jaw. "I'm sorry, Kai. I'm sure you have plenty of your own work to do without babysitting me. I don't know why Teah wants to play matchmaker." She snorted. "Why she'd imagine somebody like you and somebody like me . . ."

He swiveled his head around. "What's wrong with me?"

Laney blinked. "Nothing. I meant you and I . . ." His eyes boring into her, Laney gave a delicate cough. "You know . . . I'm—"

"You think you're too good for a non-com?" His profile hardened.

"No, of course not. That's not what I meant."

Kai braked in the middle of the road, putting the truck in park. "What did you mean then? Why wouldn't somebody like you and somebody like me . . . ?"

She'd thought she'd been giving him an out. She'd had no idea she'd offend. Laney added touchy and supersensitive to the list of cons regarding a certain helicopter pilot-cum-cowboy. "I was just trying to say that unlike the fluffy kittens you prefer, I have no ulterior designs on you. That we could agree to be friends for the duration of my visit, that's all."

He frowned. "Fluffy kittens? What are you talking about?"

Laney angled her head. "That Della person and the red-head. Persians or angoras in the cat world." She pointed at herself. "Me? I'm more like that drowned excuse for the feline we found in the ditch."

"You and the cats." He let out a breath, gave her an assessing look. "I can do friends."

Laney nodded. "Good. I just believe in laying all my cards out on the table."

He raked a hand through his hair. "I can see that."

Kai rammed the gearshift into drive. In a large clearing, he rolled the truck to a stop at the front of a white, one-story bungalow, parking underneath the shade of a towering, violet-hued jacaranda tree.

He leaped out, slamming the door behind him. "I won't be long. Maybe get yourself a refill on the coffee. I left some in the pot in the kitchen if you'd like to reheat it."

She stepped out of the truck and inhaled the heady fragrance of the white coffee blossoms. She spun a slow three-sixty, taking in the fairy-tale princess view of the orchards. "The coffee beans come from your neighbor's field?"

"No. They're my fields. You're in time for the flowers. Kona snow, we call it. Harvest begins in August. I grow only enough for the family and myself. A hobby." Kai ducked his head and took the front steps two at a time.

Kai Barnes, a regular Renaissance man. Who knew?

Green plantation shutters framed the windows. Sweet-smelling yellow ginger and the exotic orange birds-of-paradise, a bouquet for the senses, skirted the foundation of the cottage. Laney breathed in their fragrant perfume. "You live here?"

He held the carved wooden door for her as she entered the front bamboo-floored hall. "Different elevation from the ranch." He shrugged. "The land became available when I returned from my tour. Used to be Franklin land a hundred years ago. Sold to Japanese immigrants who grew coffee until the last of the family decided practicing surgery in Hilo was more to their liking. Figured I'd do my part to get it into the family's hands again. It's a work in progress."

The cat emerged from the lone hallway, twining and purring around Kai's ankles. The Siamese lifted his head at the sight of Laney, propped his bottom on top of Kai's boot, and mewed.

Smiling, she bent to rub the cat behind the ears. But he didn't move from his favored position. "See?" She laughed up at Kai. "The cat does like you."

Grimacing, Kai shifted his boot—and the Siamese—out of his path and deposited him a few inches away. "Kolohe likes anyone who puts out the water and salmon."

Laney stood tall—as tall as five foot three ever got—and rocked back on her heels, her arms crossed. "Kolohe? Thought 'we' weren't going to name him." She cocked an eyebrow at him. "Before 'we' took him to the pound?"

A sheepish, hand-caught-in-the-cookie-jar look passed over his features. He touched the tip of her nose with his forefinger. "Like you say, I seem to grow on all God's creatures. And Kolohe—" he grinned. "Means rascal, troublemaker. He seems to have grown on me. He's a good mouser. Brought me a before-breakfast gift this morning."

Laney grimaced.

"He might prove to be a keeper." Kai strode down the hallway, speaking over his shoulder. "Like his new owner. Yeah?"

She rolled her eyes. "Fo' real? No make big body, Kai Barnes."

"Very good, Ms. Carrigan. You're getting the hang of the lingo. We'll make a real Hawai'ian *kahuna* out of you before you know it." Giving her a mocking, salute, he disappeared from her sight into a bedroom.

She spent the time strolling around the public areas of Kai's home, getting to know him better. The photos of Elyse, the man she now knew to be her husband, Ben Ching, and their little boy, Daniel. Pictures on the fridge of Kai in his army uniform with his arm around Teah and an older man Laney identified as Teah's deceased husband, Pete.

Accompanied by Kolohe at her heels, Laney wandered out back to the lanai where a grove of bamboo partially obscured the tantalizing glimpse of Pacific blue. A vine twined around the latticed arbor on the side. Laney recognized the petals and scent as belonging to the pīkake jasmine. Closing her eyes, she took a long, slow breath and listened to the sighing of the wind through the bamboo forest.

"You like the view?"

Her eyes flew open. Kai, in cargo shorts and a solid green shirt open at the collar, leaned against the door frame, bare feet crossed at the ankles.

Oh, yes. She did like the view.

She flushed, scared for a moment she'd actually said that out loud. Averting her eyes from his mouth, she wheeled toward the ocean. "Bet that sunset reels in the women like sharks on the trail of blood."

Kai straightened and jammed his hands in his pockets. "Wouldn't know. I don't bring women here. I'm ready whenever you are if you want to grab your slippers." He moved aside to make way for Laney.

"Slippers?"

"First Hawai'ian lesson for today. That's what we locals call sandals or flip-flops."

"Good to know." She stuffed her feet into her hot pink Walmart special flip-flops at the front door. Kolohe darted out and disappeared into the bushes. She stopped at the tailgate of the truck, noting the rainbow Hawai'i state license plate. She quirked an eyebrow in Kai's direction.

"You like rainbows? Baby, have you come to the right place." He flung open the passenger door. "Hawai'i is the land of a thousand rainbows. Sometimes more than one a day."

Getting into the truck, she cinched her seat belt as Kai turned the key. "I like your house. Very private, and serene I imagine, after all that chopper noise."

"You do?" He threw her an enigmatic look. "*Maholo*, Laney. Most people, including my relatives, say it's too isolated. Say I'd turn into a hermit if they weren't around to drag me kicking and screaming into normal life."

She leaned her head against the backrest. "Oh, I didn't say you were normal. I said I liked your house." A flicker of a smile twitched at his lips. "Cozy, view to die for, and as a childhood book friend of mine, *Anne of Green Gables*, would say, 'plenty of scope for the imagination.'"

Laney stole a look at her companion. The same could also be said of one heart-stopping cowboy.

Kai pulled out onto the highway. "A pretend friend? Not a real one? Sounds like a lonely childhood to me."

Laney shrugged. "We moved around a lot. The Southwest. Fort Bragg. Back to Germany where Dad first met Mom. I was different from the other children. Wasn't welcomed by my mother's blond, blue-eyed nieces and nephews in Munich. Lots of different schools. Easier to keep my own company."

She gave him a slight smile. "I envy you this." Her hand swept the view out of the windshield. "And a tight, close-knit family, too."

"My life didn't start out this way. You and I have more in common than you realize." He glanced over at the wistful note in Laney's voice. "Your mom, Gisela, sounds like a great mother. You miss her, don't you?"

She sighed.. "Every moment of every day. Her sole ambition in life was to be Tom Carrigan's wife and to be my mother." She favored him with a bright smile. His heart gave a funny lurch.

"Her favorite song was 'Somewhere Over the Rainbow,' which she sang countless times to me over the years in her German-accented English. She told me I was the pot of gold at the end of her rainbow." A hint of suppressed tears laced her voice.

Feeling an unexpected surge of protectiveness, he pushed a CD into the drive on the dashboard. "Hawai'ian lesson number two. To understand the Hawai'ian soul, you must understand the late great Israel Kamakawiwo'ole."

At her look of consternation, he chuckled. "Say that five times in a row and you'll almost be a real Hawai'ian. Here's his slack key ukulele rendition of 'Over the Rainbow.' A little bit reggae, a little bit jazz. A whole lot of Hawai'ian." He pushed the play button.

The laid-back, soothing sounds filled the cab. Laney closed her eyes as the mellow notes floated in the air around them. Swallowing the lump that always formed in his own throat every time he listened to the timeless Brudda Iz, he appreciated that she wasn't one of those women who felt the need to fill space with noise.

As the music drew to its conclusion, she opened her eyes. "Maholo, Kai. That was beautiful. My mom would've loved it."

Pleased she understood his intention behind the gift, he smiled and hit the eject button. He liked being able to put a smile on Laney's face. The CD popped out.

"It's one of my favorites." He cleared his throat, ready to lighten the mood. "And if you resist the urge to rescue any more cats, I might play my second all-time Iz favorite, 'What a Wonderful World' on the way home."

She held her hand, palm up, like a Girl Scout swearing a pledge. "No more cats, I promise." She cut her eyes at him. "But I didn't promise anything about any lost dogs."

He laughed. "Got it. Forewarned to avoid any animals, period."

"Your name 'Kai' is Hawai'ian, too?"

He nodded. "It means 'sea'."

"And yet you took to the sky, not the water?"

"Don't get me wrong. I love to surf, scuba, and boogie board with the best of 'em, but the sea was my mother's thing. She followed the surfer circuit from California to here." He rubbed a hand over his face. "I've always been grateful she stopped in Hawai'i when she found herself pregnant with me."

"And your father?" Laney shook her head. "No, forget I asked. None of my business."

"Never sure, but she called the guy she shacked up with in the Waipi'o Valley my dad until she died."

She touched his arm. His heart did a treacherous stutter-step. "I shouldn't have brought up painful memories."

He took one hand off the wheel and threaded his fingers through hers, surprised and pleased when she didn't withdraw her hand. "Old pain that led to bigger blessings when Daddy Pete found me. Though I've always felt guilty she died that way . . ." His voice cracked, also thinking of his friend who'd not survived the depression. "Felt guilty my life—courtesy of Pete, Elyse, and Teah—turned out to be so much better than hers."

He pivoted toward Laney. "Sounds crazy, doesn't it?"

She squeezed his hand, an unfamiliar rightness in the gesture rendered him momentarily speechless. "Sometimes I feel guilty knowing my mom became distant with her German family after she adopted me. But they had a hard time dealing with the fact I wasn't Mom's biological child."

Kai felt a stirring of admiration for the dead woman, Gisela Carrigan. And thinking of *Kohole*, the apple—i.e. Laney Carrigan—didn't fall far from the tree. Love me, love my stray cat.

He didn't know where Laney got her fluffy kitten analogies about him. He liked strays, a stray himself.

And to his growing disquiet, he found himself drawn in particular to sleek, exotic ones like Laney Carrigan. Her silversword sharp wit. Her shoot-from-the-hip approach to life. Those large, Kona eyes . . .

With an effort, he wrenched his thoughts from taking that path. "Why did you never appear in photos with your father and mother at official army functions?"

She laughed. "Don't tell me you tried to Google me?"

He shrugged, a wry grin on his face. "You didn't Google us?"

"I Googled everyone I knew about at the Franklin Ranch. You," she lowered her chin. "Were a surprise."

"A wonderful and pleasant surprise?"

She sniffed. "Some people dwell in delusion."

"The photos?"

She fluttered her hand. He immediately missed its comforting warmth. "I wasn't exactly deposited with a birth certificate. Dad pulled a few strings for a judge to grant temporary guardianship for the emergency situation. They'd already completed the home studies, classes, and applications prerequisite to adopting."

"God's hand at work." Kai peeked a look at Laney.

Her lips tightened. "Supposedly Rose—unbeknownst to my mom—had shared her intentions with the pastor who supervised the GriefShare group to relinquish me to the custody of the Carrigans. But when presented with a social worker and the paperwork, she panicked and just up and left me one day. The pastor's testimony was key in expediting the adoption process."

"Maybe she feared if the process drew out, she'd change her mind?"

"Whatever. As far as the photos go, I think Dad was secretly afraid if Rose ever happened upon a picture of me she'd come and take me." She gave a self-deprecating laugh. "You and I know now the likelihood of that happening was zero."

He shifted in the seat. "Try not to be so hard on Rose, if you can, Laney. From the sounds of it, she did you a tremendous favor by leaving you with the Carrigans. Trust me, I know all about that. My life was no picnic though my mom kept me with her."

Laney didn't comment and for the rest of the drive she stared out the window, lost in her own thoughts. They stopped once on the way, past Kailua-Kona, at a roadside stand for a shaved ice. Part of Laney's continuing Hawai'ian crash course, he informed her. She left it to him to select a flavor for her. In honor of her newfound appreciation for Brudda Iz, Kai chose Rainbow.

Parking outside the visitor center, he let Laney dictate the pace of the tour, a quick perusal of the visitor center, a leisurely stroll through the national historic park. With her Nikon strapped around her neck—her pretty, graceful neck Kai couldn't help noticing—Laney snapped shot after shot at various quixotic angles of menacing Ki'i totems and the great wall of Pu'uhonua that separated the royal grounds from the temple complex.

"Would I have seen any of your articles before?" He stood off to the side as Laney crouched on her knees to catch the filtered rays of the sun against the recreated thatched house, the *hale*.

She pressed the button down and allowed the camera to dangle around her neck. "As Laney Carrigan, I write travel guides for magazines or for travel ezines."

He sensed he'd missed something, but he couldn't pinpoint what it was. "So your work takes you all over the globe and you like that, right?"

She shook the sand off one slippered foot. "What's not to like?"

"Bad food, lumpy beds, dealing with the TSA and their equivalent at every airport, the transience."

She elbowed him and his shadow out of the way of her next shot. She brought the camera close to her face and peered through the lens. "There's also the beauty only found in nature. The colorful dress and customs of unique people groups. I'm always learning something new. Experiencing new adventures. Finding out what's on the other side of the rainbow. You forgot about the thrill of new cuisines." He made a face. "From a man who eats Spam burgers." She threw an amused over-the-shoulder glance at him.

"At the risk of challenging long-held childhood beliefs, what if the best is already on this side of the rainbow?"

She shook her head as they picked their way across the coconut palm-fringed grove that overlooked the Honaunau Bay. Green sea turtles dozed on the sun-drenched beach. Her face lit with undisguised pleasure. She nodded toward the sea creatures. "You'd never know though, would you, unless you'd been to the other side?"

Kai peered out over the crashing surf of the incoming breakers. Out to the other side of the world, a sand-colored world of jagged mountain peaks and the desolation wrought by war. "Sometimes you don't have to go there to know."

He kicked at a pebble with the toe of his flip-flop. "As a pilot, I've often seen the rainbow at a distance and appeared to observers to fly right through it. I can tell you what's on the other side, Laney. It's all a matter of perspective. From over there you don't see the rainbow. It's only from where you stand over here," he pointed at the ground, "that you appreciate the colors."

She gripped the camera and tiptoed toward the giant prehistoric looking creature flopped upon the sand with its olive marbled carapace and paddle-like arms extended. A sea breeze wafted the coconut fronds.

"Here." Kai reached for the camera. "Let me get one of you for a change with your new friend."

Laney slipped the camera from around her neck and handed it to him.

He scooted a few feet back. "One . . . two . . . Say 'humuhumunukunukuapua'a'."

"Excuse me?"

Kai clicked and the shutter whirred. He snickered at the expression captured on Laney's face. He sand-crabbed over to the other side of the turtle, oblivious to the weird human creatures in its space. He leaned over to show Laney the digital shot. "It's Hawai'i's state fish. The day you learn to say it like a native is the day you graduate with full honors from the Kai Barnes School of Hawai'i."

Her mouth puckered. "Hoo-moo . . ."

Acting on impulse before he had time to think himself out of it, Kai placed his lips onto hers. A desire he'd resisted acting on since she'd given him what for at the airport.

She tasted of pineapple and berries, of salty sea air and something that made him want to—well, made him want to fly. And conversely, made him glad he was already on his knees, which at the moment wobbled. At her soft moan, he deepened the kiss, ready to savor a second impression. But at her quick intake of breath, Kai retracted his mouth.

What on earth possessed him to . . . ?

And they'd been getting along so well up to this point. Though not blood kin, in the ways Hawai'ians count 'ohana, she was family. If Teah ever got wind of this? Although on second thought, he had a sneaking suspicion he'd played right into Teah's hand.

He reared back, bracing himself for a smack on the face. Sleek, exotic cats had claws. Instead, in the silence that thrummed between them, he realized Laney sat cross-legged beside the honu, grinning from ear to ear.

"Do you kiss all your fluffy kittens over a turtle or doesn't this count because I'm—?"

He groaned. "Will you stop with the cat metaphors? What are you some kind of crazy cat woman?" Handing the camera over and shuffling closer to the water's edge, Kai plopped down on the sand, resting upon one elbow. His other hand scooped a fistful of sand and sifted it through his fingers. "This is one of my favorite places."

She sank down beside him. "The beach and the turtles?"

"Everything here." He scanned the temple grounds behind him. "Pu'uhonua. Know what it was?"

She shook her head.

"Place of refuge."

"Like those Old Testament cities of sanctuary?"

"Exactly. There were lots of taboos in the ancient Hawai'ian culture—*kapu*—forbidden to commoners."

"Such as?"

"Such as what we're doing right now."

Her eyes widened. He laughed at the expression on her face.

"No, not kissing. Although now you mention it . . ." He watched her squirm and blush. He discovered he liked making the independent globetrotter squirm and blush. He wondered if he could make her as weak at the knees as she made him.

Be fun to try . . .

She cleared her throat and gave him a pointed look. "You were saying?"

Kai grinned, unrepentant. "This beach, Keone'ele Cove, was reserved for royalty. Although I've always suspected the regal Tutu Mily, and hence you, might be descended from Maui kings." He tucked a tendril of her hair behind her ear.

His fingers lingered, cupping her ear. The digits on his hand had a mind of their own when it came to Laney Carrigan. The urge to touch her was overwhelming at times. His insides turned into molten liquid.

The pulse at the base of her throat quivered. A wave of pleasure spiraled through him that he inspired that sort of effect on her. But like one of his skittish colts, he decided not to push his luck. Laney Carrigan, he suspected, was one of those slow-to-warm-up creatures.

"And what happened to those who broke kapu?" With an upward tilt of her lashes, she surveyed him to see if she'd pronounced it correctly.

"It meant death. But for those who were brave and strong enough, often swimming the width of this bay, if they reached the city of refuge the priest would grant them sanctuary—restoration of the life they'd lived before. Here they received a second chance. A chance to begin anew."

Laney rotated on her side to face him, her breath inches away from him. "Like the second chance you received when the Rodrigues's fostered you?"

He dropped his eyes to the sand. Usually he avoided these conversations about his past. But the desire to know and be known by Laney ate away at his usual resolve like waves eroding the shoreline.

"My mother and so-called father were drug addicts, modern-day hippies who lived off what they scrounged from the land and government handouts. Any cash went to buy their next fix. I try to keep the few memories of my mother before the cocaine wrecked her in my mind or else all I see is . . ." He sat up.

She leaned against him.

He sighed, gazing out to where the light danced on the surface of the water. "One day they were both high. When they fought over the last hit, my father grabbed a hunting knife . . ."

"Oh, Kai."

"Neighbors who normally kept their distance called the cops. It's a case of live and let live to this day among the disenfranchised in the Valley. But her screams . . ." He swallowed past the lump. "They remembered there was a child in the house, told the first cop on the scene, a Sergeant Peter Rodrigues. There was a standoff with the police trying to negotiate him out of the house. He led them to believe he had a gun, raced out, and pretended to draw his weapon, deciding suicide by cop was better than prison."

"Where were you when this was happening?"

He wrapped his arms around his knees, drawn to his chest. "Daddy Pete found me hiding under the bed on which my mother lay dying. Her blood had dripped through the sheets and the thin mattress . . . She'd been stabbed multiple times."

She hugged one of his arms. "I'm sorry, Kai."

He relished the warmth of her comfort against his side. "I try to remember the times before. When she taught me to surf when I was five. How to snorkel. How even high as a kite that last day when she saw the crazed look in his eyes and the knife in his hand, she managed enough coherence and regard for me to shove me under the bed. She gave me what she could of herself."

Kai allowed himself to nestle against Laney, enjoying the heady jasmine essence of her. "Might heal your heart to remember the same about Rose and the quilt she made for you."

6

Laney ran her hand over the rainbow bolts of fabric that lined the walls of Auntie Teah's shop, the smooth, cottony texture playing across her fingertips. She smiled when her hand hovered over a shade of magenta similar to the bougainvillea growing at Pu'uhonua she'd seen with Kai a few days ago.

Biting her lip, she turned from the fabric at the thought of Kai Barnes to where Teah rang up the customer's purchases. Kai had been a no-show at the ranch house since that day they'd spent together. She'd spotted his truck arriving at the crack of dawn.

She'd watched him saddle his horse and ride out onto the range. Near dusk, he'd returned every evening and departed to his own solitary home without a word. No more shared breakfasts or dinners. As if after baring his painful childhood, he'd run out of words to say to anybody.

Tutu Mily had asked about him, a concerned pucker wrinkling her brow. Teah remarked he had a lot on his mind, that he'd return when ready.

Ready for what? Laney wondered.

A godsend, Mrs. K ventured to the grocer's with Mily every day because Mily enjoyed riding in the car. And although she'd lost the memory of many of her old friends, her social skills remained. She looked forward to the opportunity to "talk story" and laugh with "those nice people in town." The book of remembrance was coming along, too. And now Teah had decided to pass on the family's quilting skills to Laney.

A fruitless task, Laney feared, more comfortable with scaling mountain peaks or negotiating airport terminals. Yesterday, Teah had shown her how to fold the customary white background fabric into fourths. They spent the rest of the day—between customers and the quilt guild meeting at the store—tracing and cutting out the intricate breadfruit design.

"How did you know for sure my Lokelani quilt was the same one Mily began all those years ago?" She observed Teah center and align the appliqué breadfruit onto the base fabric.

Teah leaned over the cutting counter, careful and precise in her motions. "When the haoles came to the islands, we already had our own method of quilting, *kapa moe*, from tree bark. The missionaries introduced us to cotton cloth. Our Hawai'ian quilts are a mixture of the methods, unique and recognizable the world over for our incorporation of the beauty of our land into the design."

Laney scanned the batik fabrics—her particular favorites—their marbled, variegated colors striking.

Teah rubbed the small of her back. "I've got to sit down. I'm too old for all this standing around." She plodded over to a bevy of frond-bedecked cushioned high-back chairs. "Every family passed traditional patterns from generation to generation. Only the appliqué color on the white background varied. That Lokelani pattern is the same one my mother made for me and Mily made with Rose. Once I saw the photo, I knew you belonged with us."

Laney concentrated for the next few minutes as Teah thread-basted a half-inch inside the edge of the appliqué, beginning in the centermost part of the design.

Teah transferred the material into her lap. "You do the other side, yeah?" Teah wrapped Laney's hand around the frame.

Laney glanced over at one of Teah's smaller ongoing quilt projects stashed off to the side, the appliqué fixed in place with the tiniest pins she'd ever seen. "Why can't we use those baby pins?"

"You learn traditional way. Thread too easy to get caught on all those pins for beginner. Thread basting is more secure."

Laney sighed, studying the amount of concave and convex curves to be anchored. "I'll be a grandmother like Tutu before I ever finish."

Teah patted her shoulder. "Not many want to learn today. I fear it's a dying art unless your generation learns to see the value of the old ways. I never could get Elyse to sit still long enough to try." Her lips crinkled. "Too busy with schoolwork." Her chin, both chins, fell forward. "I failed in my duty."

Laney bit back a smile. "You must've done something right, Auntie Teah. She became a Hawai'ian cultural historian, after all."

Teah poked out her lips. "Head knowledge. At least she allowed Mily to teach her some rudimentary hula." Her face lit with enthusiasm. "Say, that would be a fine thing for Mily to teach you, her only grandchild."

Laney groaned. Delicate and graceful no one had ever accused her of being. "Tutu may not be up to it . . ."

"Some things you don't forget. The story of the music—in Mily's case, Mrs. K told me—is so deeply embedded in a person's mind and soul that it's often retained long after much else is lost." She tapped her brow with her index finger. "Mily's still got plenty of moves."

Laney extended the quilt top out from her as far as her arm reached. "And why this breadfruit pattern?"

Teah withdrew a small needle from the pineapple-shaped pincushion she wore about her wrist. "Easiest to learn."

Laney rolled her eyes.

Squinting, Teah threaded the ochre-colored thread through the eye of the needle. "And the one, due to tradition, beginners first tackle. Each pattern tells a story. The breadfruit, the *'ulu*, is said to bring a fruitful life, and the quilter who finishes it will never lack wisdom or knowledge. I figured with the changes the Lord has brought in your life, a little wisdom from Him might be helpful."

Laney cut her eyes at Teah. "You can say that again." She glanced at the honu sea turtle appliqué hanging on the wall over the cash register. At the memory of that afternoon kiss, heat rose in her face.

Teah demonstrated how to fasten the first stitch a quarter inch under and performed a few more slipstitches to lock the leaf in place. "Your turn." She shoved the quilt top toward Laney.

Hunching her shoulders, she copied Teah's deft handiwork. Teah's stitches appeared almost invisible. Hers . . . not so much.

She thrust the fabric at Teah. "I'm never going to be any good at this. I'm messing this up."

"Nothing worth having was ever gained without hard work and effort. Appliqué is like life. You learn when you trust in the Lord, and you and your stitching get better." Teah balanced the needle across her forefinger. "You watch closer this time. I do three stitches, you do four. Practice will make perfect. Yeah?"

She bent her head over Teah's exquisite needlework and took her turn. The last one barely better than her first.

"Plenty of prayers go up with every stitch I take when I make a quilt for someone."

Laney paused, the needle and thread between her thumb and forefinger.

"I pray for God's blessing on that anniversary couple or for the birthday child's coming year. God's watch-care over the newborn. God's plans to be accomplished for that bride."

She waited as Teah, lifting her face toward the rattan ceiling fan, searched for the right words.

"Mily and your mother, Rose, prayed for you while you nestled in Rose's belly. Rose loved you and wanted you to know your heritage so she gave you a Hawai'ian name, Alana. God has brought you back into our lives for a reason. God's reason." Teah blinked, moisture creeping into her eyes.

She clasped Teah's hand. "Thank you for allowing me to come and know my family. For opening your home at the ranch to me."

"Your home," Teah insisted. "Your family, too."

Not everyone, she suspected, as thrilled as Teah that a long-lost cousin had returned to the fold.

"I'm afraid it's my fault Kai has kept away from the house. Me he's been avoiding at Mily's expense this week. Does he feel I'm trying to take his place?" She let the quilt top fall into her lap. "Because I never would, you know. He's the one who belongs. Not me."

Teah took Laney's hand in hers. "You belong or else he would've never told you about his childhood." She nodded at her surprised look. "He told me he shared with you the story of how he came to the family. The story about how we found each other. You could count on one hand the people he's ever opened up to after what he . . ." A pained expression crossed Teah's face. "If you had seen the filth and squalor Pete found that child in."

"How old was Kai when Uncle Pete rescued him?"

Teah's voice trembled. "He was seven, but he hadn't been fed, as best we could tell, in a week. Never been to school, he was skin and bones."

Though the image of Kai once being the vulnerable, little boy Teah described wrenched Laney's heart, the man he'd become resurfaced, never far from her thoughts these last few days.

"Well, he's certainly filled out now." Her cheeks pinked as she realized what she'd let slip.

Teah gave her an amused smile. "So you've noticed, huh?"

She arched her brows and stabbed herself with the needle. "Me and every wahine on the Big Island, I imagine." Wincing, she sucked the blood off her finger.

"First rule," Teah tsk-tsked. "Don't get blood on the quilt top. And you are not every wahine."

She watched Teah wet the end of a long, wooden toothpick with her lips and with a dexterous twist, turned under the edge of a leaf. "Right. I'm the one that makes him uncomfortable."

"Women don't make Kai Barnes uncomfortable." Teah laughed. "He's been surrounded and outnumbered by us most of his life."

Laney sneered at her awkward attempt to duplicate Teah's small, hidden stitches. "So you're saying it *is* just me." She squirmed, trying to fit her posterior more comfortably on the wicker chair.

"You and he are both on a journey to discover what is of first importance." Teah removed the fabric from Laney's hands and took out a stitch. "Kai makes himself uncomfortable." She shot Laney a sharp look. "You and he are a lot alike. High walls. Self-protective barriers between you and the rest of the world."

"Now wait a minute . . ." She and Kai Barnes were nothing alike. Okay, they both had lousy biological mothers, she'd grant Teah that.

"Did Kai tell you it took three hours and multiple chocolate bars before Pete coaxed him out into the light?" Teah squinted at Laney's last few stitches and took them out, too. "That scared little boy has never managed to crawl all the way out from underneath the bed upon which his mother died. He trusts few. He allows himself to love even less." A tender smile played at the corners of Teah's full lips, her dark eyes gentle. "Am I wrong in thinking that about sums up Laney Carrigan, too?"

The bell over the front door jingled. Laney whirled, relieved to see Tutu, clutching the Lokelani quilt like Linus with his blanket, and "Rose" enter the shop laden with a large, canvas bag.

Saved by Mily.

Mily strolled over to Laney, her skinny hips as graceful as the professional hula queen she'd once been and offered her cheek to kiss. Laney obliged with a smile. Mily settled into the circle of chairs and gestured for Mrs. K to join them. "Kiss your mother, too, Laney."

Laney's head snapped. Teah's mouth hung open.

"No, Mother." Mrs. K, her face red with embarrassment, dropped to the chair opposite Laney. "Laney's occupied right now. Busy helping Teah with the shop and learning to appliqué."

A mutinous look entered Mily's usually mild eyes. She crossed her arms.

Teah exchanged a chagrined look with Laney. Swallowing, Laney rose and leaned over to Mrs. K, giving her a quick peck on the cheek. She smelled, Laney noted, like a ginger blossom. A nice, motherly scent.

Mrs. K gave her hand a quick squeeze, the look on her face grateful.

Teah cleared her throat. "What's in the bag, Auntie? What have you two been up to today?"

Mily drew out the scrapbook from the bag at her feet and beckoned Laney. "Come see what we've added."

She peered over Mily's shoulder as her tutu balanced the book in her lap. Mily pointed at the picture of a young auburn-haired man standing beside a youthful Mily in a Polaroid snapshot. "Your grandfather, Jared."

Laney worked her fingers under her hairline. She let out a puff of air.

Mrs. K edged forward on her seat. "What is it?"

She lifted a portion of her hair above her ear, exposing her scalp. "It's easier to spot in the sunshine, but I'd always wondered why someone like me had reddish roots."

Mily clapped her hands in delight. "Jared would've been so pleased to know his only grandchild inherited more than—"

"What's on the next page?" Teah lumbered up, catching the scrapbook before it slid to the floor.

Laney scowled, not so sure she was pleased she'd inherited anything from a man who'd wished to end her life and sent her mother away to exile.

Mily flipped the page where strands of leafy *lauhala*, used in hula skirts, had been tacked. She pointed out various poses of herself performing at luaus all over the islands. Photos followed of Mily and Jared on horseback on a cliff where wild lokelani roses bloomed overlooking the ocean.

"Jared and I got married there." Mily tapped the picture with her finger. "Right on the ranch." Smile lines radiated from her eyes.

Teah nodded. "A beautiful spot for weddings." She patted Mily's shoulder. "Where Elyse dreams of one day bringing couples from all over the world to get married at Franklin Ranch."

Mily shook her head. "Did you ask Jared? I'm not sure he'd approve of strangers on the homestead." She swiveled to Mrs. K. "I forget, Rose. Is that where you married Pastor K?"

Mrs. K's face crumpled. Teah flipped to another page, distracting Mily with reminiscences of family luaus and community roundups in the old days.

"Why are there no pictures of my mother?" Come to think of it, Laney didn't remember a single photograph of her mother anywhere in the house, either. Had Jared in his rage ordered all pictures of his wayward daughter destroyed?

A secret part of Laney had always yearned to know what her birth mother looked like, whether she got her height—or lack thereof—from her mother, whether the curve of her smile resembled Rose.

Mrs. K took the book from Mily's lap and closed it with a snap. "Umm . . ."

Her grandmother smiled. "Rose and I will work on that tomorrow."

The bell jangled again. Teah bustled off to attend to a stout lady with a Texas-sized accent asking for quilt kits. Mily plucked Laney's project from the coffee table and began to take tiny, even stitches.

"Oh, Tutu . . ." She reached for the breadfruit top.

Mrs. K laid a gentle arm on Laney. "It's okay. As long as one of us monitors, I don't think she'll hurt herself. After a lifetime of sewing, she misses having something to do with her hands."

"I'd like to see some photos of my mother." Laney hated the wistful sound in her voice. "To see if I inherited more than red hair from a cantankerous old man."

"Don't judge him too harshly, Laney. In his own way, he felt as betrayed by his daughter as she did by him. In the end, he came to deeply regret his actions."

Laney snorted. "Too little, too late." She cocked her eyebrow into a question mark. "How do you know he changed?"

Mrs. K clutched the book to her chest. "Teah said . . ." She waved a hand in the direction of the New England style white-steepled church down the block from the shop. "At the church, on his gravestone."

Frowning, Laney whispered so as not to upset Mily. "Do you know if they buried my mother there? Or," she gulped. "Did they leave her to a pauper's grave on the mainland?"

Her eyes full of anguish, Mrs. K sank into the chair beside Mily. "Two headstones in the Franklin plot," she mouthed over Mily's folded head.

Laney moved toward the door. "Tell Auntie Teah, I'll be back soon. I have a pilgrimage to make first."

It wasn't often Kai admitted to being nervous. Rounding the side of the lava rock walls of the church, an unfamiliar anxiety squeezed the air out of his lungs as he approached the small cemetery. Under the shade of a candlenut tree, he stopped, taking in the small figure of Laney kneeling between two headstones.

Laney Carrigan and the turmoil she'd created didn't figure into his plan to recover from his own PTSD and Hank's suicide, and turn the ranch back into a profitable enterprise. He grappled with doubts that he could, indeed, save the ranch. Or were his efforts just postponing the inevitable? But ready or not, Laney had come, tearing massive holes in the tapestry of his hitherto well-ordered life.

Especially after more research on his part revealed something he'd begun to suspect from his conversations with her, her veiled attempts to distract him from talking about her writing, her occasional lapses regarding prior assignments.

She'd been smack in the middle of what little mind he had left since Kandahar. He'd thought of her and nothing else in the days since he'd last seen her. Nothing but that soul-stirring kiss with its enticing possibilities of a future he'd sworn would never be his destiny. He enjoyed the ladies, make no mistake, but he'd never allowed anyone to get as close as Laney.

What had he been thinking? That maybe he'd scare her off with the revelation of the genetic curse he carried from his violent, drug-addicted parentage? And after his experiences in Afghanistan, he understood all too well the dark forces that led his friend to take his own life before he proved a danger to others.

He feared the same dark forces within him as well. Problem was, for whatever reason, Laney's arrival seemed to have triggered one of the more insidious symptoms of his affliction. He'd not slept much this week, plagued by insomnia made more acute with wide-awake dreams of sandy beaches, green turtles, and soft mauve lips.

So he'd tried to spend himself, riding the fences, checking the small herd that grazed on the hillside, riding himself and his trusty horse, Muffin, to exhaustion each day. And yes, he'd done his level best to avoid a certain intrepid reporter.

To no avail. Time, he decided this morning, for a new approach. Maybe avoidance wasn't the right tack. Maybe spending more time with Laney, letting the "new" wear off of their relationship, would do the trick. As they got to know each other better, no doubt the passing fascination akin to a shipboard romance, would wear off with time.

Because he wasn't about to start something he had no intention of ever finishing.

Clearing his throat so as not to spook her, he eased open the iron-scrolled gate. Startled at the sound of screeching hinges, Laney pivoted on her haunches and fell onto the grass. At the sight of him, she grimaced, her face flushing.

This was already going so well.

He strode over and offered her a hand. When she placed her hand in his, a small tremor of desire traveled through him. Her eyes widened, but she dropped her gaze as he heaved her upward.

"Mahalo." She dusted off the bottom of her denim, hip-hugging shorts.

And yes, he noticed. Little about Laney escaped his notice. He swallowed. Fences, he scolded himself. Solid boundary lines made for good neighbors.

She glanced at him, a question in her eyes.

"Mrs. K told me I might find you here when I came looking for you at the shop."

She pointed to herself. "You came looking for me?"

His turn to flush, he dug the toe of his Sperry into the turf. "Yeah, thought you might want to go body surfing with Daniel and me today. Surf's calling."

Surf wasn't the only thing calling him, but he shrugged, striving for a nonchalance he didn't feel.

For a moment, silence reigned and he worried after an absence of days she'd refuse his overture of—whatever it was?—friendship. But in the time it took for his blood to congeal in his veins, she nodded.

"Okay."

"You're really going to go?"

She crossed her arms over her royal blue t-shirt—hey, he was a pilot, trained to observe details. "Didn't you just invite me to go or was that my imagination? You know we writers are capable of imagining all kinds of things." The barbed sarcasm of her tone wasn't lost on him.

He deserved that. Kai gave a nervous chuckle, sounding like a braying donkey. He stifled the sound, hand over his mouth. Donkey, he figured, wouldn't have been the word Laney might have chosen.

And as a writer, she could impale him with her words if she chose. She gestured to the tombstone of Jared Franklin. "Did you know him?"

Change of topic. Good thing.

Kai resisted the urge to wipe the beads of sweat forming on his brow. He'd gotten off lightly. She could give as good as she got.

"He lived only a few years after I came into the family. I remember him as a kind, but sad, grandfather figure."

Laney snorted.

He rubbed the symbol of the cross etched at the top, a chiseled stone lei draped around the cross bars. "Mama Teah says he changed after he learned of Rose's death. Surrendered his pride, bowed his knee to God."

"The cross on the headstone resembles the twelve-foot wooden cross on the ranch overlooking the ocean where Mily told me they were married."

A smile flitted across his lips. "After he learned of Rose's death, he insisted on hand hewing the beams himself and erecting the cross as a sign of how he'd surrendered his heart to God. He invited me, a scared, eight-year-old boy, to help him. I remember he told me he had a granddaughter." Kai glanced at Laney's shuttered face. "About my age, he believed. We—mainly him—placed it where it looked across the water to where he hoped his granddaughter would one day see it and return home to her people."

Laney angled her body toward the adjoining headstone. Lokelani Rose Franklin carved into the granite. "His timing stinks. He missed his opportunity to make things right and save Rose's life."

He gripped her shoulder. "My timing's not been great so far this week, either."

Laney's rigid stance softened under the palm of his hand. A teasing smile lifted her cheekbones. "Hate to tell you, Cowboy, but timing *is* everything."

He jammed his hands into the pockets of his blue swim trunks. "Anyway, can we call a truce? For Daniel's sake?"

"Just Daniel's?" She gave him a sideways glance.

Exhaling, he grinned. "Mine, too."

Laney tossed her hair over her shoulder. "In that case, you've got a deal."

7

Kai flopped onto the beach towel beside Laney, her eyes closed beneath her sunglasses, as sleek as a cat in the afternoon sun. A gentle trade wind rustled the bamboo grove that separated the ocean from his bungalow. He shaded his eyes with his hand making sure Daniel stayed out of reach of the lapping, crystal blue waves at the shore's edge.

It had been a great day. One of the best he could ever remember. His favorite nephew—okay, his only nephew—beside him, the smartest, most intriguing woman he'd ever met hanging onto his every instruction—and his waist, too, he recalled with relish—as he demonstrated the proper way to catch waves.

The protected bay, shaped like a crescent moon fallen to earth, was unusually placid for an April day. Perfect for beginner surfing, boogie boarding, or whatever your poison.

He showed Laney how to catch a wave, how to swim out to where the swells were just beginning to break. His hands on her shoulders as the waves slapped at their bodies, he positioned her toward the shore.

"When the next wave comes, lie on your board," he'd instructed. "Kick like crazy and catch it. Feel the push of the wave. Surrender your power to it. Put your arms," he demonstrated. "Over your head. Make the letter *A* with your index fingers."

And the lithe woman who somehow always managed to surprise him did just that. Caught the next wave, gliding all the way in front of the foaming surf to the shore. Her knees scraping the black sand, she stood to her feet, laughing in exhilaration at the ride. Jumping up and down on the beach awaiting his turn, Daniel clapped at his new cousin's victory.

The remains of a quick plate lunch they purchased from the roadside stand on their way out of town awaited proper disposal at the house. Lounging on the towel underneath the aquamarine sky, Kai thanked God for today, a gift, a much better day than any he'd experienced since leaving Kabul three years ago. He flicked a glance over to Laney whose creamy complexion gleamed amidst layers of cocoa-butter sunblock.

His heart did a tango at the thought of how he'd helped apply the lotion to her back. He grinned.

"What's so funny?"

He lay back, his arms folded underneath his head. "Nothing. How'd you like bodysurfing and boogie boarding?" How did she manage to read his mind, gauge his emotions like she did? Was she as aware of him as he was of her?

She flipped over to her belly and propped on her elbows. Her hair slicked back from the ocean water, red tints glittered from the roots of her scalp. "Good. Now I'm a real Hawai'ian? You said a real Hawai'ian—"

"I know, I know. Has to love bodysurfing. You're well on your way, I'd say." A trickle of contentment parted his lips in a sigh. She was scrappy, but strays like them had to be, he reckoned.

Daniel's head, a few feet away, popped up at the sound of their voices. Daniel called for them to admire his architectural masterpiece—okay, the kid actually said "fort." Kai threw up his hand, curling his middle fingers and extending his thumb and pinkie. Daniel returned his *shaka* greeting. Laney cheered him on to add a few more buttresses.

He'd enjoyed watching her interact with Daniel. Her dark head bent over Daniel's as they'd carved a moat around the perimeter of the sand structure. A natural-born mother despite her self-admitted, limited experience with children. A warm, loving woman who deserved a forever home with an emotionally healthy husband, not some damaged cowboy, and plenty of sloe-eyed, happy-faced children.

Kai shook off the unpleasant, intrusive thought. Today was meant for joy not sorrow. Keep it light, Cowboy, he reminded himself. "You trying to turn that Hawai'ian boy's work of art into some medieval monstrosity?"

She placed her hand under her chin. "Nothing wrong in expanding his horizons."

He jerked his head toward the splendor of the Pacific. "Nothing wrong with this horizon."

Truce or no truce, he decided, with Daniel occupied, it was time to switch gears and confront Laney with the truth. He fingered his smartphone lying on the edge of the towel. "Got another email notification this morning from Hoffmann's blog. Post about dodging pirates off the coast of the Seychelles."

She swiveled, avoiding his eyes, and fell back prone.

"I take it 'A. Hoffmann' is a pseudonym for the real writer, Laney Carrigan."

Her lips tightened. "Hoffmann was my mother's maiden name. Different journalistic genre. Different audience."

"Why didn't you tell me it was you who interviewed my buddy Hank? Your pieces were insightful and inspiring."

"My pieces and the accompanying publicity may have ruined any chance Hank Turner ever had for healing."

He sat up. "You made sure Hank got a chance to tell his side of the syndrome, put a human face on a malady the American public barely acknowledges. You brought exposure to the dirty little secrets the military machine prefers to sweep under the carpet."

"Like my father, the brigadier?"

He bit the inside of his cheek. "I wasn't trying to slam your dad, Laney."

She pushed herself up to a sitting position. "He was the one who pulled the strings that got me placed with Hank's unit. That's why the *Herald* agreed to publish the articles when he and I convinced them of the good that could be accomplished." She gave a half-mocking laugh. "Some good for Hank and his widow."

"You did a lot of good, Laney. Thanks to that series, the VA began to offer debriefing geared to soldiers returning home, and counseling for wives and families awaiting their wounded warrior's return. Your exposé spawned valuable research into treatment options for effective and timely interventions."

"Like my grandfather, too little, too late for Hank."

He shook his head. "I've talked to his widow. The guy you captured in your first article before the demons of his fear took over will be forever in print when his children are old enough to understand their dad. I, on the other hand, had seen how shaky he already was before he went stateside. I should've made him get help. Turned to his commanding officer with my doubts about his stability."

"Survivor guilt. For your mom and Hank."

He frowned.

"Understandable, but misplaced. I viewed his files—" at his surprised look "—I have my sources. The brass were aware, recommended counseling, which Hank, once home, ignored."

A relieved feeling loosened some of the kinks in his back. He fixed his eyes on Daniel, keeping track of his whereabouts. "Thank you, Laney, for sharing that with me. I've felt so helpless, so responsible."

She hugged her knees, her eyes on Daniel, too. "You weren't responsible. We make our own choices in life. To seek help or not. In my research, I discovered that the veterans who are able to talk about their experiences heal more quickly."

"Oh, there's no cure for PTSD. It's always there, lurking like a yawning black pit, threatening to swallow you whole."

She gave him a sharp look. "You speak as if you've experienced PTSD yourself."

He shrugged. "Don't let this ruggedly handsome—" He grinned as she made gagging sounds. "—too cool for school exterior fool you." He sifted the black sand between his fingers, bulldozed it with his hand into a mound. "I was never as on-the-ledge bad as Hank, but the black thoughts come sometimes out of nowhere and for no reason."

"Nightmares?"

Kai fought to keep his voice from wobbling. "Not in a while. But the anxiety and rootless fears . . . ?" He flashed her a cheeky grin. "The mood swings and irritability you imagined were a normal part of my sparkling personality."

Her arm fell to the sand beside his. "Teah told me about the financial stresses on you as the acting manager of the ranch in this economy. The anxiety you're feeling could be a natural response to real pressures."

Kai let out a gust of air. "Yeah, everybody believed we'd go under a couple of years ago. The whole island got scared when the tourists stopped coming for a while."

"That was about the time you got home."

"Home was what helped me." His gaze connected with hers. "The soothing sound of the waves. The clean, bracing ocean breezes. The relaxing rhythm, the oneness that comes between a horse and his rider."

"Equine therapy."

He shot her an amazed look. "You've heard of it?"

"Since Hank's death, I've tried to keep up with the latest treatments for PTSD cases. I've read the few scholarly journals on the research so far. A promising course of treatment. Visited a horse farm in northern Virginia where they've met with some success."

His eyebrows curved. "I can't believe you know about it. Read about it. I've studied everything I could get my hands on. There's so little like that here on our side of the world even with the thousands of active and non-active military personnel in the islands. I've dreamed . . ." He dropped his gaze, suddenly shy.

At the water's edge, amid squeals of laughter, Daniel dug his toes into the sand resisting the tidal pull out to sea. Like how he'd felt last week after Pu'uhonua. Before it was too late, he'd jammed his proverbial toes into the black sand. Maybe it was already too late.

Laney's breath hitched. "An equine center? Here at Franklin Ranch? Why Kai, I think that's a wonderful idea. Good for the veterans. An answer to the ranch's financial future." Her smile dazzled him. Addled him at the speed she'd grasped his vision.

"Not so fast. Takes money to get the property up to code. Not to mention the red tape for zoning permits."

She straightened. "You'd need to provide more riding rings. Update the stables and equipment. Get the trails upgraded. Train staff as wranglers and mental health aides." She held her hands, shoulder width apart, her thumb and forefinger in an L, framing the future she envisioned. "A website. Promotional materials."

He laughed. "Whoa, there, cowgirl wannabe. None of that's possible without a serious influx of cash. Not to mention the endorsement and referrals of Veteran Affairs."

"And how does that work with Elyse's dream of making the ranch a wedding destination?"

He chuckled. "I see Mama Teah has been talking. This ranch has plenty of room for everybody's dreams. Ben plans to get in on the act as well, opening his own business to cater those millionaire weddings Elyse has planned in her head."

She sighed. "I think it all sounds wonderful. Who wouldn't want to get married here?" She bit her lip and blushed.

He frowned. "Not me. After what I saw the PTSD do to Hank and his family, I'd never risk—especially with my father's genes running through my veins—putting a wife and children through that."

"Is that what you're afraid of? That the PTSD would bring out some hidden DNA gene for violence? I don't think it works that way. You're nothing like your parents, Kai. I've seen your gentleness with Tutu and your patience with Daniel. I don't believe that about you."

"Believe it or not. I'm not willing to take the risk." He hunched his shoulders. "I've got my hands full running this ranch, trying to keep a roof over our heads. The equine center, like Elyse's wedding fantasies, is just that. Fantasy, seeing as neither one of us has any legal right—"

"Uncle Kai?" A spray of gritty sand heralded Daniel's approach as he shuffled over to them clutching a snorkel mask and fins. "You promised we'd go out to the black rock."

He rose, towering over Laney. "So I did, little buddy. So I did." Saved from a quagmire best left to Teah to explain.

Daniel bounced on the tips of his toes. "Cousin's coming, too, isn't she?"

His eyes surveyed her modest jade tankini. Contrary to the Hawai'ian tourist culture, Kai, brought up to be a good Christian man—a rededicated Christian man thanks to Pastor K—appreciated that while she most definitely to his way of thinking had *it*, she didn't flaunt it. Certain aspects should be off-limits to the viewing public and private for a husband's eyes only.

Not that he was in the market for a wife. He figured he'd made that abundantly clear. "Think you can handle a little underwater exploration?"

She jumped to her feet, putting her hands on her hips. "Bring it on, Cowboy. I can handle anything you care to dish out."

Of that one thing, he was certain.

With Daniel, for safety's sake, encased in a florescent yellow life vest, Laney and Kai kept him between them. They dog-paddled out to a cluster of black rocks at the mouth of the secluded cove to an area Kai assured her wasn't too deep that at any point in their adventure they couldn't stand on their feet. She'd watched in amazement minutes earlier when Kai squirted a stream of baby shampoo onto the mask lens from a travel-size container he'd secreted in his duffel bag.

"What in the world are you doing?"

"Travel tip for a travel writer." He smudged the liquid with his finger along the inner portions of her mask. Trudging over to the water, he splashed it in the waves, wiping the remains away on the leg of his surfer-length blue trunks. "Keeps the masks from fogging underwater."

She tilted her head. "Good to know. Mind if A. Hoffmann quotes you in the next blog?"

He grinned and handed over the mask. "Be my guest."

For a moment, she saw stars, blinded by the grin exposing strong, white teeth and highlighting his firm lips. The tactile memory of the feel of those lips on hers caused her heart to palpitate.

Get a grip, she scolded herself. She donned her mask, adjusting the straps behind her head.

"Coral reef's great here," he promised. "Just be careful not to touch or damage it."

"Not to mention," she interjected, her eyebrows arched, "the damage it could do to bare flesh."

"Right." Smiling, he stroked his chin. His eyes, with the light blue centers bleeding out to darker shades of blue to black, reminded her of the cobalt tidal pools along the beach surrounded by the black lava of the rocks.

"Isn't Daniel a little young for this adventure?"

Kai rolled his eyes. "No, Mother. Hawai'ian kids are practically raised in the water. And besides . . ." He ran a line from a hook on his own personal flotation device to the D ring attachment on the back of Daniel's life jacket. "His Uncle Kai is out to make sure no SARs are needed today."

"Always good to have a professional on board."

Kai snorted. "This professional intends to stay out of the search and rescue business."

Upon reaching the rocks, each of them gave the others a thumbs-up and sank beneath the luminescent surface of the waves. Sun-kissed beams of translucent turquoise filtered to their position. Schools of azure blue fish floated past the coral outcropping.

She didn't know which way to look first amidst the rainbow cloud of tropical sea life. At the sunny yellow tang? Or the comical-looking parrotfish?

Kai led the way around the jagged underwater shoreline. He gestured at the funny, long-nosed butterfly fish and the zebra-striped ones swimming past in a kaleidoscopic blur of movement and motion.

Coming up for air, Kai pointed at the spray of water in the distant horizon. "Spouts." Grabbing hold of the surface of the rock, he lifted Daniel onto his shoulders. Fluttering her fins in rhythmic motions, she rotated her body in the direction of a trumpeting sound followed by a gigantic tail fin wave. The ebb of the water brought her into close contact with his bare shoulder. She shivered.

"A humpback," Kai whispered, his lips against her ear.

Daniel sucked in an excited breath, but remained motionless and silent atop Kai's shoulders.

"I wasn't sure we'd see any this late in the season. Thought they might have returned to Alaska by now. Keep your eyes peeled. Wait and we might get to see the whale breach the water."

Hardly daring to breathe, she inched closer to Kai, steadying herself with one hand next to his on the rock, his chest at her back. Moments later, their patience was rewarded. The magnificent sea creature rose out of the water, arching his enormous body. With a resounding thump that echoed across the waves, he splash-landed into his Pacific birthplace.

Daniel wiggled his body, trying unsuccessfully to reign in his pleasure. "Wow, Uncle Kai."

"Wow, indeed, Uncle Kai," she whispered.

Kai turned, his chin grazing her jaw line. His eyes shone. "Say a prayer. And if we're blessed today, let's stick our heads under the water and see if he's in the mood to sing to us."

Daniel hopped off Kai's shoulders and with the tiniest of human splashes broke the surface of the water. Reinserting her mouthpiece, she followed Kai, diving toward the ocean floor. And then, she heard it.

A series of whistles and screeches. A low groan. Clicks and creaks. Magical. Hauntingly beautiful. Amazing how it traveled over miles of ocean to reach their ears.

Later, when they'd returned to their towels on the grainy, black beach, she thanked Kai for including her in the excursion as she released Daniel from the safety harness. Not an easy task, she soon realized, with an energetic, wiggly little boy.

"Whale make big body, right, Uncle Kai?"

Kai laughed and ran his hand through his short hair, flicking rainbow drops of water.

She glanced up from her vain attempts to towel off a struggling-to-be-free six-year-old. "What does he mean?"

Kai broadened his chest, the sight of his six-pack abdomen rendering her momentarily speechless. "The sounds are made by whales establishing their territory."

Daniel waggled his shaka hand at Kai. "Da whale get choke chicks, brudda."

Kai doubled over. Daniel fell over on the sand, enjoying Kai's mirth.

"Did he just say . . . ?"

"Choke, Auntie Laney. Means much, many." Daniel slapped his own thigh, amused at himself. "Like Uncle Kai."

Kai stopped laughing. "Now wait a minute, little buddy. I do not—"

"Do tell, Daniel." She rounded her eyes at Kai. "I'll just bet he does."

"Mom read me a book about the whales. They know one song and they sing the same song over and over."

She handed him the towel. "Yeah?" And in a singsong mimicry of Teah, chanted, "Just like your Uncle Kai."

Daniel swiped at his face. "I know more songs than one. Wanna hear?"

Kai dropped to his oversized towel. "You're killing me here, man."

Plucking her damp towel off the sand, she took hold of both ends and rattailed it into a twist. Flicking one end in the direction of Kai's exposed back, she whipped it where it landed with a resounding snap against his flesh.

"Ow!" he howled, leaping to his feet. He grabbed one end and yanked, jerking her forward. "You want to play dirty, do you, Laney Carrigan? I'll show you dirty."

At the look on his face, her eyes widened. She let go of the towel and stepped back. Dropping the towel between them, Kai took a step forward.

Despite herself, she couldn't stop the high-pitched squeal that came out from her lips.

His hands on his hips resembling a mini-avenger, Daniel stood by Kai's side. "Screams like a girl, Uncle Kai."

Kai looked at his nephew. His lips twitched. "She is a girl, Daniel."

Glad he'd noticed, she took advantage of his moment's distraction to sidestep and dodge his outstretched hands. Kai made a grab, but he was a second too late. She took off running down the beach.

Snatching up the towel and turning on his heel, Kai gave chase. Daniel followed, whooping and hollering. "We'll get her, Uncle Kai. We'll show her who's the boss."

"No fair," she screamed over her shoulder. Her feet pounded against the sand, splashing at the water's edge. "Two against one." Kai, with his longer legs, gained on her.

"Nobody ever tell you all's fair in love and war?" He called after her within an arm's breadth of reaching her. In a sudden move, he grasped her shoulder and swung her around. Pinning her arms to her side, he bundled her round and round with the towel like the Hawai'ian Spam burrito Teah had served last night.

Spam, like a lot of things, she'd begun to acquire a taste for.

"And which would this be?" she gasped, his hands atop her shoulders. His gaze flickered from her eyes to her mouth. His breathing as ragged as her own. His face, close enough to . . .

Daniel caught up to them. "Got her right where we want her, Uncle Kai."

She cocked an eye at Kai. His hands slid to her waist. She took an unsteady breath.

"Brudda? Is this what you do when you take my son on an outing?"

Kai's head jerked toward the tree line. Daniel waved. Laney's eyes darted to where Elyse in her tourist-friendly aloha wear stood with folded arms. Kai dropped his arms and took a step back. Teah, a coy expression on her face, waggled her fingers. Laney felt like oozing into the sand at the sight of Mily, Pastor, and Mrs. K standing beside her, broad grins on their faces.

Daniel trundled off to greet his mother. With a sheepish look, Kai released her from the straitjacket, spinning her around slowly. Weaving on her feet, she took the towel from him. Raking a hand through his hair, Kai marched up to greet his guests.

Laney draped the towel around her shoulders, noticing for the first time how low in the horizon the sun appeared. A great day. Maybe her best day ever. She cut her eyes toward Kai where he talked with Pastor K.

She'd longed her whole life for extended family, for the 'ohana she'd discovered here on the Big Island. She just hadn't known they came with strings, strings attached to a certain helicopter pilot with dangerous blue eyes. Dangerous to her plans. And to her heart.

No matter what he said to the contrary.

She took a step toward her family, her eyes fixed on Kai. "You're killing me, man," she whispered. "Killing me."

8

Unable to locate the ladies inside the ranch house, Kai followed the sound of their voices past the giant elephant ear plant at the corner of the house, beyond the gnarly, gray-limbed banyan tree, to the open, level patch of land that ended abruptly at the cliff overlooking the broad Pacific. One false move and next stop Maui. As he drew closer, he detected the unmistakable sounds of John Cruz's "Island Style" classic. The sight that met his eyes both pleased and surprised him.

Underneath the hewn wooden cross he'd helped Jared Franklin erect, Mily and Mrs. K endeavored to teach Laney the basic moves of the traditional hula. An apt pupil, Laney's eyes were narrowed in concentration, observing Tutu's every instruction.

"Feet flat on the ground," called Mily, sitting on a bench surrounded by the fragrant wild lokelani rose bushes. Mrs. K's iPod rested beside her. Mrs. K stood shoulder to shoulder with Laney for moral support. Though the older ladies were clothed in casual island capris and sandals, they'd gone all out on Laney's costume for authenticity.

He leaned against the massive banyan tree, not wanting to miss the show. He noted the multiple strands of fragile pīkake around Laney's neck, worn in place of pearls by island brides. His heart did a funny lurch.

Kai was pretty sure Laney had no idea of the significance of that particular lei Mrs. K and Mily probably purchased from the Foodland in Waimea. But he was also sure Teah wasn't the only one with an agenda.

"Knees bent. Displays the hip motion. Side to side," Mily yelled. At Laney's perplexed look, Mily rose to her feet, extended her bony arms and demonstrated the swaying cant of the hip action. "Over the foot you've put your weight on. Like this."

Decked out in one of Mily's old traditional skirts—a loose, rainbow blend of fabric gathered around the waist—Laney raised her arms and attempted to copy Mily's movements to the relaxed, acoustic guitar sounds of Cruz. Amazing, he recognized from old photos, how much Laney resembled Mily at the same age. The leafy wreath garland that encircled her head, the head lei *po'o*, glistened in the late afternoon sun.

Mily strolled behind Laney and straightened her shoulders. "No hunching. Relax shoulders. Relax hands and arms. Not so high." She lowered Laney's extended arms below shoulder level.

She turned her drill sergeant attention toward Mrs. K. "No bouncing, Rose. You know better. And that face?" Mily let out a snort of undisguised disgust. "The face reflects the emotion of the story. And it's not a story about constipation."

Exchanging amused glances, Laney and Mrs. K giggled.

"Tut, tut, tut." Mily clapped her hands. "None of that. Focus, ladies." She frowned, turning Laney's chin in the direction of her flowing left hand.

Mily made a *V* with two of her fingers—and in a move he remembered seeing John Travolta do once in a movie—pointed the *V* inward at her eyes and then jabbed the *V* out toward Laney. "Eyes always follow the lead hand."

The song ran down. Mily gestured to Mrs. K who scurried to hit Play.

The melodic, rhythmic strains filled the air. Her eyes closed, Mily, with her hands in front of her face and as graceful as the undulating rhythm of the waves caressing the sand, began the story with the gesture for "speak." Her arms arched high over her head like the sun. She steepled her hands like a house. She wafted both arms up, one higher than the other.

He wasn't a hula expert, but over the years he'd picked up enough to know that move meant mountains. Mily crossed her arms over her chest and extended them out to where Laney gazed entranced.

Mily's hips stopped. "Now you," she barked, the mini-drill sergeant in play once more. Her hands lifted in front of her face. Laney and Mrs. K obliged the same.

In old Hawai'i, it had been common to compose *mele*—songs—for every occasion. Births, funerals, weddings . . . His breath caught.

And then, he understood the story Mily told with her body.

A story of homecoming.

The arms over her head for sun, many suns, he interpreted. Many mountains crossed. Mily drew her arms over her chest and extended them to Laney and Mrs. K.

Love to you, Laney and Rose, Mily's body sang. Mily brought her hands over her heart. *Love back to me.*

Mrs. K stopped. From a distance, he watched her shoulders shake. She, too, understood Mily's swan song of love. He shrank back under the canopy of the tree. As the song concluded, Mily put them through their paces one more time.

Kai backpedaled, not wishing to disturb the *mana*—spirit—of the moment. He'd wait for the ladies to return to the house in their own time. There was always paperwork to keep him busy until he could speak to Laney.

He sighed, ducking under a low-hanging avocado branch. Piles of paperwork. Another clue when he'd returned from Afghanistan several years ago that something was desperately wrong with Mily who'd always acted as the ranch's accountant. To their dismay, they'd found unpaid, past due notices and the books in a terrible mess.

Letting himself through the screen door off the lanai and taking off his black sneakers, he hurried to the ranch office down the hall from the kitchen. Pushing open the door to the shelf-lined study, he pulled out the leather desk chair and plopped down. He moved the mouse to activate the bookkeeping program. It'd been a long time since the ranch made any profit.

Ten minutes into recording receipts in the computer ledger, his thoughts drifted to Laney. He glanced at the clock at the top of the screen, surprised he'd been able to keep his mind on anything other than her for ten minutes. The corners of his mouth turned up at the memory of Laney's graceful, swaying movements. He scowled at his image in the computer screen.

This would not do. This would not save Franklin Ranch. Maybe his idea to share another part of his life and Hawai'i with Laney tomorrow was a bad idea.

But the notion of giving Laney his bird's eye view of his beloved island refused to leave, teased at the fringes of his mind. That causing her to fall in love with the land of her forebears might cause her to stay, to put down roots.

Unease niggled at his conscience. He squirmed, gripping the armrests of the chair. Was that all he truly was trying to make her fall in love with? For Mily's sake? Not his own?

He set his jaw. For Mily's sake. For Laney's own good.

Kai didn't do the L word. He was shaka fine with his house, his 'ohana, his horse, and the sky. He pulled back his ragged feelings from falling over the edge of a cliff he feared above all else—including losing the ranch.

He'd congratulated himself after the sortie on the beach a few days ago. He'd kept it light. He hadn't given into the temptation that day to kiss her until they both had to come up for air. He'd kept it fun. Daniel had proven a great chaperone. It'd started to get dicey at the end when their horseplay strayed to another level, but—Kai shot a silent thank-you to the ceiling—he'd been rescued by the family.

His heart remained safe. Laney and the feelings she aroused in him corralled behind the fences of his determination. The twinges of fear—that made him want to throw up in the middle of the night tortured by the never-can-be's—told him he needed to stop, to run to the farthest corner of the ranch and stay there.

But the thought of Laney's first sunrise over Kilauea with him as her guide compelled him.

Kai raked a hand over his head. He'd be fine. His emotions were under control. He'd handle the Laney dilemma like he'd handled the other women over the years who'd gotten too close for this cowboy's comfort.

He reached for the next receipt to be logged. Bank statements to be balanced. Bills to juggle. The proverbial robbing Peter so Paul would get paid.

But as long as he followed certain parameters like with his PTSD, the Laney problem was entirely manageable.

And that you could take to the bank.

Laney poked her head around the frame of the study door. "Kai, Mrs. K—" She came to a dead stop on the threshold at the sight of Kai's head across his folded arms.

"Oh, Cowboy . . ." she whispered, her fingers tugging at her pearl earring.

He stirred. She stepped back, determined to beat a hasty retreat. But at the sound of her footfall, his head shot up. He blinked at the sight of her in the doorway. Stretching his arms above his head, he gave her a slow, sleepy grin.

"A guy's got to find his beauty sleep when he can." His eyes teased.

She pursed her lips, giving him a sideways glance. "Some more than others."

He twisted his torso, putting a hand to the small of his back. "You came looking for me?"

She'd come looking for a family. She glided around to his side of the ebony desk. She'd not apprehended until now she might also have come looking for something more.

His face flickered with pain.

"What's wrong with your back?"

He inhaled and let it out through his nostrils. "Occupational hazard for chopper pilots. Long hours in the cockpit hunched over, the constant vibration, not enough seat padding." He gave a short laugh. "It's made an old man out of me."

She placed her palms flat on the bunched muscles beneath his shoulder blades. "Let me make you a young man again."

He stiffened at her touch, but relaxed as her hands kneaded out the knots beneath his black t-shirt. He rolled his head around and from side to side.

"Your neck muscles kinked, too?" She placed her hand on the side of his neck against the telltale pulsation of his heartbeat.

Kai shot out of the chair.

Her hand in mid-air, she gaped at him. "What's wrong?"

Kai put the desk between them. "We're not doing that, Laney."

"Doing what?"

He wagged his finger from himself toward her. "This thing we do, you and I."

She folded her arms. "What thing?"

He let out a huff of air. "You know what thing. We're friends. Nothing more."

She nodded. "Right. Friendly cousins." Laney made a move in his direction.

His jaw dropped and he held up his hand. "Stop right there." His lips poked out. "And we're not cousins."

She cocked her head. "So you've drawn a line in the sand." She advanced, a credit to the brigadier. "What are you going to do if I step over this imaginary line of yours?"

He backed up, his eyes wide with alarm. "Stay over there, I said."

She tapped her big, fuchsia-painted toe over the edge of the rug and smirked. "I had no idea, Kai Barnes, you were such a scaredy cat."

He retreated another foot and crossed his arms over his chest. "I'm warning you, Laney. You'd better behave or . . ."

She leaned her head forward over the invisible divide and batted her lashes. "Or what?"

He rolled his shoulders back. "Or I won't take you on a sunrise copter ride with me tomorrow." He jutted his chin at her and stamped his foot on the koa floor to show her he was serious.

"Umm . . . ." Retracting her foot, Laney, with her finger on her chin, pretended to consider his proposal. "Let me get this straight. We're not friendly cousins, you say." She gave her best round-eyed I-Didn't-Realize-My-Foot-Was-So-Heavy-Officer look.

He retreated one more time, the look in his eyes wary.

She smiled. Sweetly. Barracuda sweet. "Which would make us maybe kissing cousins instead, yeah?"

He growled.

She slipped around him to the door. "Mrs. K sent me to ask if you'd stay for dinner. She told me," Laney laughed. "Because she loved me and she wanted to save my cholesterol levels, she's going to stay and cook her lomi salmon specialty."

She fluttered her lashes at him as he stood in the middle of the room, clenching and unclenching his hands. "And I'd love to go with you tomorrow, Kai."

"We. Are. Not. Cousins," he shouted at her back.

She moistened her lips as she hula'd her way toward the kitchen. "No," she whispered. "But we do kiss. Oh, Cowboy, do we kiss."

9

I still don't see why we had to leave the house at three a.m.," groused Laney. She shoved the brown paper bag of Hawai'ian sweet bread at him. "Here's your breakfast, courtesy of Ben."

Beside her in the cockpit, where the copter rested on the tarmac, Kai smiled that smug, infuriating smile of his and opened the bag. He inhaled and smacked his lips in appreciation. "A real morning person, aren't you, Carrigan?"

She sniffed and settled her bottom in the co-pilot's seat making sure the lap belt and shoulder harness were securely fastened. Over her legs, she repositioned the baby-size Lokelani quilt Tutu—like a wheel stuck in a rut—had insisted she bring with her today.

With the bag clutched in one hand, he fiddled with the instrument panel with the other. "It's a balmy sixty-five degrees outside. The cabin's fully equipped with heat and air. You didn't need to bring that, Laney."

"Tell that to Mily this morning. She and Teah got up with me for a quick cup of coffee—Kai's Kona, Mily calls it—and said I needed to remember my roots when I took to my namesake."

"Ah." He leaned over and fingered the label on the underside of the quilt.

She darted a look at him. "My name, Alana, means . . ."

He gave her one of those looks that sent her heart into overdrive. "Sky. I remember."

To give herself something to look at beside those tidal pool eyes of his, she peered out the panoramic glass vista into the inky black darkness. A full moon hung, refusing to surrender to the morning's light. Was it her imagination or did the stars and the moon gleam brighter and more luminous here on the Big Island?

But then again, maybe it was the company she was keeping these days. "It's dark outside."

"So we'd have time to drive to the heliport, gas the chopper, and get to Kilauea before sunrise." He bit into one of the rolls.

"I thought there'd be other passengers."

"Nope. Just wanted to show you my personal version of Hawai'ian hospitality."

She chortled. "I think you've done your best already to show me the true meaning of aloha, Kai Barnes."

"Now, Laney, you agreed . . ." He arched one brow. "Don't make me 5-oh you."

She rolled her eyes. "This seems like an expensive way to say aloha. Unless this is some pilot perk, can you afford—?"

He crumpled the bag in his hands. "Can't you just say 'Thank you, Kai' so we can be on our way?"

She bared her teeth. "Thank you, Kai. Now get this bird off the ground."

He bowed from the waist. "Your wish is my command."

She flicked her hair over her shoulder. "Hardly."

He ignored her. "Get ready for me to take you on the most spectacular ride of your life." He donned his headset.

"Oh, you've taken me on a ride, all right."

"What?" he called, adjusting switches. He pointed to the headset wrapped around her neck. She complied and found the sound of the rotors blessedly muffled.

"That's better," his voice tinned in her ear as she sensed the aircraft lift off and hover momentarily before gaining altitude and speed.

Her tummy somersaulted and for once, it had nothing to do with the cowboy-cum-former-army-rescue-pilot by her side. She grabbed hold of her seat. "Are you sure this thing has been cleared to fly?"

Kai shot her a wicked grin. "This coming from a woman who floats down the Amazon with former headhunters and chases ivory poachers in Africa."

She snorted. "You call this flying? You just beat the air into submission."

He rolled his eyes.

She didn't let loose her grip on the seat cushion. "How fast are we going?"

"One hundred fifteen knots per hour. A great cruising speed till we reach the lava fields."

She shuddered. "What's 115 in English?"

"That's one hundred and twenty-five miles per hour for you landlubbers."

She shuddered again.

"Relax, Laney. Don't you trust me?"

"Should I?"

His laughter rang in the cabin. She forced a small smile from between her clamped lips. She was glad this copter had the state of the art two-way communicating capacity.

So she could harass the pilot, of course.

He tapped the windshield where streaks of light threaded the April skyline. "Not much to see as of yet. I'll give you the grand tour on the way home." His expression turned solemn. He cut his eyes over to her. "One rule, though."

She tensed. "What's that?"

"Don't try to get out before this whirlybird comes to a full and complete stop."

As he chuckled at her outraged expression, she peered skyward through the wraparound windows, folding her hands in prayer. "And dear God, when you strike down this strutting peacock named Kai Barnes, please don't cause me, this humble servant of Yours, to plummet with him, too."

He laughed out loud. "Always interesting being with you, Laney Carrigan. You keep it real."

She snorted. "Somebody's got to keep that colossal ego of yours grounded."

In response, Kai pressed a lever on the console. Strains of Bobby McFerrin's "Don't Worry, Be Happy" floated through her headphones. At his smirk, she stuck her tongue out at him.

But as they followed the windward coastline toward Hawai'i's Volcanoes National Park, the rhythmic throb of the rotors lulled her into letting go of her death grip on the seat. At first, all she could distinguish of the *terra firma* were glowing, orange bands.

He gestured below them. "Lava flow."

Laney followed the trail of his finger where pulsating veins ranging from papaya to burnt umber thrummed and percolated across the moon-barren landscape of the lava desert. Spurting streams diverging from flaming rivers of fire gushed and cascaded like atomic hot rapids of a searing inferno.

Swooping along, he jerked his head at the spouts of steam rising from the crater beneath them. "Pu'u 'Ō 'ō vent." He nudged the copter forward, soon skimming over the surface of the water.

Plumes of steam rose where the smoldering, liquid rocks met the cooling waters of the ocean, sending glowing, red clouds into the sky. And in that moment, the moon's pale dominion of the night yielded its supremacy to the golden orb of the sun. She caught her breath, unsure where the fiery brilliance of the lava ended and the ascendancy of the other began. He grinned a satisfied—like he'd ordered it just for her pleasure—smile.

"Welcome to Creation," he murmured in a voice as full of awe as Laney felt. "Not a bad way to spend a sunrise. Watching God fashion and shape the world again."

"There was evening and there was morning . . ." she whispered, her eyes glued to the latest forging of land as the first rays of light streaked across the sky.

He lingered a second longer. "A new day."

"'And God saw how good it was.'" She suppressed a sigh. Whenever she was with Kai, life seemed very good.

Better than good.

He turned the chopper toward the coastline. She kept her gaze fixed on the glorious display of the new dawn as long as she could.

The e-ticket crinkled in her pocket. Her hand trailed to finger the quilt. She'd sent off her piece on the city of refuge to her travel editor. As well as a short article geared toward family magazines about sea turtles and snorkeling with children.

Had she at last found the right place to land and put down permanent roots?

She glanced over to Kai, intent on maneuvering the chopper toward home. He gestured for her to observe the silvery-coated, Hershey-like kisses that oozed and dribbled across the terrain.

Part of her longed for a repeat of that kiss at Pu'uhonua.

Part of her was scared to death he would.

She was the scaredy cat now. But had she found the right man to love and trust to never walk away? The L word hovered on the edge of her lips and her heart. The L word brought with it obligations, a commitment to clip the wings she'd spent a lifetime cultivating.

What about her career? Her next big assignment that would put her on the cutting edge of photojournalism?

She nestled into the warmth of the quilt. Perhaps that dream no longer held the allure for her it once had, replaced by deeper longings for stray cats and green-shuttered bungalows surrounded by coffee orchards.

Or maybe she was as mixed up as the signals Cowboy kept sending?

Help me, God. Stay or go? Is there a future here for me? She slid her gaze over to Kai's preoccupied form. *With him?*

Her hand drifted to the escape route wrinkling in her pocket. Go or stay? Fight for what you wanted the most or turn tail and run?

She glanced over her shoulder as rays of rosy pink flooded the sky and came to a sudden decision. She'd email her editor this afternoon and ask for an extension on her departure.

Seeing Laney's rapt face at the sunrise of a new creation had been worth every penny Kai wouldn't get to spend on a new irrigation line for the coffee trees. He'd been praying most of another sleepless night for a way to entice Laney to put down roots and stay. And she'd understood his not-so-subtle suggestion that wings and roots weren't mutually exclusive.

Just like she got him. Fears and all.

Kind of scary sometimes how much she got him.

Approaching the Waipiʻo Valley, he dipped lower over a channel, weaving around the magnificent sea rocks. Laney's breath hitched in wonder as they ascended a mist-shrouded ridge from which a curtain of water cascaded from a hole in the face of the rock. They swooped over emerald green hanging valleys and soared over the precipitous peaks of fluted sea cliffs.

One of the many things he loved about Laney. A man who craved the quiet places, he'd surprised himself over the last few weeks at how much he'd wanted to spend time conversing with Laney, getting her perspective—coupled with her penchant for opinions galore—on every topic under the sun.

He caught the echo of his own thoughts. Loved? Since when? He didn't do that word. He couldn't be in love with Laney. He'd worked so hard not to be in love with anyone.

Friends . . . ? Love was okay between friends, he reasoned. Between family. Like his feelings for his sister, Elyse.

Liar.

His feelings for Laney were nothing like his feelings for Elyse.

Wending his way closer to home, as a special added bonus, he buzzed over the rolling pastureland of the ranch. Judging from the rain-drenched forest, he surmised it had rained in their absence. On his coffee trees, he hoped.

She clapped her hands at the sight of the distant red-roofed ranch house beneath the monkey pod trees and the blossoming grove of coffee plants at his nearby home. He hit a button, causing Brudda Iz's haunting rendition of "Over the Rainbow" to fill the cabin.

Laney smiled at him. He smiled at himself in the windshield. For Mily's sake, he reassured his reflection.

And to show you couldn't upstage the Creator, a double bowed helix of color arched across the sky above the hills to the east of the ranch.

He sent a silent thanks skyward. It didn't hurt to have a divine helping hand on the case, either.

She swiveled, incredulous. "How ever did you manage that, Kai Barnes?"

"I told you two weeks ago you'd come to the right place for rainbows." His chest expanding, he reached for his polarized aviator glasses. "Timing, my dear Laney. Like you said the other day, it's all about timing."

" 'There's a season for everything. And a time for every matter under the heavens . . .' " she quoted.

"Ecclesiastes." He saluted her with one finger against his forehead. "A time to plant. Roots, Laney girl."

"A time to embrace healing and to mend," she responded with a pointed look in his direction.

He decided to ignore her unauthorized excursion into his psyche. Bidding a reluctant farewell to the rainbow melting amidst a flood of sunshine, he headed toward the heliport. Time for a change in topic.

"You know your Bible. Sounds like Rose left you with good people. Talked to your dad since you got here?"

She shifted in her seat, her eyes dropping to the toes of her Nikes in the floor of the cockpit. "No."

He blinked, angling his head at the strange sound in her voice. "Don't you think you ought to?" He threw her a teasing grin. "Ease his mind you've not been devoured by Hawai'ian serial killers?"

She glared at him. "Since when did you become my keeper?"

He shrugged and made a note to himself. Dad—a touchy subject.

"Besides," she averted her face toward the lush, green slopes below. "He knows where I am and how to reach me. If he wanted to."

"I was just saying—"

"I'm just saying he doesn't want to. He's busy with his new wife, Wendy . . ."

She said the name of her stepmother with an expression reserved for changing diapers.

"You don't like her?"

She grimaced. "She's okay. I'm not selfish enough to wish for my dad to spend the rest of his life alone. But the speed at which he remarried? After all those years of moving around the world with my mom having to say good-bye to church friend after church friend, he marries a woman—" her voice rose "—only a few years older than Elyse, mind you. And suddenly he throws over a career he's spent a lifetime building and retires?"

"Maybe he believed it was time to gather stones even rolling army ones?"

She scowled. "What happened to a time to mourn?"

He'd know in the future, Kai vowed, to leave this topic alone.

"And there's the new stepson . . ." Her agitation betrayed her escalating discomfort.

He scrutinized her, surprised at the tinge of bitterness in her usually upbeat voice.

"The son he never had. The son he always wanted, but instead, he got me. The little brown baby left on his doorstep." Her fist clenched on top of the quilt.

His eyes widened. "Laney." He touched her arm. "I'm sure your father doesn't feel that way."

"More like a time to scatter stones in his mind." She grunted. "Who do you think sent me on this mission of discovery?"

Her shoulders hunched. "When I was twelve and helping my mother pack the house for another transcontinental move, I accidentally found a copy of the adoption application papers they'd filled out years earlier. They'd checked the box for 'Boy Preferred'."

"Perception isn't always reality, Laney. I think maybe you've read way too much into it than your father or mother ever intended." He stroked her petal-soft cheek, trying to reassure her and rewarding himself with an impulse he'd denied himself all morning.

And then again, he swallowed hard, sometimes perception *was* reality.

He found himself unable to look away from the little girl lost look on her face. "When you came into their lives, and your dad gazed into those big, coffee-brown eyes of yours, it was probably love at first sight and a case of 'a time to keep.'"

She stared at him, an uncertain look passing across her features. But she relaxed against his hand. "How do you do it for a man of such few words, Cowboy?"

He withdrew his hand, steadying his control over a bumpy patch of air. "How do I do what?"

"Always know the right thing to say to make me feel better."

He could've asked her the same question.

Laney's clenched posture loosened a notch. Her lips curved in a weak smile. But still, a smile. "Okay, I'll give him a call later. I needed to talk with him about something else anyway." Her hand opened on top of the quilt.

Hovering over the helipad, he stuck the landing as smoothly as the liftoff.

"Your permission to unbuckle and disembark the aircraft, Captain Cowboy?"

How he did love the light in her face when she looked at him. A look just for him?

Kai pushed back the Bose headphones and allowed the rotors to wind down. "I never made it to captain." He plucked her earphones off to dangle around her neck.

Mainly for an excuse to feel the silken threads of her hair against his fingers, he rubbed a wisp of her hair between his thumb and forefinger before tucking it behind her ear. "But flattery could earn you another ride next week to those waterfalls you wanted to check out. Maybe chase some more rainbows for real, A. Hoffmann."

He grinned at her, mentally justifying how he could always dip into his rainy day fund.

Make that a rainbow fund in Laney's case.

10

There followed for Laney idyllic days—days like a fragile dream. A dream come true of family, belonging, and roots. Question was: Should she lose herself in the moment or wait for the other flip-flop to drop?

Because sooner or later in her experience, reality had a way of intervening in the most wonderful of rainbow dreams. Nothing, not even home, remained forever.

A. Hoffmann's editor hadn't been thrilled to postpone the trip to Jakarta, but Laney Carrigan's travel editor had been pleased with her short articles about her Hawai'ian adventures including surf lessons with Daniel, courtesy of Kai. Even Ben did his part to educate her to the culinary delights of the Big Island, starting with a tour of a pineapple plantation and behind-the-kitchen-door scene at the Moana.

She spent her days doing what she could to lighten Kai's workload at the ranch. He'd reluctantly agreed to let her help with the exercising and grooming of the horses.

"Dad's last post was D.C.," she explained. "And Virginia's horse country. After Mom died, I spend a fair amount of time doing my own version of equine therapy."

"English saddle?" His lip feigned a sneer of paniolo arrogance.

"Don't you worry about me." She poked his Stetson back on his self-assured head. "I can scoop poop with the best of 'em."

"I know," he said with a wicked gleam in his eye. "I read your fluffy kitten post on Hollywood celebrities."

When she reached for the pitchfork stuck in a hay bale, laughing, he beat a hasty retreat.

Each Sunday, Ben, Daniel, and Elyse made a day of it at the ranch with the family following the service at the little white-steepled church in town. Kai appeared to accept her presence in his life and the family's. His face more relaxed, his eyes no longer looked as haunted. And he'd shared what Pastor K had meant in his life since his return from war.

Her respect and admiration for Pastor K grew, as she noted the love and devotion in his eyes when he picked up Mrs. K from her duties at the ranch each evening. A devotion that caused an ache in her own heart as she wondered if she'd ever find that kind of love in someone's eyes for her. So far, her track record wasn't so good, at least in regard to her biological mother. Laney appeared all too easy to walk away from and forget.

Pastor and Mrs. K also reminded Laney of her dad and mom and . . . her dad with Wendy. She'd had a long, overdue conversation with her dad, some nagging childhood questions answered easing a piece of her heart. There'd also been a flurry of emails between her and some of her dad's Pentagon buddies.

This Sunday, she took special pains with her dress before church. Not that Sundays, like the other six days on the islands, were anything but casual. Still, it was hard to break the traditions of a lifetime. Not to mention a certain cowboy who never missed a service. She contented herself with a flowing, pink sundress, winding her hair into a neat chignon at the nape of her neck. She stood back, her hand fondling the gold cross at her throat, to survey the result.

Not fluffy kitten material exactly. But it would do. The best Laney Carrigan could do.

She followed the Chings, Teah, and Tutu, carrying the quilt along with her Bible, into the small, koa-pewed sanctuary. Once again, she found herself answering the inquisitive questions of her grandmother's old friends as well as the younger families who continued to farm this region. She answered their questions in the age-old way she'd observed the Hawai'ians employed to establish a connection, a shared history with each other by way of the all-important family ties.

I am Laney, she'd say, *daughter of Rose, grandchild of Jared and Miliana Franklin*.

When it came to more probing questions regarding the place Laney considered home, she fell silent, made polite excuses, and drifted away.

She'd come to love the peace contained within the church's walls and the walls themselves, painted with Bible stories by long-ago missionaries—a distant Franklin perhaps?—in an endeavor to share their faith with a then-illiterate people. Daniel and the lion's den. Noah's ark. Her favorite, Moses in a basket among the bulrushes.

The old organ, in a life struggle against the humidity of a tropical climate, struck the chords of the opening hymn. Out of the corner of her eye, she observed Kai slip into the pew across the aisle from them. He looked tired today, she thought, and wondered why. Wondered what images from a dry, barren land haunted his sleep in the land of abundant water. He'd not—and that seemed significant—chosen to share that part of his past with her.

Pastor K mounted the pulpit with a fire in his eye, an intensity on his mocha brown face. He read from the text of Mark about a man who came to Jesus with a withered hand. "All of us come to the foot of the cross with our own unique disabilities and dysfunctions. Physical, emotional, relational, or spiritual."

His eyes scanned the congregation. "Don't be afraid to bring to Him your fears and your anger, the root of bitterness, your guilt at moral failure, or the sorrow of your loneliness. But first, you must come."

She stole a look across the aisle and found Kai's eyes on hers, his mouth pulled downward. He studied her with a searching scrutiny before facing forward again.

"Come with expectancy," Pastor K cajoled. "The man with the withered hand had an aching need for God to do something, anything to make him whole."

Kai's head went down into his hands, propped upon his knees. She longed to make him better. She knew only God could restore to Kai and to herself the gaping, empty places in each of their hearts.

"Jesus told the man to stretch out his hand and his response was obedience. He stretched out his hand and his hand was restored." Pastor K gripped the edges of the pulpit. "In the midst of our disability, we find His divine ability. He comes to us with grace and healing."

She let the words soak into her own parched soul, her longings for a forever home. Her desire to be there for her grandmother. Her yearning for a true love.

"Guilt meets His forgiveness," Pastor K promised. "Confusion meets His peace."

She peered down the pew at Mily's serene countenance.

"Loneliness meets His companionship. The lost," Kai's head popped up. "Find direction."

Pastor K gestured for the organist to play. "What is withered in your life today, my friends? What is hurt and wounded? Is there a need for restoration, *ho'oku'kahi*, reconciliation, in your relationships? Come," he beckoned. "Do not delay. *E ho'i mai*, come home. Your *pilialoha*, your beloved, awaits."

At the closing strains of the final hymn, she watched Kai hurry away only to be caught at the door by Pastor K. With the Chings retrieving Daniel from children's church and Teah and Mily engaged in an animated conversation with a couple she recognized as neighbors, Laney slipped out of the pew and made her way over to the mural of baby Moses.

"He's always been my favorite."

She glanced over her shoulder to find Mrs. K at her elbow. "Mine, too. I've spent a lot of time over the years thinking about him. Identifying with him." She gave a short laugh. "Abandoned in a basket or in my case, a car seat. Maybe he came with a quilt, too?"

Mrs. K bit her lip. "All his life in God's hands, though." She pointed at one end of the drawing. "His new, adopted mother bathes just there on the other side of the reeds." Mrs. K sighed. "And there on this end," she gestured. "His sister sent by his mother to watch to see him safely into Pharoah's daughter's arms. A woman who can protect him. A woman who can provide for Moses what his own mother, Jochebed, cannot."

She angled toward Laney. "Can you not see it as the ultimate act of love?"

Laney stiffened. "Are we talking about Moses or me? Gisela Carrigan found a sick, asthmatic, undernourished infant. What sort of woman walks away and forgets her own child?"

Mrs. K gave her arm a light squeeze. "A desperate one?"

Her lips thinned. "I'd have loved to be a fly on the wall when Moses met his birth mother for the first time." She turned her back on the mural. "Something it doesn't look like I'll ever get the opportunity to experience."

"Laney . . ."

She wrapped her arms around the woman. “Don’t mind me, Mrs. K. This ‘ohana stuff dredges up things I thought I’d overcome a long time ago.”

Mrs. K took hold of Laney’s chin, looking deep into her eyes. “I sense you’re at a turning point, Laney. A *huliau*. But I fear until you do, *ho‘oponopono*, and set things right, you will never be free of this pain and find God’s best for you wherever He leads you. Let go of the blame. Forgive your mother, I beg of you. Embrace what she gave you.”

“I’m working on that, Mrs. K. I want to stay here for Mily’s sake. But long-term?” She cut her eyes at the foyer, gazing after Kai’s retreating, broad-shouldered back. “There are extenuating factors to consider.”

Mrs. K patted her hand. “I understand, honey. Maybe better than you know. But I’m keeping both of you in my prayers. *Pule*. You can add that word to your Hawai‘ian family dictionary.”

She smiled. “You’ve been a true friend to this mainland outcast, Mrs. K.”

Mrs. K drew her in, her arms tightening. “I’ve always been your friend, Laney, and I always will be.”

Laney stayed to have lunch with Pastor and Mrs. K, who’d promised no Spam in a can. After lunch, Pastor K retired for a quick nap. She and Mrs. K lounged on the parsonage lanai as Mrs. K examined Laney’s latest handiwork on the breadfruit pillow top.

“You’ve finished the appliqué.” Mrs. K held the less than perfect stitches to the afternoon light. “You’ve made remarkable progress in such a short time.”

Laney leaned against the white wicker settee and sipped her tea. To make it fun, Mrs. K had propped a tiny, pink parasol at the edge of the glass. "No TV at the ranch. Mily goes to bed early. Teah or I rotate night duties. Teah tells me the next step is to make something called a quilt sandwich and do this echo thing she showed me to sew the layers together. I get a lot done in the wee hours of the night."

She gazed at the lokelani rose bed in the yard. "Too much time to think. To wonder what's going to happen in the future, to me and to Mily."

"No problem with thinking," Mrs. K nodded. "As long as you don't let it drift into worry. Time alone is also good for prayer." She cocked a look in Laney's direction.

"Yes, Mother. I know, pule," Laney teased.

Mrs. K flushed. "I did not mean to—"

She slapped at a mosquito. "No worries, as Kai would say. Be happy."

Mrs. K draped the quilt top on the whitewashed ottoman. "I pray for your happiness, Laney. Truly I do."

She blinked back sudden tears. "I am, Mrs. K. Maybe happier than I've ever been. And it scares the lava out of me."

"Happiness that lasts," Mrs. K placed a hand over her heart, "in my own experience must begin here with peace between God and yourself."

"*Na'au*. Heart . . ." Laney sighed. "That's the part that's the most confused."

Mrs. K's eyes crinkled. "Men are slow creatures, Laney. A sad, but true fact. He'll catch up."

Laney laughed.

"Give him and the Lord time to do His work in both of you."

"How did you get to be so wise, Mrs. K?"

Mrs. K's faded brown eyes teared. "By making so many mistakes."

After another helping of *haupia*, a creamy coconut pudding, Mrs. K volunteered to run her back to the ranch. They returned home to find Teah wringing her hands, Daniel clinging to his mom and Mily infinitely worse.

"What's happened, Auntie?" Laney cast a look around the living room as Mrs. K rushed to Mily's side. Ben dabbed at one corner of the Lokelani quilt with a sponge.

Mily jerked away from Mrs. K. "When is Jared coming? When is Jared coming home?"

Teah's lips trembled. "When she lay down for a short nap, she was fine. But she awoke like this. Her coordination's not so good. She spilled her coffee on the quilt. And . . ." She burst into tears.

At Mily's agitated pacing, Laney shot a fearful glance to Mrs. K who'd followed Mily to the other side of the room. Mily craned her neck out the bay window watching for Jared in the driveway. Laney clutched the quilt while Ben made valiant attempts to blot out the light brown stain. She flipped the corner over to the label and traced her name, Alana, with her fingertip over the swirling, cursive letters.

"It's called a catastrophic reaction." Mrs. K held out her hand to Mily. "Won't you sit, Mother?"

Mily savaged the assembled group with a scathing look. "When is Jared coming home? Where is Jared? What have you done with him? With my quilt?"

"What's wrong with Tutu, Mama? Who's she calling for?"

Elyse bent her head over Daniel. "Hush, honey. It's okay." But the look she sent Laney said that it was anything but okay.

Ben looked up from his ministrations on the quilt. "Maybe you better take Daniel to the kitchen for a while, Elyse." She nodded and, her arm around the frightened little boy, departed.

Teah sank onto the sofa beside Ben.

"Here, Mother," Mrs. K continued as if she'd not been rejected a moment before. "Sit in the chair by the window where you can see Father come home from the barn."

Mily calmed a fraction, allowing Mrs. K to seat her. "Riding his black stallion?"

Teah's voice wobbled. "Shouldn't we tell her he's . . . ?"

Mrs. K shook her head. "These types of outbursts are usually triggered by too much information or stimulation for her disoriented brain to sort through all at once. The memory is a complex and sometimes contradictory organ. Her need for her husband expresses her search for something she feels is lost. Her memory of Jared Franklin is stronger than her memory of his . . ." She leaned over Mily, smoothing her snow-white hair from her face. "I will take care of you, Mother. It's going to be all right. I will take care of you."

Mily's constricted face relaxed at the soothing touch of Mrs. K's fingers.

Teah slumped. "I suppose we should be grateful we've had the old Mily as long as we did. God's grace for you, Laney, these last three weeks to get to know Mily before she . . ." She put her hand over her mouth to cover the quivering of her lips.

With the quilt in hand, Laney approached her grandmother, kneeling at her feet. "It's going to be okay, Tutu." She draped the quilt over the old woman's knees. "See, Ben erased the stain. Good as new." She rested her hand on the sleeve of Mily's petal pink robe. "I won't leave you, I —"

Mily flung off her hand, a frightened look in her eyes. "It was you!" She jabbed a finger in Laney's face. "You ruined my quilt."

Her shoulders tightened. "No, Tutu. I didn't. I didn't."

Mily's brows furrowed and her nostrils flared. "She stole it and ruined it." She stuck her face inches from Laney's, venom shooting sparks out of her eyes. "Who are you? What are you doing in my house?"

She reeled back. "It's me, Tutu. Laney."

Mily shook her head from side to side resembling a frenzied dog.

"It's Alana, Tutu. Rose's baby."

"Rose's baby is gone," Mily shrieked. "Rose's baby is gone. My quilt is gone." She shoved Laney backward.

"Mother," Mrs. K grabbed at Mily's flailing hands. With a strangled cry, Laney scrambled out of harm's way.

Ben jumped to his feet to assist Mrs. K. Horrified, Teah heaved herself upward. "Auntie Mily," she cried. "Stop. Don't do this."

Mily writhed. "Get away!" She jutted her chin at Laney who clung to the door frame. "You've ruined everything. Get out of my house!" She dropped her face into her hands, sobbing. "Make her leave, Rose. Make her go away. She ruined everything."

Turning on her heel, Laney raced for the door, not bothering to retrieve her sandals or respond to Mrs. K and Teah's cries to wait. Blinding tears pouring down her cheeks, she bolted without thinking, without stopping, straight into the bamboo grove.

Anguished sobs choking her breath, she plunged headlong into the dense jungle, driven by an overpowering urge to escape. She ran until a stitch in her side left her gasping for breath. But she couldn't go back. There was no going back.

The leaves slapping her cheeks, the sharp lava rocks cutting into her bare feet, she wondered if perhaps her mother, Rose, once fled along this same path. If Rose had felt as driven from her home, rejected and unloved as her daughter did today.

But like the humpbacks who returned home each season, Laney burst into the open not twenty feet from Kai's front door. She stopped under the shade of a tamarind tree to catch her breath, willing the raking sobs to quiet.

Sanctuary? With Kai? What was she thinking? Showing up on his doorstep like some woebegone . . . She stepped back when a phone rang inside the house.

The front door flung open. Kai vaulted off the porch to the ground, the phone in his hand. His face tense and . . . Scared?

Laney shook her head. She'd probably imagined scared, projecting her own jumbled emotions on him. She retreated another surreptitious step toward the rainforest.

Striding toward his truck, his eyes darted in her direction at the flicker of motion. "She's here," he barked into the phone, clicking OFF. Without losing a beat, he veered toward her.

And now, Laney realized, there was nowhere left to run.

11

Panic-stricken when Teah called and told him what happened, Kai's first thought had been to search the beach or follow the road to town until he spotted her. His relief to see her standing in his own front yard under the tree that used to hold the Hayashi children's swing had been so profound as to almost drop him to his knees.

Then, he noted the streaks of blood on her arms. Observed the tear tracks salt-dried on her cheeks. Her swollen, pain-filled eyes gouged his soul. He rushed forward and enfolded her within his arms.

"Laney." Her hair smelled of pīkake. Just this once, he promised himself, he'd comfort her. And allow her to comfort the hole inside him.

She burrowed her face in the fabric of his old polo. And he noticed how perfectly her petite form fit within the circle of his arms. How the top of her head fit at just the right spot into the hollow underneath his chin.

Her body convulsed with the lingering remnants from sobbing too long alone. "Sh-she doesn't remember who I am, Kai. She's forgotten me, too."

A shudder went through him. Her arms wrapped around his waist.

"I'm so tired of being everybody's mistake," she whispered.

Kai pulled back so he could see her face. He nudged her chin with his finger. "You were never a mistake."

Her knees wobbled, as weak as a newborn foal. Scooping her into his arms, he carried her into the house and out to the lanai where the sun blazed a molten gold path to the edge of the horizon. Settling her into the rattan love seat, he winced at the condition of the soles of her feet.

Closing his eyes, he placed a gentle kiss on her cheek. "I'm going to get some water and clean those cuts. It's not going to be fun."

She leaned her head upon the backrest, her eyes fixed on the sunset. "I'm tougher than I look. Survivors like me just keep going and going and going. From abandonment to cancer to Alzheimer's and rejection . . ." Her body jerked on a sob.

Kai retrieved a basin, cloth, and water from the kitchen. He prayed the beauty of her homeland would seep into her soul in this hour of her need, healing and restoring. The depth of his feelings for her shocked him into silence as he gathered his first-aid supplies. His feelings deepened every hour they spent together. The part of his heart he'd closed off frightened and beckoned him at the same time.

He returned to the lanai to find Laney's first Hawai'ian friend curled in her arms and offering an intuitive solace only Kolohe could provide. After a moment's annoyance with the stray, Kai recognized the stupidity of his jealousy at a cat in a place the secret part of Kai longed to be, too.

She bit her lip to keep from crying out when she slid her feet into the lukewarm water of the basin.

"You don't have to play the hero for me." Kneeling beside her, he dabbed at the cuts on her arm. "You're already the bravest person I know."

She tilted her head. "Me?"

"You came here, didn't you? To reach out to people you'd never met. Offering your heart and all the wonderfulness that is Laney Carrigan."

She laughed and touched the top of his head. "You're the hero. Just can't help rescuing people, can you?"

His chest rose and fell. He leaned forward, a hair's breadth from her face. Her mouth parted.

But releasing her hand, he backed away. "Don't get the wrong idea, Laney. I'm nobody's hero. Least of all yours."

Her face shuttered. She cast a long look toward the mauve clouds lining the sky. "I've probably stayed too long as it is. I've stayed longer than I intended. Longer than any place since Mom died."

A knot in his stomach formed. "You're leaving?"

She kept her gaze trained on the sunset, looking everywhere but his eyes.

Hoping for a rainbow?

She shrugged. "I told Teah about it. I have another assignment, a big one. One I've been working toward for months. I should've flown out weeks ago."

His heart lurched sideways, swaying like a disjointed hula. "I thought you'd come to stay, to get to know the family."

She fidgeted, darting a look at him. "I am. I did. But the timing of this . . . Mily . . ."

He sank into a chair across the lanai. Safer over there.

She cocked her head, listening to the noises of the dusk, the ever-present chirping of the geckos. "It's an opportunity of a lifetime."

Kai narrowed his eyes and gestured at the upland forest. "This is a life, Laney. You'd be missed."

Her look sharpened. "Would I? Who would miss me, Kai? Would you?"

Kai drummed his fingers on the wooden arms of the chair. "Mily and Teah. Daniel and Elyse. We'd all miss you."

"What do you think I should do, Kai? Stay or leave?"

His fist clenched. He refused to meet her searching gaze. "I think you should do whatever you want to do, what God tells you to do."

"What's God telling you to do, Kai?"

He got to his feet in a quick, jarring motion. Restless, he moved over to the steps. "I'm going to save this ranch and this family. I'm going to enjoy the peace and serenity of my life."

"Alone." Her voice sounded tired, sad. A sadness, his fault. A sadness for her own good, from which he wouldn't try to rescue her.

He perceived the statement in her voice, not a question. He nodded, peering into the deepening night. "Where?" he whispered.

"Where what?"

"Where is your assignment?" At a sudden, uncomfortable thought, he wheeled. "I'm assuming this is a Laney Carrigan piece, not an A. Hoffmann one." He'd reread the Afghanistan articles Laney had filed. Imagining her dodging snipers and IEDs made him physically ill.

"Jakarta."

His eyebrows rose. "But you'll be back after you finish the travel guide or article or whatever, right?"

She ran her fingers over a purring Kolohe.

He frowned at the lucky, stupid cat.

"If I can. It's going to be a long assignment."

"Several months?"

"Several years."

He made a growling sound in the back of his throat. "What about Mily? You're going to get her hopes up, make her come to depend on you and then vanish out of her life?"

Laney set her jaw. "She doesn't remember me anymore. Last person in her memory, first person out. It won't matter one way or the other to her. Like you, she'll get over it."

"She's having a bad day, Laney. She'll be better tomorrow."

"Not that many tomorrows left for her memory, Kai, and you know it. Might as well get out while I can."

He released an explosive breath. "You sure sound an awful lot like that birth mother you claim to despise."

She surged to her feet, dumping Kolohe on the wooden deck. He landed on his paws. She winced as her yet-to-be-bandaged feet made surface contact.

"Doing everybody a favor. Especially you." Her nose crinkled. "You and me, fluffy versus stray, roots versus wings. Ridiculous, huh?"

That statement was best left alone. The silence stretched between them, broken only by the shrill crowing of the mynah bird that called his property home. "There's that much to tell about Jakarta that you've got to stay several years?"

"Not just Jakarta. I'll be going into the interior and living in a remote village."

He crossed his arms. "No internet access I'm betting. How do you plan to get your stories to your editor?"

She remained silent.

"What would be of interest to travelers in a primitive region populated by militant guerrilla factions and . . . ?" His eyes grew enormous. His gut twisted. "Tell me you're not planning to infiltrate a group of Indonesian extremists, Laney Carrigan."

"Laney Carrigan isn't. Laney Carrigan writes, as you so eloquently pointed out a few days ago, fluff pieces. A. Hoffmann writes reality." She jabbed at her face. "You forget I'll blend in. And I've been studying the dialect for months."

"Does your dad know what you're planning? Still trying to prove to your dad you're as good as the son he never had?"

Her eyes blazed. She squared her shoulders.

Kai shook his head, unable to stop a grisly dread of Laney captured and alone at the hands of bandolier-clad terrorists. "Unacceptable risks, Laney. Way too dangerous."

She snorted. "This from a man who makes his living flying over erupting volcanoes." She stomped over to where he stood, leaving a tiny trail of bloody footprints. "A man too scared to open his heart to what God might have in front of his stupid, stubborn nose."

"My way nobody gets hurt."

She angled her neck to face him, toe-to-toe against him, all up in his space. "Least of all, you."

"I know what I'm doing."

"So do I," she countered.

"I'm in control at all times."

"Thought that was God's job. And maybe that's what's wrong with the both of us."

He clenched his teeth. He didn't ever want to leave this place.

She couldn't wait to.

"When will you leave?"

Her shoulders lifted and dropped. "A few days. A week at most."

"After I bandage your feet, I'll take you home."

"Not home." The look she gave him almost broke his heart. "But you can take me to the ranch."

Kai's prediction proved correct. Mily awoke in a better, if more fragile, state of mind the next morning. Mrs. K instituted household changes. All activities were to be posted daily on the fridge as a point of reference for Mily—for as long as she retained the ability to read and comprehend.

Mrs. K planned outings for the morning hours, Mily's best hours of the day. Her meals were served on a large, white plate set on a bright, orange raffia mat with utensils and cups designed for the disabled or those losing muscle skills. Mily greeted a wary Laney the next day as if they'd only just parted and amicably at that.

Cutting back on her research trips, she resolved to spend the remainder of her time with Mily. Alongside Mily on the sofa, Mrs. K on the other side, they'd sit companionably, hand in hand. Unable to deter Laney from rescheduling her flight, Teah, with the family's help, decided to throw Laney a going-away aloha luau and invite close friends and neighbors.

Aloha, good-bye.

The story of her life. One goodbye after another. She'd hoped this trip would be the start of a long hello. But somewhere in the journey, she'd foolishly started yearning for so much more.

She was determined to finish the small breadfruit cushion project now encased in a wooden hoop for quilting if it killed her. Or her fingers. Whichever came first. Mrs. K lent a hand in one section when Laney's eyes watered from hours of concentration.

"Am I doing this right?" Laney asked as Teah emerged from the kitchen where Ben organized the evening's buffet. She'd watched them dig the earthen pit and lower the ti-wrapped pig into the smoking oven before shoveling sand and fronds to enclose the heat.

Her glasses perched on the end of her nose, Teah examined the arched, echo stitches radiating from the curves of the breadfruit design resembling ripples of water on a pond. Or the bow of a rainbow.

"Fine for a beginner. You get better next project, yeah?"

"Thanks, but I think I've been insulted." Laney wasn't sure how a next project would work in the jungles of the Indonesian archipelago. If she'd stayed though, her next project might've been a replication of the green sea turtle on Teah's shop wall.

Or one day another baby-size Lokelani quilt for a child with amazing blue eyes and creamy brown skin?

She shook herself. Futile line of thought. No sense in daydreaming the impossible. No use trying to recapture a moment that meant more to her than to Kai.

"No, Laney. Good work." Teah pointed to the section on which Laney and Mrs. K collaborated. "Good as the work Rose did on her first project with the Lokelani quilt."

Sure enough. She glanced over to the baby quilt Mrs. K had convinced Mily for once to leave behind as they made their daily trek to the languid waters of Kai's cove. For the first time, she experienced a rush of pleasure to be compared to Rose.

Teah patted her knee. "We'll miss you. Kai's got a burr in his boots. There's so much I need to tell you." She sighed, lines wrinkling across her forehead. "I wish . . ." Her head swiveled at the sound of a truck in the driveway.

Laney, stupid idiot that she knew herself to be, didn't have to turn her head. She'd long ago learned to distinguish the sound of that lone engine winding its way past the house toward the barns.

She wondered if he'd have the guts to tell her good-bye before she left. If he'd avoid her at the luau tonight.

The clock's ticking, Cowboy.

And not just ticking. Booming . . . Tolling . . .

"Uh, Laney?"

Laney jolted at the sound of his voice in the doorway.

His eyes looking bloodshot and stubble shadowing his jaw line, Kai fingered the suede brim of his Stetson. He cleared his throat and shuffled his feet.

"If you two will excuse me, I'm sure Ben is longing for my *poi* Spam recipe for tonight." Teah scooted with surprising speed past Kai.

Laney's cheeks reddened.

At the uneasy silence, he inserted a finger between the collar of his plaid Western shirt and his neck. "I wanted to see if you'd take one more trail ride with me this afternoon."

"Why?"

He ran a hand over his face. "I've not been fair to you from the get-go—"

"Ya think?"

He flushed. "You've got to make everything so . . ."

"Difficult?" She sniffed. "How about honest?"

He drew a deep breath. "I think you deserve to know what happened to me in Afghanistan."

She straightened. "Kai, you don't have to—"

"I want to. So you'll understand and not leave here angry with me." He rammed the hat on his head. "I wish you wouldn't leave here at all," he muttered to the air between them.

"If wishes were horses, we'd be riding rainbows in the sky."

"Please, Laney," he whispered, an earnestness coloring his face. A look smoldered in his eyes, darkening the blue of his pupils.

Why not? her treacherous heart responded. Why not seize the time with Kai while she could?

"Okay, Cowboy." She swallowed. "I'll go."

His stance relaxed, smile lines crinkling at the corners of his eyes. "Be sure and wear your swimsuit under your jeans."

"On a trail ride?"

His smile broadening, his left cheek dimpled. "We live on an island, wahine. You're never truly far from the sea."

But in two days' time she would be. Far, far away from eyes as blue as the sea.

One more trail ride—all he was willing to offer, all they'd ever have. Would a few more memories be enough to last a lifetime? She blinked away tears.

They would have to.

12

Kai cinched the saddle belt tighter under the sorrel's belly. Mango was a big blowhard, puffing out her stomach to fool the unsuspecting into leaving the saddle too loose and threatening to unseat those naive enough to believe her tricks. He knew the feeling.

His entire world had upended since Laney arrived on the island. His stomach tied in perpetual knots like a lassoed calf, robbed of all common sense. The orderly, quiet life he cherished gone down a lava tube whose name was Laney.

Kai gave Laney a boost into the saddle and handed her the reins. To give himself something to do—anything but look into those melted chocolate drop eyes that haunted his dreams—he bent to adjust her stirrups to fit her short stature. A lot of power encased in such a small package.

Laney flexed her heels in the stirrups. "Thanks."

He loped over to untie his horse's reins from the fence rail outside the barn. "I'll get Muffin and we can be off."

"Muffin?" She snickered. "As in Stud Muffin? Really?"

He swung into the saddle and grinned. This was the Laney from the early days. "Only stating the obvious." He let his brows rise, striving to match her lighthearted tone. "Or so the ladies tell me."

Making sure she had his attention, Laney pantomimed gagging motions. She clucked her tongue to urge Mango forward. Kai squeezed his heels into Muffin's side and came alongside Laney as they left the ranch house and outbuildings behind. Ahead of them wide, open waves of pastureland rolled. The darker green lushness of the forest covered the surrounding hills. The ocean lay on the other side.

His body relaxed in the familiar and comforting rhythm of rider and horse. Unwound in the jingle of the harness and the creaking of the saddle. Muffin gave an appreciative snort. Mango whuffled in response, flicking her ears back and forth.

Life was good. A horse beneath him, under the open sky with God's bounty around him. He cut his eyes over to Laney's denim-clad figure. Her ponytail swished in cadence with Mango's blond tail. His eyes stung. Maybe the best friend he'd had since Hank—maybe ever—by his side.

He rubbed the side of his nose. No doubt about it—spending time with Laney was better than therapy, equine or otherwise.

She pushed the brim of her straw-colored Stetson back a few inches from her face. "I put on sunscreen, but the sun sure feels good on my skin."

"It'll be cooler in the shade of the rain forest. I hope you also doused yourself with insect repellent." He glanced at her. "Or you're about to get up close and personal with one of Hawai'i's most annoying creatures."

She gave him an arched look. "Should I try to guess who, in your esteemed estimation, might be another annoying creature?"

He removed his hat and slapped it back on his head. "No comment."

"Don't get me started," she warned. "And just for that," she dug her heels into Mango's side, enticing her into a fast trot. "Let's see if your skill matches that Mauna Kea-size mouth of yours," she called over her shoulder and nudged Mango into a canter.

At the surprised look on his face, she let out a yee-haw, a cross between a rebel yell and a Maori war cry. Her hair, loosening from the turquoise squash blossom clip, streamed behind her. She raised one hand in the air, letting Mango have her head.

"Yahoo!" Her face lit with an inner glow. "Watch *me* fly."

"Both hands on the reins!" he yelled. He clicked his tongue and drove Muffin, chomping at the bit in his mouth, into a full gallop. This girl scared him worse than the Taliban. "At least hold one hand on the saddle horn."

"That's for greenhorns," she called as he gained on her, racing across the grassy turf, hooves flying.

But he reveled in her sheer enjoyment of the horse, the way she attacked each obstacle in life. How nothing in her world was insurmountable. At the singular delight with which she managed to savor each moment as a supreme gift.

"Slow down, Laney," he yelled. "I'll never catch up to you at this rate." He hunched in a forward position over Muffin to spur him to greater speed. "No fair. You got a head start."

"All's fair in love and war." She echoed his own words weeks earlier. But she gave a gentle pull on the reins, slowing. "Which is it?"

And it hit him. No matter what he told himself, no matter how he guarded his heart. It was love. Maybe since the moment he'd spotted her perched and defiant on top of a suitcase. Or maybe since she'd had the courage to rescue a stray like Kolohe.

Catching up to where she waited for him at the edge of the forest, he jerked Muffin to a full stop. He kicked out of the stirrups and hurtled off the horse. "Laney Carrigan, you are the craziest wahine, I've ever . . ."

Laughing, she swung off Mango. "You've ever what?" She let the reins drop.

He took off his hat and wiped his arm across his brow, willing his heartbeat to slow to normal speed. Or as normal as it ever got around her. "You about gave me a heart attack."

She crossed her arms, thumbs out on the upper arms of her white chambray shirt. "That all I do to your heart, Kai Barnes?"

Muffin whinnied behind him. Reining in his emotions, Kai bit the inside of his cheek and busied himself by tucking his shirttail into his Wranglers.

Smirking, she twirled her hat.

He wiped a hand down the side of his jeans. "Come on." He grabbed hold of Muffin's harness and headed for a trail into the brush at the foot of the mountain. "I've got something to show you."

Once under the canopy of trees, the sounds of the earth-scented forest engulfed them. The sighing of the wind across the prairie land replaced by the sound of an *'elepaio* on a branch over their heads. He smiled at the song of the Hawai'ian rain forest bird. He stopped Muffin, put a finger to his lips and motioned with his eyes for Laney to see and listen.

Her eyes widened, and he could almost see her ears straining to hear. Laney, he reflected, not so unlike the bold, curious little bird. Not as visually striking as a blue jay or cardinal, but oh, the song the 'elepaio sang. First song to greet a Hawai'ian sunrise and the last aloha at the approach of sunset.

The throaty bass response of a pesky *coqui* frog croaked in counterpoint. Co-key. Co-key.

He ventured on the little used trail until the leafy six-foot ferns and banana fronds became too troublesome for the animals to pass through. He gestured for her to stop and he looped the reins over a forgotten, tilted log, rotting in the humid jungle climate.

"We'll go on foot from here." He removed his saddlebag strapped to Muffin and hung his hat on the saddle horn.

She patted Mango's shoulder. "Will the horses be okay?"

He pointed at the small stream. "They're within reach of the water and after that wild run," he shot her a wry grin, "they're probably in as much of a need of a nap as me. They'll wait for us." He looked back over his shoulder.

Swatting at a mosquito, she followed him into the undergrowth as the terrain sloped uphill.

His conscience had been bothered this week by his unkept promise. He refused to make promises he couldn't keep. He wasn't that kind of man. But this one, this promise he consoled himself, he would fulfill.

Laney picked her way behind Kai through the leaf-carpeted path sprinkled with red heart-shaped anthuriums. Laser rays of sunbeam dappled the forest floor. Orchids thrived among the tropical vegetation. The rushing sound of water filled her ears. Kai pushed aside a curtain of vines and peering over his shoulder, her eyes widened at the cascading water falling from a precipice at the top of a forty-foot cliff.

At the look on her face, he grinned. "Your own personal Franklin waterfall. Just like I promised."

"Wow," breathed Laney.

"Not as wow as the four-hundred-foot Akaka Falls or maybe on your next visit the eighty-foot Rainbow Falls." His arm swept the entire mango grove including the tumbling curtain of water that spilled into a sparkling pool surrounded by wild, white clumps of fragrant ginger. Their sweet perfume filled her nostrils. "But a private piece of Paradise for those of us in the Franklin 'ohana who steward this land."

His eyes shimmered with a hint of moisture gone so rapidly she wasn't sure she hadn't imagined it. "I thought it was time you joined the rest of the Franklin initiates."

She swallowed, her gaze ping-ponging between his face and the place of dreams before her. "A true Hawai'ian at last?"

He held out his hand. "From the first, I think your heart was always in its essence, Hawai'ian. Come and see."

She placed her hand in his, and twining his fingers through hers, they ambled into the glen. The roar of the water reduced them to silence. Clouds of mist spiraled up from the churning water at the base. A million fragments of rainbows danced in the mid-afternoon sky.

He led her over to a flat portion of ground at the edge of the small pool where the translucent water remained calm. He withdrew a blanket from the saddlebag.

"No need to chase rainbows." He spread the blanket over the level woodland floor. "They were here, all the time."

She said nothing, folding her legs underneath her. The rainbows were here, she conceded as she watched him remove a Ziploc bag of sliced fruit from the leather satchel. Problem was, would these same rainbows chase her dreams for the rest of her life?

"You came prepared."

He smiled and plopped down beside her. "Better than a Boy Scout. I've even got water bottles in here at your service."

She lifted her chin. "Boy Scout, my great-aunt Petunia. You were never a Boy Scout, Kai Barnes. If anything, you're the product of Uncle Sam's finest."

He sank his teeth into a slice of passion fruit. "I like that about you, Carrigan. The loyalty to your dad's troops. I don't know about your Carrigan kinfolk and I hate to have to be the one to tell you this, but there are no great-aunt Franklin Petunias."

She smiled and bit into a chunk of pineapple.

He threw the bag between them. "Now for the fun part." Jumping to his feet, he wrestled out of his shirt, his muscles flexing. When he caught her staring, warmth crept up her neck.

"What are you doing?"

He pried off his boots. "That's why we brought our swimsuits." The jeans came off next, leaving him bare-chested in his tropical blue surfer shorts.

She fingered the buttons of her J. Crew work shirt. "So we can swim in the lagoon? Sounds like a great plan." She kicked off her riding boots and stepped out of her jeans.

"That," he gestured upward. "And dive from the top."

She fell backward onto the blanket. She pointed. "Up there?" she shrieked. "You've got to be kidding me."

"It's fun." He leaned down and tugged at her arm.

She resisted, letting gravity and her inertia have its way. She shook her head. "No way, Barnes. Contrary to popular opinion, I," she jabbed her finger in her chest, "do not have a death wish."

He planted his hands on his hips. "It's safe. I promise. I wouldn't let you dive if it wasn't. Franklins have dived here for generations. It'll be fun, you'll see."

She continued to shake her head.

Exasperation laced his voice. "Look, I'll go first. I'll show you how fun it is."

He scrambled up a footpath along the side of the cliff face, a barely discernible trail wide enough for only one foot at a time and scrabbling handholds. He stopped about ten meters from the top—the height of Olympic diving platforms she remembered from her dad's plum assignment on the staff of a five-star during the Olympic Games in Australia.

Kai crept to a lava-formed ledge, his toes wiggling over the edge. He raised his hands above his head. "Watch," he called.

But she couldn't. She hid her face behind her hands.

"Baby," he jeered, forcing her to look between her fingers. He pushed off and leaped into the air.

Laney gasped and held her breath as he plunged headfirst into the languid water with hardly a ripple. She counted to five and still he didn't emerge.

She hastened to the water's edge, hanging her head over the rocks. With a mighty thrust, he vaulted out of the depths with a spray of water as he flung his head from side to side dashing the water from his face.

Laney reared back, landing with a thud on her bottom. "Kai, you big idiot. I thought you . . ." She sputtered while he grinned at her, his head bobbing above the water.

"Piece of cake, I told you."

"Show off."

Grabbing hold of a boulder-sized rock, he heaved himself out of the pool, rivulets of water streaming from his body to the ground. "Come on."

She crab-walked backward. "Oh, no. I'm not going up there."

"What happened to my crazy wahine cowgirl?"

She opened her mouth and closed it again. He'd called her his wahine?

Perhaps sensing he had her on the run, he pressed his advantage. "We don't have to go so high. We can go to another spot only halfway."

"I don't think this is a good idea."

He extended his hand. And like the fool she apparently was in his presence, she took it. She allowed him to pull her to her feet.

"I'll be right there with you the whole time."

She huffed out a sigh mixed of resignation and frustration.

"Come on," he coaxed, like she was Mango. "It's not as high as it looks."

"No, it's probably worse."

But true to his word, he led her to a promontory only half-way up the slope and stepped aside. Murmuring words of encouragement, he cajoled her forward.

Her neck craning at the bottomless water pit below her, she stopped inches from the edge. Adrenaline and sheer terror raised chicken skin on her arms. "This is nuts." Her heart pounding, she backed into his chest.

Kai wrapped his hands around her waist and staggered back to keep them both from tumbling over the edge. "We'll do it together the first time."

"First time?" She snorted. "Won't be much left when the EMS divers pull my dead body from that watery grave."

He crinkled his eyes at her. "Don't you trust me, Laney?"

"Should I?" But it was no use against the pleading look in those blue cow eyes of his. And he knew it, hateful man that he was.

He let go of her and pried her death grip off the coiled muscles of his arm. He walked out, handsome as you please, to the end of all sanity. Without a word, once again he held out his hand to her and waited.

Ungluing her body from the rock face, she tottered forward. Her heart in her throat—she'd never realized the anatomical possibility of that until now—her mouth went dry. She rested her hand and her life in his.

Strong, warm fingers wove into hers.

"It's deep," she whispered and shivered.

"Don't look down. Keep your eyes on mine." His eyes pinned her. "Nothing the two of us can't handle."

Laney took a deep breath but kept her gaze fixed on him. His eyes reassured her. He cocked an eyebrow into a question. She nodded.

Squeezing his hand, she jumped with him, the safety of the land falling away. For a moment it seemed as if time stopped and they hung suspended. But in a rush, her stomach dropped as she and Kai hurtled through space as time sped up once more, free-falling as if they were in the chopper.

Laney had only a second to draw in a breath before their bodies broke the surface of the water. Her hand still in his, they drifted to the bottom, tiny bubbles of air escaping from their nostrils. Her hair floated like a brown *kapa* cape around her shoulders.

He grinned at her, his smile as wide as one of those Ki'i totems at the place of refuge. Releasing her hand, he gave her an underwater thumbs-up. Joy gurgled in her chest and like a rocket, she jettisoned her body to the surface. Her head bobbed above the water, her feet tangoing a desultory dog paddle.

Kai sprang from the liquid depths beside her. "You did it." He dashed the water surging over his face. Treading water with one arm, he pulled her closer.

"We did it." She held up her hand and high-fived him. "Humuhumunukunukuapua'a."

"What did you say?" He stood, his brow wrinkling.

"Hoo-moo-hoo-moo," she repeated. "Noo-koo-noo-koo-ah-poo-ah-ah." She grinned. "You said if I ever learned to pronounce that fish I'd graduate with honors from the Kai Barnes School of Hawai'i."

And for fun, she repeated it to him again, faster just to show him she could. "Do I pass the exit exam, Captain Cowboy?"

"With flying colors." His eyes darkened as he stepped forward, his voice a husky murmur.

Laney's heart thudded. She was leaving in three days. Unless he changed her mind for her, gave her a reason beyond Mily to stay.

He strode toward her, his legs rippling the water. She found her footing on the sandy bottom. He lowered his head, his chin on his chest.

"Laney . . ." A tremor of longing threaded his voice, a filament of light in his eyes when he said her name. He took a shaky breath and raked a hand through his damp, glistening with sunlight hair.

She froze, staring at his mouth. His hands gripped her upper arms and he lifted her until her toes dangled in the water. He drew her in, his arms entwined around her waist, her mouth a mere breath away from his. She could feel the hammering of his heart. She savored the smell of him—the leather of the saddle, the clean sweat of Muffin, the hay of the stables, and the ginger-scented aroma of the water—that mixed and mingled into the making of the total package that was Kai Barnes.

"What are we doing, Laney?" He sighed. "What am I doing here with you . . . ?"

Laney caressed his jaw line. Her arms encircled him, her fingers touching the soft black curls at the nape of his neck. No matter the outcome, she resolved to confess the truth, the aching yearning harder and harder to subdue.

She couldn't face the future—as alone as it promised to be—she couldn't live with herself unless she faced her own fears and told him, without strings, what she felt inside.

"I love you, Kai. I understand your PTSD and I'm not afraid of it or of you because I love you."

A groan escaped from between his lips and his mouth found hers, ravenous and devouring. She melded her lips into his with the relief of sharing feelings she'd kept too long cork-screwed inside. She drank him in like a parched lava desert soaked in a rain shower.

With a sudden wrench, he released her and stared at her, the opaque blueness of his eyes reflecting surprise, a barely controlled passion, and turmoil. He lowered her to the water and she slid down his chest, her mouth already missing his, leaving her feeling bereft.

"I'm going to stop now." His chest heaved. "While I still can."

She nodded and moved past him toward the blanket. He followed her and handed her a towel before he yanked his shirt over his wet back and with trembling fingers misbuttoned it. He gave a disgusted shake of his head, his breath ragged.

Laney made no attempt to help him. She plopped down and reached for the bag of fruit. Some puzzles you had to untangle for yourself.

He sank down beside her and stretched his long legs using the saddlebag as a cushion for his head. "We need to talk."

She shrugged. "So talk. Nobody's stopping you, but you."

But instead, he closed his eyes.

A few minutes later, Laney detected the even, steady breathing that told her he'd gone to sleep. Turning on her side, propped on one elbow, with the clock ticking, Laney decided to enjoy the view.

Maybe, like that one last aloha kiss, for one last time.

13

With a jerky start, Kai awakened to find Laney gazing at him, an intense awareness of him in her eyes. He flushed and ran a hand over his jaw. "I'm s-sorry. I can't believe I fell asleep."

She smiled, those luscious lips of hers arching. "I'm not sorry or surprised with the load you manage every day." She angled her head. "What can I say? Story of my life. I put 'em to sleep every time. That's me, B-O-R-I-N-G."

He snorted. "Not hardly. Of all the words I could think of to describe you, Laney Carrigan—stubborn, plucky, independent, courageous, insane—boring would never apply."

Kai sat up, leaning on his elbows as he glanced at the small sliver of blue sky above the pool. "How long was I out? Teah's probably getting worried."

"I have a feeling worry isn't the primary emotion Teah feels when you and I are together." She offered him the fruit. He shook his head. "You weren't asleep long. Maybe an hour."

"An hour?" His eyebrows raised. "I'm sorry, Laney. Not the best of company for you."

"Oh, I found ways to keep myself occupied." She wrapped her white shirt around herself, tying the tails into a knot at her waist and rolling the sleeves. "What were you dreaming about?"

He twitched. "Nothing. Did I say something?"

"No, I just wondered."

Nothing he wanted to share with her. For the first time since he'd returned from Afghanistan, his dream had been pleasant. No sounds of grinding crashes into hard-packed earth, no cries of wounded men. Nor the terrifying blackness and dripping sounds from that long-ago time as a boy.

His dream beside the crystal blue lagoon had been more than pleasant, something he'd not wished to awaken from. An impossible dream of him at this same pool and a small, brown-skinned girl he'd been attempting to teach to swim. A very pregnant Laney had lounged on a blanket, where she lay now, watching and cheering them on.

Kai dashed the cobwebs from his mind. If he ever shared this particular daytime fantasy with Laney, she'd be like purple on poi. That kiss alone earlier . . . He had no defenses against more of that—no walls high enough to deflect his heart's yearning for the sweet possibilities with this woman.

He glanced over to Laney bunching the strands of her hair into an untidy ponytail.

Time for him to bare his soul. Tell the ugly truth about why there'd never be a future for her with a man like him. She deserved a whole man, a well man, who'd give her tropical dreams come true like the one he'd just entertained full of lovely children and golden afternoons.

But not with a man who was one aftershock away at any given moment from an eruption that could destroy her and everything in its path without warning.

He drew his knees to his chest and wrapped his arms around his legs. "We received an SAR call to locate and retrieve a group of three soldiers who'd managed to get separated from their platoon during an ambush in a hitherto friendly village in the Helmand Province."

She stilled, her hands dropping to her lap.

"They'd managed to radio their approximate location in the hills behind the village. One of them had taken a direct hit with an IED. He'd lost his legs. They were attempting to keep him stable until help arrived."

She scooted closer to him, but she didn't touch him. She mirrored his position with her knees.

"I flew the unarmed medevac. We were as always escorted by an Apache." He gazed out over the lagoon. "My crew had located the trio on the ground below when . . ."

He sighed, moistened his lips. "Hell broke loose. The Taliban spotted us. Launched a surface to air missile. We were hit under the belly of the chopper near the front end. The aircraft was spinning. I was fighting like crazy to bring us down in one piece."

Laney's breath hitched.

"We *were* going down. There was no doubt about that and the Apache could do nothing to help us. They were being bombarded themselves in a fight for their own lives."

He visualized again the billowing smoke and the fire. He heard the savage yell of victory from the throats of bearded warriors as the jolting impact reverberated through his body.

"I crashed a multimillion dollar piece of equipment and signed the death warrant for my crew." His lip raised in a sneer. "I emerged, as usual, without a scratch. Or at least, ones you could see."

"You brought the chopper down safely," she whispered. "You gave your co-pilot and the medics a fighting chance."

He darted a look at her. Her shoulders hunched, she stared ahead, her lips drawn in as grim a line as his own. And somehow he was consoled by the knowledge that she—of all the people in the world—did understand.

Kai had read the dispatches she'd sent from the field when she'd been embedded with Hank's squad. How the convoy in which she'd been riding had been ambushed on the highway outside Kabul. How surrounded by soldiers from her father's command they'd fought off the insurgents until reinforcements arrived. The thought of what she'd seen, what they'd both witnessed in their tours, chilled him.

To comfort himself as much as her, he drew her clenched fist from where it lay on top of her knee. He warmed her ice-cold hand between his palms.

"Nolan, my co-pilot, was critically wounded from shrapnel. One of the medics took a sniper's bullet when we scrambled out of the burning aircraft."

"And you and the other medic dragged your co-pilot and the dead sergeant to cover."

His eyebrows rose. "You finally got around to Googling me?"

A wry smile tugged at her lips. She lifted one shoulder. "What can I say? I'm trained, like you, to be resourceful."

He let a breath trickle out. "We spent the night fighting off pockets of incursions against our rudimentary position. The platoon spent desperate hours trying to free themselves from the vise they found themselves in at the village. Another team pushed as fast and as hard as they could from our base of operations. Irony is, we crashed almost on top of the lost trio's location. Though little good we did them."

"You were decorated, you and the medic for bravery, Kai. Against impossible odds, you never gave up. You protected the men in your charge."

"You *have* been reading reports about me." He released her hand and waved his in a gesture of dismissal. "You of all people know you can't believe everything you read. Highly inflated version, I assure you."

She shook her head, tendrils escaping from behind her ears. "You're a hero whether you admit it or not."

He scrambled to his feet, the suddenness of his motion rocking Laney backward. "The heroes, like Nolan, died giving their last full measure of devotion. Nolan died without regaining consciousness. That other poor soldier—the one we were supposed to rescue—bled out on the red desert sand minutes after we crashed. There was nothing I could do to save him."

"You can't save everybody, Kai. Nobody expects that of you, least of all God."

"I expect it of me."

Rising, she brushed the sand on her hands against the bottom of her swimsuit. "That's the survivor guilt talking. Give it to God, I beg you, Kai, before it destroys you. I've been praying for you to let God heal the broken places in you like Pastor K talked about. Let God take care of the yesterdays, the todays, and forever."

His brows furrowed into a V. "*I've* been praying somehow God would convince you to stay."

She searched his face for answers he couldn't give her. Her mouth quivered before tightening. "Maybe that's the one thing you can control."

Kai dropped her gaze and stuffed the towel and the fruit inside the saddlebag. "As much fun as this always is with you, Laney, this thing we do, I'm too tired to argue and you have an aloha luau to attend."

"Have it your way." She flipped her ponytail over her shoulder. "Aloha hello. Aloha goodbye. Your choice, Kai Barnes. Your choice."

Laney stared out the bay window at the shiny red convertible and the balding middle-aged man with whom Kai stopped to converse. After untacking the horses and running a currycomb over their sides, at the sight of the convertible in the driveway, Kai had scowled and suggested she might want to get a move on getting ready before the guests arrived.

Feeling dismissed, she entered the house and paused long enough to see the man arguing with Kai before thrusting a brown manila envelope at him. Not any of her business, she reminded herself.

Her heart cramped at the memory of what Kai had said. And, what he hadn't. Though his eyes . . . his eyes said what his lips would not. She wasn't sorry she'd told him the truth of her own feelings. But the familiar wave of insecurity, of not belonging, crested in her heart.

Who was she kidding? Perhaps he hadn't responded because he didn't feel the same depth of emotion for her.

She brushed her fingertips across her lips, reliving his tingling caress. Maybe the simple truth remained that she was good enough to kiss, but not good enough for anything more, no matter what excuses he voiced.

At the sound of Teah's raised voice, she shuttled that unhappy conclusion from her mind and made her way toward the kitchen. When she recognized her name on Mrs. K's lips, Laney halted on the threshold.

"We should tell her." Mrs. K stood in the center of the kitchen, wringing her hands in her hibiscus red dress.

Teah's head shook. "Let's not spoil tonight. It may be too much for her to handle."

Were they discussing Mily or her? Some instinct caused Laney to shrink into the shadows.

Mrs. K's brow puckered. "How will she feel when she learns the truth? It's not fair to anyone, least of all her. I think I should—"

"Absolutely not." Teah grabbed hold of Mrs. K's sleeve. "Leave it. One more day won't matter. Let the 'ohana tell her. All of us together. Tomorrow, I promise."

Had Mrs. K decided she could no longer handle Mily's care alone? Was the family getting ready to place Mily into a care facility on a full-time basis?

She'd known in the back of her mind this day was bound to be inevitable, considering the progression of Mily's disease. But she'd hoped, coward that she was, she'd be gone by then and not have to witness more of Mily's slow disintegration.

Laney beat a quiet retreat toward her bedroom, pain at what awaited Mily lancing her heart. She took a quick shower, scrutinizing her reflection in the bathroom mirror as she finger-combed the wet tendrils of her hair into a chignon. She rummaged in the armoire for the brand-new dress Elyse talked her into buying in a mad moment of retail therapy in Kona last week.

Pulling it over her head, she smoothed the folds of the soft, buttercup fabric and tied the halter-style bands behind her neck. She did a three-sixty in front of the full-length mirror. The flirty rolled edges of the dress cut just above the knee swirled around her.

Would Kai notice her new dress? She wondered why she was such an idiot to care if he did or not. Had her forever-young mother once wondered something similar in front of this mirror?

Tonight's for happy memories, she berated herself. Memories she'd hoard and live off for the unhappy alone times that lay in her future, far away from this tropical land of dreams that never came true. She slipped her feet into the fancy gold flip-flops

Elyse also insisted she purchase. Checking her scant makeup one more time, she rubbed her lips and the shimmering coral lipstick together.

Show time.

Laney followed the sound of music and voices out the lanai and through the winding path past the avocado grove and banyan tree to the open land at the foot of her grandfather Jared's wooden cross to where Ben had erected table after table piled high with luau food. The roasted smell of the Kalua pork permeated the air. Ben had explained the traditional luau fare to her this morning as he and his friends prepared the evening meal.

Bamboo mats lined the table topped with choices of lau-lau—pork, chicken and fish steamed and wrapped in ti leaves. Walking over to the table, she spotted the lomi salmon dotted with tomatoes and green onions. She waved at a small cluster of people she recognized from church. The lokelani roses glimmered in the fading rays of the setting sun. Pastor K waved to Laney. Mrs. K gave her a weak smile, her features pinched.

She inhaled the aroma of the shredded pig, noted the sweet potatoes, taro chips, and steamed breadfruit. She admired the colorful display of the fruit centerpiece, a tiny replica of Mauna Kea tiered with papayas, guavas and passion fruit topped by a pineapple. Standing by the table, she observed Kai in deep conversation with Ben. Elyse moved from throng to throng, greeting the Franklin guests. Daniel greeted each guest with a red puff lei for which the Big Island was renowned. And, under Elyse's duress and with much eye-rolling on his six-year-old part, a kiss.

Teah sidled alongside her. She placed an arm around Laney's shoulders and planted a quick kiss on her cheek. "It's been a long time since the ranch had so much to celebrate with our friends and neighbors. It was a blessed day when we found each other again, and you made your way home."

Home?

She glanced over to where Kai stood with his arm around Mily's frail body. Her face alight with joy, her foot tapped to the traditional ukulele music the praise team from church played. Tonight, Laney prayed, would be a good night for Mily. No catastrophic reactions.

Teah pointed to a pie at the end of one of the tables. She smacked her lips. "Mac Pie. Mily and I did that together." At Laney's involuntary concerned look, Teah laughed. "Mily's old recipe. Like pecan pie but with macadamia nuts and Maui sugar. Only other thing I'm actually any good at in the kitchen." She cocked her head, a half smile coating her lips. "That and my famous Spam recipes, of course."

Laney's lips quirked. "Oh, of course."

Mily and Kai joined them. But she'd felt him approaching before she even turned around. Would it always be this way? Feeling this connection? She bit back an inward groan. A non-issue for her in three short days.

Wearing a blue aloha shirt, Kai pointed at the hollowed-out coconut shell filled with poi. "Be sure you get your fill of Hawai'i's most beloved dish." His eyes twinkled.

She gave a mock sigh, striving to match his light tone. "Another acquired taste you forgot to warn me about, Cowboy?"

Mily draped a lei around Laney's neck. Laney bent to receive Mily's proffered peck. "My granddaughter."

Laney squeezed her hand.

Mily leaned in to whisper in her ear. "Don't mind, Kai." She patted the pocket of her orchid purple muumuu. "I always bring a few packets of sugar to sweeten the poi for myself." She winked at Laney. "I've brought enough to share."

Teah punched Kai in the muscle of his arm. "Just don't let my son get into your stash, Auntie Mily. That boy's sweet tooth would wipe you out."

Kai rubbed his shoulder and faked a grimace. "Everybody's a comedian in the 'ohana."

Teah's eyes traveled around the kiawe-enclosed glen. "Poi from the taro plant. With its heart-shaped leaves the staff of life for the ancient Hawai'ians." She rotated toward Laney, her expression intent. "Symbol of the ideal 'ohana, did you know, Laney?"

Laney—not sure where this was going—shook her head.

Teah's hands rounded in front of her waist. "Grows in clumps of stems, *'oha*. And the younger stems," the circle of her hands expanded. "Like children, stay near the older core, yeah?"

Laney bit her lip. Kai looked away, stuffing his hands into the pockets of his black cargo pants. "I hear you, Auntie Teah. But I've got a job to do right now."

Kai kicked at the turf beneath his feet.

Mily patted Laney's bare arm. "Give the girl some room, Teah. When our Laney bird needs a rest from her flying, she'll know where to land, recognize where her nest is now."

Grateful for her understanding, Laney managed a smile that faded when Kai pivoted on his heel and walked away toward the musicians.

Amid much good-natured ribbing among the assembled guests, at the droning call of a conch shell, dinner was served on the grounds. Everyone had brought their own beach chairs from home. Teah, Elyse, Ben, and his crew piled every plate high with delicious offerings. Kai and Daniel iced and filled glasses with fruit juices. Laney, uncomfortable to be the center of attention, was made to sit on her own green canvas chair and was not allowed to help.

Pastor K supervised as the other men built a roaring bonfire. Laney's lips trembled at the sight of the many smiling Hawai'ian faces illuminated by the flickering flames of the fire. Should she stay?

Kai stood alone and remote at the perimeter of the gathering, his face in shadow, his eyes hooded. Should she reconsider that perhaps God had another, better plan for her? Could she bear to stay with the constant reminders of Kai and what was never meant to be?

Mily performed a small solo number to an enthusiastic round of applause, her hips swaying as gentle as the calm surf of low tide. Music and laughter filled the night. As the band of light faded at the edge of the horizon, Laney gazed at the stars beginning to glimmer against the heavenly soft texture of a blue velvet sky.

She watched Kai stroll over to a plumeria plant at the edge of the garden where he plucked a small yellow blossom. Twirling it between his fingers, he wended his way toward her. Kneeling beside her chair, he held the fragile flower, his face wistful. Her heart turned over.

"For the guest of honor." He held it out to her, a question in his eyes, his palm open.

She remembered what he'd said earlier. And what he hadn't said then or now. Steeling herself, she took it from him and placed it over her right ear.

His face constricted, but he cupped her cheek with his hand. She stilled, her eyes closed.

"*Wahine nani*," he murmured.

She felt him rise and move away. She opened her eyes to find Teah staring a black hole through her body. She frowned at Laney and gave a slight shake of her head. Heaving herself from the chair, Teah crossed over to Laney.

"Why you put in that ear?" Teah's hand reached toward the flower at Laney's right ear. "You probably don't know—"

Laney's hand halted Teah's in mid-air, before she could pluck the blossom. "I understand, Auntie Teah. I've done my research." She flicked a look at Kai's stiff back where he stood, his hand posed on Daniel's shoulder. "Kai understood, too. He gave it to me to choose." Her gaze returned to Teah's. "He left it up to me. No commitment on his part."

"He'll come around, Laney. If you'll just stay, yeah?"

"Maybe. Maybe not. Most likely, not. All of you," she gestured. "Have shown me how important roots and family are. He offers me family, 'ohana, but not himself."

She touched the delicate, sweet-scented flower with her fingertips. "Left ear if you're taken. Right ear if you're still seeking." She squeezed Teah's hand. "Still chasing those rainbows, I guess, for a little while longer. Till I find my Pete or my Ben."

Teah blinked, moisture welling in her eyes.

"It's not enough, Auntie." She peered into Teah's face. "You know that wouldn't be enough for you or Elyse." She let out a deep, shuddering breath. "It wouldn't be enough for me. Not in the end."

Teah placed a sympathetic hand on her shoulder and made as if to move away.

"By the way, Auntie?"

Teah paused.

"What does *nani* mean?"

A gentle smile curved Teah's lips. She bent and kissed the top of Laney's head. "It means," her lips whispered against Laney's hair, "pretty one."

14

Elyse clapped her hands and brought the group to attention. "Time to talk story." Grabbing a University of Hawai'i Warrior stool, Elyse huddled closer to the light of the flames. Her face, Laney observed, lit with an ethereal glow.

She proceeded to tell of a time before Captain Cook and the haoles arrived to the Hawai'ian lands. When ancient Polynesian mariners using the stars followed the migration of the golden *kolea* bird and traversed the great blue divide, the boldness of their *huaka'i*, journey, amazing even today. Her face animated, she employed a studied motion with her hands Laney had seen her utilize at the Moana's lavish weekly luau. Elyse told her rapt audience of the great Kamehameha—how as a young man he took up the challenge of the sacred two-ton Naha Stone.

Daniel and the other neighbor children's eyes grew large as Elyse imparted the legend that foretold whoever moved the stone—in an Arthurian/Hawai'ian version of strength—would one day be king, conquering and uniting the islands. Laney found herself holding her breath with the children as

Elyse recalled the fourteen-year-old Kamehameha who not only moved the stone but who later fulfilled his destiny.

"And that stone still stands in Hilo." Elyse's voice dropped to a whisper, a slight smile crossing her features in the fire-light. "Awaiting Hawai'i's next great king." As one, Laney and the children released their breath in a gust of air.

Pleased at the effect of her story, Elyse laughed and sat back. The other adults gave her a round of applause. "And would you care to hear the rest of the story?"

The children's heads wobbled like hula girls on a dashboard.

Elyse swept her arm toward Pastor K. "They're all yours, Pastor."

Pastor K took his place before the fire, his hands clasped, his head bowed in a moment of prayer. When he looked up, his toffee eyes swam with love at his beloved flock. Laney watched the faces transform around the fire as Pastor K shared how another stone had been moved on a long ago day in a land far removed from their tropical home. "And a great king shall one day return. Your king. My king. The King of kings and the Lord of lords, who fulfilled His destiny, conquered sin and death, and who unites all whose hearts yearn to know Him."

His gaze swept over to Mily. "Now we know only in part. Maybe just the next baby-sized step in our personal *huaka'i*. But one day . . ." He gave a great sigh. "One day . . ."

A chorus of "Yeah?'s" and "Amen's" floated up from the circle of light. And for the first time—maybe ever in her life—she understood the true meaning of belonging. Not limited by ties of blood, but bound together as one by strong cords of love from the heart.

"Then, my dear brothers and sisters," Pastor K's tender glance traveled over to Kai. "And then 'the earth will be full of the knowledge of the Lord's glory just as water covers the sea.'"

A moment, a holy moment, suspended time. Moonlight sparkled over the inky black waters below.

"Habakkuk," Mily chirped.

The moment passed as chuckles broke out. Pastor K grinned. "Good to see you know your Bible, Miliana." He stepped aside. "And now I think, if we apply a little pressure, Teah might be willing to favor us with a story, too." Teah shook her head.

Elyse tugged her mother into the light. "I'm not the only one in this family who has stories important to pass along to the children."

Surrendering to the inevitable, Teah told of a time when she was a small girl and a great air force attacked the *'aina*, homeland of the Hawai'ian people. She spoke of how the fish were rationed and boys left the villages to defend a nation that wasn't yet officially theirs. Recalled how the poor who worked the pineapple plantations, as her mother and Mily's had, lived off the imperishable, ubiquitous Spam to supplement their diet.

The old ones straightened, nodding their heads in remembrance of Teah's stories. Soon after, as the night sky, studded with breathtaking constellations, deepened as the hour grew late, the guests packed their chairs and murmured their mahalo's and aloha's.

Kai assisted Ben in making sure the *imu* was completely extinguished. She and Elyse helped Pastor and Mrs. K tote the platters into the kitchen to be packed for leftovers the next day. Seeing Mily adrift, she offered to help Mily get ready for bed while the others completed the cleanup.

In Mily's master bedroom, she noted the masculine touches of a life lived with a beloved spouse, Jared's presence never far from Mily's thoughts even after all these years. She wondered, not for the first time, if Mily's loyalty and love had been misplaced in such a man.

As she helped her grandmother into the frilly pink nightgown, she wondered the same about herself.

She drew the quilted counterpane around Mily's chin. There was the sound of car doors shutting in the driveway signaling Pastor and Mrs. K, the Ching family, and probably Kai, too, had departed for the night. Mily brushed her hand over the appliquéd cotton fibers. "This is the wedding quilt Teah made as a teenager on Maui with my sister, for my new home with Jared."

Laney admired the rich batik shades of green. "I think Teah also talks story with her needles."

Mily smiled.

"As you do with your hula." Laney sighed. "Tutu, I'm sorry I must leave you for a while, but—"

"Teah pieces the fabric of her life into the bolts of cotton. I with my music." Mily touched her hand to her chest. "The music in here." She held her hand over Laney's heart. "You stitch your life with your words. A quilt of words still in the making. I know you'll come back when you can."

"I will, Tutu. I promise you I will."

Mily glanced around the room. Her face puckered. "Where is Rose's quilt? You know how I like to keep it near."

She rose. "Don't worry, Tutu. It's around here somewhere. I'll find it for you."

Hearing Teah rattling around in the kitchen, she checked the front living room first, then the dining room.

Standing in the foyer, she noticed the door to the study ajar. She pushed the door open with her shoulder. Her cheeks lifted as she spotted the baby quilt draped over the leather desk chair.

Teah or Kai must have picked it up somewhere and dropped it here when they got busy with ranch business before the luau. Scurrying around the desk, she plucked it from the chair. She swung it over her arm and as she did so, the flutter of air sent a brown manila envelope on the corner of the desk into an avalanche. Neatly stacked printed pages floated like gossamer wings to the rug.

"Great." She gaped at the scattered papers lying helter-skelter across the floor. "Kai and Teah will kill me when they see the mess I've made in here."

She squatted, duck-walking from one page to the next. Her hand froze as she scooped up the last one. A document headed with "The Last Will and Testament of Jared Reece Franklin."

Laney frowned. Standing, she bunched the papers together and straightened the edges against the wood grain of the desk, jostling them into a semblance of order. Retrieving the envelope, she deposited it where she'd first seen it, attempting to duplicate its original position.

"There." She tidied the desk to make sure everything was back in place when an unfortunate thought occurred to her for which she hadn't made allowances: perhaps the pages were numbered.

With the rose quilt draped over her arm, she sank into the chair and grabbed the papers again. Flipping through the stack, she was glad she'd taken the time to check when she noticed a page out of order. Removing it, she thumbed through the rest of the pages to insert the errant page once more.

And sighted the words, "To my beloved wife, Miliana Kanakele Franklin, and to my equally beloved granddaughter, Alana, whereabouts unknown . . ."

Her breath hitched as she scanned the rest of the page. She shrank into the chair, the papers clutched to her chest. Her grandfather, the man who'd threatened her pregnant mother, the man who'd wished her unborn self dead, had left the entire Franklin estate in the joint custody of herself and her grandmother.

She peered at the oil portrait of the proud, redheaded cattle baron on the opposite wall. Her lips trembled. Mrs. K had been right about Jared. Rose's death had triggered an abrupt change of heart for the old man.

Laney remembered the cross carved onto his tombstone in the cemetery. She stared out the window, seeing in her mind's eye despite the darkness outside, the wooden cross the ailing, bereaved man had hewn by hand and erected at the spot where he'd spoken his marriage vows to Mily. A beacon, acknowledging Kai's earlier words, for a lost granddaughter to return one day.

She closed her eyes, her chin bowed to her chest. "He did regret what happened," she murmured. "He did want to make things as right as he could."

The sting of tears hovered on the edges of her lashes. She took a shaky breath and laid the papers on her lap, smoothing out the wrinkled surface. Why had no one told her about this legacy? Not that this inheritance changed anything for her.

Her fingers sorted through the pile, aligning the edges on all four sides. Placing the papers atop the envelope, she noticed another document sticking catty-corner inside a red folder. Her eyes darted from left to right. Her heartbeat sped up. She had no business looking through other people's private papers.

But maybe this bequeathal did change things. Maybe this *was* Laney Carrigan's business. She withdrew the folder. The words, *Franklin Ranch*, appeared on the tab at the top.

She opened the folder and stiffened. A loan application from the bank in town. A loan using the ranch as collateral. On the lime green sticky note affixed to the top someone in a sloping, slanted hand had written, "Signature awaiting notarization."

Her eyes skittered across the page. Her breath caught at the amount of the loan request. She noted Teah's signature using Mily's power of attorney beside one line for *Owner*. Across from her signature, a blank line and Alana Rose Carrigan's name typed below.

She crumpled the application in her hand as realization struck her. She'd been used. Brought here under false pretenses. To further someone else's ambitions at the expense of her own. Crystal clear now why a man like him would be interested in someone like her. Why he'd offer her a flower at the luau, not for himself, but for the family.

"There you are, *keiki*," Teah huffed and popped her head around the door. "Mily's been calling for you. And we—" Teah's gaze traversed to the folder in Laney's hand. "Oh, Laney. We were going to—"

Laney's mouth tightened. "When I got ready to set foot on the airplane? When I'd done what you wanted, and I was out of your way, Auntie Teah?"

She stepped toward Laney. "It wasn't that way, child. Let me—"

Laney scrambled to her feet. "I think I've heard and seen about all I need to hear."

Teah put a hand to her mouth. "It's not what you think, Laney. Kai has been after me to tell you about your grandfather's will from the moment you got here—"

"Which you conveniently forgot to mention . . ."

"This loan thing came up after you'd already arrived. Kai's been trying to find a way to dig us out from the economic hole we're in without resorting to involving you and the bank. He didn't want you to think we'd run your heritage into the ground."

She folded her arms. "No, you just thought you'd wait and see if I truly belonged to the 'ohana before you handed over the key to the ranch. Waited to see if I proved trustworthy."

"It's my fault, Laney. I kept Elyse and Kai from telling you, but it wasn't that I questioned your belonging. From the moment Elyse recognized the Lokelani quilt you and your dad posted, we knew you belonged with us. But I feared the will and its obligations might be too much at once for you to handle. That and—"

"What's going on here? I heard raised voices and Mily wanted. . ." Kai pushed his way into the room. He came to a screeching halt when he spotted the folder. "What are you doing with that?"

Bristling, her back ramrodded. "Only what I should be doing. Taking care of property you neglected to tell me belonged to me." Tears threatened, prickling at her eyelids, but she hardened her heart and freeze-dried them on her cheekbones. "So just for informational purposes, whose idea was it to lure me here and—?"

"Nobody lured you here, Laney." His teeth clenched.

She raised her brows. "Oh, really? Clever of you to spot the quilt on the website and contact me. Running out of time, weren't you? Getting desperate to find the long-lost heir so you could save the ranch." She grabbed a pen from the cup holder on the desk.

"Was it Elyse who came up with the plan?" Her eyes ping-ponged between Kai and Teah. "Or Teah?"

A muscle jumped in his cheek. "Stop making it sound like some sort of Hawai'ian conspiracy against you. You heard Teah." He ran a hand over his head. "If you'd shut your mouth long enough to hear her out—" Laney snorted "—you'd know Elyse posted on the website in all innocence as she told you. That when she and Teah spotted that quilt photo they knew they'd found you."

"So you say now." She sashayed over to him, gripping the pen in her hand like a spear. "Maybe it was your idea, Kai Barnes." He refused to give ground. "For your information, all of this was so unnecessary. Apparently I'm more like my real father, Tom Carrigan, than I ever suspected. Together, he and I have managed to pull a few strings from his pals at Veteran Affairs. Franklin Ranch is on their radar now as a potential site for an equine therapy center. I have the papers Dad emailed me yesterday in my case. I planned to surprise all of you tomorrow with the news."

Hunching her shoulders, she gave a derisive laugh. He winced. "Well, surprise, surprise, Kai Barnes." She waved the papers in his face. "The surprise is on me. Veteran Affairs has scheduled an interview for you in Hilo next week. I sent them glowing reports of the operation. Thanks to my dad's influence, the interview is a mere formality. But the paperwork, I warn you, will be endless. They've agreed to fund the ranch on a year-long trial basis before committing themselves further."

Teah grasped Kai's arm. "It's your dream come true, Kai. And Mily can stay here as long as she's able."

Laney flung the papers against the rock solid wall of his chest. He flinched.

She scribbled her signature across the blank line for Owner. "Here. All done. You're a notary. So notarize this." She jabbed the pen in his hand. "Signed, sealed, and delivered. I'll leave the papers with you. In fact," she drew the quilt to her chest. "If you want me to sign over all rights to this property to you, Elyse, Teah, or anybody else on this stupid island, I'll be happy to. Have your fancy attorney draw up the papers, and you can email them to me." She moved toward the door. "If you can find me next time."

Teah took hold of her arm. "No, Laney . . ."

She shook Teah off.

His nostrils flaring, Kai flung the papers on the floor. "Will you just stop, Laney, and listen?"

The despicable, gut-searing tears were going to have their way. And she knew if she didn't get out of this room this very minute, she'd lose it completely. Lose whatever shreds of self-respect remained.

She shoved him aside. "Must be a bitter pill to think I would've done all this for nothing, doesn't it, Cowboy?" She gulped back a sob. "No need for you to have put yourself out there and romance the ranch out of me, after all."

"Romancing the ranch?" He choked, a strange sound in the back of his throat. "You can't believe that?" His pupils dilating, his face darkened with anger. "How dare you say that to me, much less think that of me. Of us." He shook his head. "It was never that way between you and me. Not after all we've—" He lunged at her, but she darted under his arm into the hallway.

Kai slammed his hand against the wall, and the door frame reverberated. Mily stood motionless, a pale ghostlike figure in the doorway to her bedroom. She reached for Laney.

"You and me, we keep each other company tonight," she cajoled as the tears cascaded down Laney's face.

"Oh, Tutu. It's all a lie. Everything is a lie."

Mily pulled her inside and shook her head at someone in the hallway behind Laney before shutting the door. She patted the quilt clutched in Laney's arms. "You and me and the quilt. We will be all right, yeah?"

She fell across Mily's bed. "Nothing is ever going to be right again, Tutu."

Mily climbed on top of the bed, her skinny varicose-veined feet poking out from her nightgown. "It will be all right. Sunshine makes everything better. We will pray tonight, you and I. God gets us through it all." She cast her gaze over to the silver-framed picture of Jared on the bedside table. "He will get me through this last part of my journey, and He will get you through yours."

She wrapped her arms around her grandmother, burying her face in Mily's rose-scented bosom.

Mily cupped Laney's face between her dry palms. "You came back to me. And Rose, she will pray, too. Your mother will be back to us, my keiki, in the morning."

But she sobbed harder against Mily's shoulder because her mother was never coming back.

Neither of them.

15

When Mily fell asleep in the early hours before dawn, Laney opened the door, holding her breath lest the door squeak and betray her presence. Half of her expected—hoped?—to see someone waiting on the other side for her to emerge. The other half of her scolded for being a fool.

She crept down the hall to her own bedroom and shut the door. She dragged her black duffel from the armoire. Early or not, if she had to camp out at the airport an extra two days until her flight departed, she wasn't spending another night in this house.

Her house.

She rubbed her eyes. She'd chased this rainbow right to the pot of something less than golden. Time to move on. She contemplated calling her dad, but she didn't trust herself to speak to her father in her present state of mind.

Better to wait until she was airborne, she decided, stuffing her clothing—dirty laundry and all—into the bag. No need to let him know what an idiot she'd been. On second thought, as she dumped her bathroom toiletries on top of the clothes, she thought she might wait until she landed in Jakarta. Take advantage of an internet cafe and save a phone call.

That way, a small voice chided, *it'd be too late for him to try and change her mind.*

Laney took a long, hard look at her puffy eyes in the bathroom mirror. Was Kai right about her? Was her life consumed with the need to prove something to her father? Was Jakarta what God was telling her heart to do, where to go next?

Kai Barnes wasn't right about anything else on earth, why would she suppose he'd be right about this? She abso-flipping-lutely wouldn't live her life bound by his opinions of her.

But God's?

She cast a glance at the ceiling. She'd pray as soon as she got to the airport. If God had other ideas for her life, D.C. or Italy or Timbuktu for that matter, she'd change her flight.

Only—she spotted a pair of sandals underneath the four-poster bed—she couldn't think straight here. She needed to get out of this place.

Bending to snatch the shoes, as she straightened the air whooshed out of her lungs and she tottered against the mattress. She put a hand to her head. What was the matter with her?

Maybe lack of sleep and an empty stomach?

She planted her hands on her hips. They owed her breakfast. She'd take a quick shower, finish packing and be out of here so fast that—as one Southern belle high school friend from her Fort Bragg days used to say—the screen door wouldn't hit her on the way out.

Donning her laundered navy blue skirt and pink shirtwaist blouse, she discovered she lacked some basic toiletry necessities that might be impossible to obtain once she landed in Jakarta. Ramming her pink tortoiseshell glasses onto her face, she yanked open her bedroom door. Taking a deep breath for courage, she sailed into the kitchen—dragging with a great deal of noise for emphasis—her suitcase by the strap behind her.

Coffee cup halfway to his lips, Kai froze from where he leaned against the wooden countertop. All conversation ground to an immediate halt between Mily and Mrs. K seated at the kitchen table. Teah pinched her lips together.

Mrs. K scrambled to her feet and gave Laney a quick hug. "Teah told me what happened last night," she whispered into her ear. "You and I need to talk."

Laney, her eyes sparking fire in Kai's oblivious direction, returned her hug in a grateful squeeze. Mrs. K, her one true friend. Maybe she and Pastor K would lend her a bed tonight and save Laney's back from the airport floor.

Mily pushed a plate of grainy bread topped with homemade guava jam. "Have some toast." Mrs. K opened a cabinet to locate a juice glass.

She plopped herself where she could keep a wary eye on that great deceiver named Kai Barnes. If looks could've killed, he'd have been reduced to volcanic ash by now. She sank her teeth into a triangle of toast.

Teah cleared her throat, wringing her hands in her apron. "Laney, I'm afraid we didn't leave things well between us last night—"

She held up her hand. "I need to restock my supplies before I get on the plane."

Mrs. K drew in a sharp breath and darted an anguished look from Teah to Kai. Teah grabbed at the back of the chair in front of her. Kai muttered something under his breath Laney didn't catch.

Teah's mouth trembled. "But your flight doesn't leave for another couple of days."

Kai set the mug down with a thud on the countertop.

Her lips tightened. "I wondered if it wouldn't be too much trouble for me to borrow a ranch vehicle and run to town for those supplies. I'll call a taxi from there and maybe later you and Kai or . . ." She swallowed. "If Pastor and Mrs. K would be willing to return the car, I could leave it outside Nagoto's." She glanced from Teah's shuttered face to Mrs. K. "It should be safe there, don't you think, for a few hours?"

Digging his hand into the front pocket of his Wranglers, Kai clomped across the koa floor in his boots and thrust a set of keys in her direction.

She shrank back. "Those are the keys to your truck, Kai. I didn't mean for you . . . Not your truck . . . I meant one of the ranch Jeeps."

"Take it." Nostrils flaring, he jingled the keys in front of her face. "It belongs to you anyway. Everything Teah, Ben, and I own is mortgaged to the hilt to keep this ranch afloat. Your ranch, as I believe you so eloquently pointed out to us last night." His jaw hardened and the look he sent her way scorched her cheeks.

Which only made her madder.

"Fine. I will." Her lip curling, she scooted her chair across the floor and wrapped her hand around the keys he held in his palm. The moment her skin made contact with his though, she regretted the impulse.

They both jerked at the sizzle of electricity that shot like a lightning bolt between them. His brow puckering, Kai massaged his hand. He jutted his chin and stepped around Mrs. K.

Grabbing his Stetson off the spindle of a chair, he clamped it down on his head and headed for the door. "Work to do," he growled, his eyes narrowing into ice blue slits. The screen door slammed behind him.

"Laney," Mrs. K's soft voice wobbled. "I need to . . . I should've—"

"Didn't you say you had a list of things Mily needed from Nagoto's, Mrs. K?" Her cheeks flushing, Teah inserted herself between them, plucking a piece of paper off the table. "Perhaps, Laney, you'd be so good as to purchase these on Franklin credit and bring them to the house for us?"

Laney started to shake her head.

"I called Elyse this morning. She's on her way with Daniel. He'll be heartbroken if you leave before he has a chance to say goodbye."

So not fair, she groused, to play the kid card.

Teah's eyes pleaded with her to say yes. Mrs. K couldn't bring hers up from the floor.

She let out an explosive sigh. What, after all, would it matter next week? She'd no desire to hurt a small child.

Laney examined Mily's puzzled face. Or hurt her grandmother, either. Mily's fingers twiddled restlessly at the Lokelani quilt in her lap. Her index finger like a needle jabbing up and down at the fringes of the quilt. After the typhoon of emotion last night, no wonder Mily wasn't having one of her good days.

This was no way to behave. Her mother—probably both of them—would be ashamed at the way she was reacting. Taking out her displeasure with Kai on the rest of them.

Perhaps Teah had been telling the truth about the will and the loan application. Perhaps she'd jumped to erroneous conclusions based on her own insecurity and inability to trust.

She sent up a swift plea for wisdom and forbearance. "All right," she conceded. "I'll be back." She ambled around the table to Teah. "I promise."

Leaning over, she planted a kiss on Teah's cheek. "Don't worry. Families work through these kinds of issues all the time."

A single tear rolled down Teah's plump, brown face. She squeezed Laney's hand, giving Mrs. K a long look. "You're a credit to your parents, Laney Carrigan."

Mily harrumphed. "And her grandmother, too."

Laney released a laugh, breaking the tension. Now, if she could prove as much a credit to her God in handling a sticky situation known as Kai Barnes.

Laney filled her green plastic shopping bin with travel size containers of shampoo, toothpaste, and a small bottle of aspirin. This whole situation had given her a giant-sized headache.

Hadn't aspirin been on Mrs. K's list, too?

She gazed about the country store, which also functioned as the local post office. A few village grandmothers chatted with the elderly Mrs. Nagoto and the young man she recognized as Mrs. Nagoto's grandson stocking the narrow-aisled shelves. He gave Laney a cheeky grin and waved, almost toppling a pyramid of Purina dog food.

He reddened, but he jerked his head in the direction of his grandmother and put a finger to his lips. She resisted the urge to laugh.

Lotion, she remembered from the list. She headed toward the beauty section. Cotton balls, too. She stashed the bag in the bin.

Q-tips? She withdrew the crumpled list from her purse. Those peanut butter cookies Mily loved. Kitty toys.

She and Mily had made it a point to visit Kolohe every afternoon so he wouldn't get lonely there by himself until Kai returned from a tour flight or from working the ranch. Mily wanted a few playthings to keep Kolohe entertained on her next visit. Kolohe had a soothing effect on her tutu. As if he understood the old woman's confusion. Though thoroughly independent, he liked to rest on Mily's lap and be stroked.

Laney moved toward the aisle with the dog food. She smiled at the sight of rainbow-colored wicker balls and the six-pack assortment of toy mice. Kolohe would love these. Reaching beyond the top can in the dog food pyramid, Laney reflected on how much she'd miss Kolohe.

Though Kolohe wouldn't be the only one she missed. Or, her mouth trembled, the one she'd miss the most at a certain green-shuttered bungalow.

She set the toys in the bin, her treat for Mily and Kolohe. That was everything . . . Except—

Laney held the list to the light. She ticked the items off in her head and perused the basket to make sure.

Aspirin.

She'd forgotten to pick up the aspirin Mrs. K wanted. She laid the list on top of the groceries, settling the basket in the crook of her arm.

And froze.

She shook her head. Couldn't be. Her eyes played tricks on her, her mind and heart exhausted with the events of last night's revelation.

Laney took a step toward the front of the store and the cash register. She stopped. The unsettling thought refused to go away, niggling at her brain. She sidestepped the dog food display and deposited the basket on the planked wooden floor.

Only one way to be sure.

Silly. Ridiculous. Crazy.

It couldn't be true.

Don't be such an idiot.

Bending, she retrieved the list. She squinted at the capital *A* in aspirin, written by Mrs. K who'd learned cursive handwriting in a day when penmanship mattered.

Gripping the paper, her hand shook as she lowered the list to eye level. With her finger, she traced the curlicues and flourishes of the *A*. An *A* she'd learned to copy as soon as she'd been old enough to write her own name, Alana.

Her mouth opened into a circle. Her body quivered.

And suddenly every half-heard conversation, every unfinished remark, every glance since she'd arrived made sense.

The conversation between Teah and Mrs. K last night. She'd believed they spoke of not telling Mily the news about placing her into a long-term care facility.

But it wasn't about Mily. It was *her* Teah warned Mrs. K not to tell until after the luau.

Not fear that she'd discover the truth about the bank loan.

They'd feared when to reveal to Laney the truth about her mother.

Her knees buckled. Her hand groped behind her. Gravity rushed up to meet Laney as she swayed and fell into the stack of dog food. With a roar of crashing metal, the cans toppled and rolled, colliding like doggie-faced pinballs against each other.

"Ai-ai-ai!" Mrs. Nagoto scurried around the counter, her hands in the air.

The grandson emerged from the end of the aisle.

Mrs. Nagoto, padding in her tabi cloth footwear, reached Laney first.

She peered dumbstruck at the old woman.

"Missy Franklin, Missy Franklin."

"I'm not—" Gulping, she shook her head to clear her ringing ears. Old habits died hard in the village. She was Miliana Franklin's granddaughter and to the villagers, she'd always remain Miss Franklin.

Mrs. Nagoto, not one hundred pounds soaking wet, socked her teenage grandson in the arm. "I tol' that grandson of mine . . ."

"Ow, Tutu!" he howled, rubbing his muscle.

"I tol' you no put stack . . ." She raised her hand to the height of her head. "No put stack so high. You no heard of gravity?" She angled toward Laney and nudged her grandson with a sharp, pointy elbow.

Laney shot a look at the grandson. Sheepish, he extended his hand, which Laney took. Once on her feet, she weaved.

Mrs. Nagoto placed an arm around Laney's waist. "Take easy, little lady. Not so fast."

She gaped at the destruction at their feet. "I'm-I'm so sorry for the mess I've caused, Mrs. Nagoto. Let me help—"

"Grandson do better this time." She tugged Laney's arm and pulled her to a stool beside the counter. "He do what his tutu say is right next time."

At a glare from his tutu, her grandson suppressed a groan and scuttled down the aisle, roping runaway cans into a pile.

Mrs. Nagoto patted her shoulder. "You okay, yeah?"

She stared at the paper clutched in her fist. "Mrs. Nagoto?" Her voice rasped. "Would you happen to know the given name of Pastor Kahanamoku's wife?"

Mrs. Nagoto's brow wrinkled. "Village tradition not to call first names of the reverends. Use last names. In respect."

She moistened her lip with her tongue. She took hold of the elderly woman's hand. "I know, Mrs. Nagoto. But I need to know. To be sure." Her eyes welled. "Would you tell me, please? Surely as the postmistress . . . ? Do you know?"

Mrs. Nagoto frowned. "Sure, honey. Sure. No get so upset."

Laney pressed her hand and scanned the woman's lined face. "Her name?" she whispered.

"Mrs. Kahanamoku's name?" Mrs. Nagoto shrugged. "Her name is Rose."

16

Driving like a maniac, Laney was never quite sure afterward how she managed to get from Nagoto's General Store to the ranch in one piece. Her mind, in an endless loop of deception and betrayal, replayed every encounter with Mrs. K—Lokelani Rose Franklin—over and over again.

Careening down the lane toward the house, she jammed her foot on the brakes of Kai's truck, stopping just shy of the front porch. Clouds of dust billowed, the brakes screeching. The yard empty, Elyse and Daniel hadn't yet arrived. Grateful for that, she jumped out of the truck and slammed the door shut.

Teah stepped onto the porch, wiping her hands on her apron. "What's wrong, Laney? Did you forget—?"

She marched past Teah straight into the house. The front room empty, she stalked past an empty dining room. She found the Lokelani quilt draped where Mily left it at breakfast. Teah lumbered with heavy footfalls behind her.

Laney plucked the quilt from the chair and held the grocery list next to the quilt label on the backside. The screen door to the lanai squeaked open. Her head snapped up.

Mrs. K—Rose—tiptoed in, a welcoming smile on her face. "Mily's taking a midmorning nap after the festivities last night. Did you have any . . . ?" The smile froze on her face. "What's wrong?"

Nostrils flaring, she raised the list in the air. With her other hand, she lifted the quilt. "Perhaps you'd introduce yourself to me more formally this time, Mrs. K? Or should I call you Rose like Mily does?" She threw the paper on the table. "But you can be sure I won't be calling you Mother. Ever . . ."

Rose flinched.

Teah reached for Laney.

She shook Teah off, her nose wrinkling. "And you, Auntie Teah? Lies just roll right off your tongue as smoothly as one wave after the next."

Teah turned a pasty white. She backed into the nearest wall, her hand on her throat. "I didn't mean . . . I wanted Rose to wait until today when everyone gathered here to tell you so we could be there to cushion the shock for you."

She reared. "Does everyone in the village know but me? Everybody at the luau last night know what a big fool I've been to trust any of you?"

Gasping, Teah grabbed the wall for support.

Rose came around the table and steadied Teah. "Sit down, Teah. You didn't take your blood pressure pill this morning, did you?" She dragged out a chair for Teah. "And you, Laney, need to lower your voice. No need to upset Mother, too."

Laney stiffened. "You don't get to tell me what to do." She jabbed her finger at Rose. "You gave up that right when you abandoned your own baby like a piece of unnecessary baggage on a stranger's doorstep."

Rose whirled. "Not a stranger. A good friend I left my infant daughter with when I had to work." Her mouth drooped. "A Christian woman who longed for a blessing like the daughter I had. A daughter I couldn't afford to take to the doctor though she cried hour after hour with repeated ear infections." Her voice rose several decibels. "A woman whose prominent husband would ensure my beloved child never went hungry or lacked for anything ever again."

The screen door creaked. Kai poked his head inside. "What's going on in here? I can hear you all the way to the barn." At the sight of their set faces, he glanced from Laney to Rose and back to Teah seated at the table, her breathing labored with repressed sobs. "What's wrong?"

His face tightening, he strode to his foster mother and grasped Teah's shoulder. "Mama Teah? Are you all right?" Receiving no answer, he sidestepped the table to where Laney clutched the quilt. "We explained about the ranch and the loan. What did you do? What did you say to her?"

The blood gurgled in her veins. "What did *I* say? What did *I* do?" Her eyes strained forward. "What about what she didn't say to me? What all of you've known and failed to tell me about my mother, Rose?" Her arm gestured at Rose, frozen in place behind Teah.

"Your mother? I don't understand. She died a long time ago in Las Vegas." He swiveled to Teah. "Right?"

"He didn't know, Laney," Teah whispered, her lips bloodless.

Rose rushed to the cabinet and rooted out a brown prescription bottle. She dumped one pill into her hand and extended it to Teah. She dropped the blue pill in Teah's open palm.

"No one knows. Not in the village. Nowhere. None of them remembered me from so long ago." Rose filled a small glass with tap water. Her hand wobbled, sloshing the water. "Not even my Maui cousin Teah, who'd not seen me since I was a little girl. Not until yesterday before the luau, when Mother showed Teah the page in our book of remembrance. One of the last pictures taken of me before I left the ‘ohana to go to college.”

Rose handed Teah the glass. “I’m not the same prideful teenager that left here all those years ago.” She watched as Teah put the pill in her mouth and raised the glass to her lips.

With a finger, she traced the deep wrinkles etched in her features. “The grooves in my face. The whitened hair. I look ten years older than my actual age. Lines carved from living homeless for a few years.”

She pivoted, staring out the window over the sink. “The ravages of what alcoholism does to a person who drinks, not just to forget but to end their worthless existence. A person who has no home, nowhere to belong, no child to hold anymore for whom to fight to go on living.” Her hands wrapped around the porcelain edge. “A person who’s lost everything and everyone they ever loved.”

Kai’s eyes widened. “You’re Lokelani Rose Franklin? Laney’s mama?”

Laney’s lip curled. “Not my mama. My biological mother. And me an accident she’s still too ashamed to acknowledge.”

Wheeling, Rose met her gaze. “Never ashamed. When Scott received the call to the pastorate here, I knew it was time to face my past and make amends. Amends too late for my father but still in time for my mother. And when I learned Elyse and Teah found you . . .” She swallowed.

“Does Pastor K know the truth?” Kai raked a hand through his hair. “He must know. Doesn’t he?”

Rose dipped her head. “He’s known the truth about me since that moment twenty-six years ago when he and a group of seminary students from an inner-city mission found me face down in my own vomit in the gutter.” She rubbed one hand over her shoulder blade. “Stabbed and left to die by the prostitute turned heroin addict who stole my wallet with my driver’s license and the last ten bucks I had to my name for my going-to-finish-the-job bottle of whiskey."

His eyes probed Teah's. "The addict? The woman they found with Rose's identity? The one they buried in the cemetery beside Jared Franklin?" Teah dropped her head to her hands.

Rose nodded. "Scott's wrestled day and night with his conscience and the truth. He wanted me to tell everyone right away."

Laney entwined her arms around the comforting presence of the quilt. The anger, thank God for the anger. It kept the tears at bay. "So why didn't you? Was it common curiosity that brought you here as Mily's caretaker posing as my friend, or—?"

"I am and have always been your friend, Laney." Rose sighed. "But you were so angry, so hostile every time anyone mentioned your birth mother." She gripped the chair. "I was a coward. I hoped maybe with time, if we had the chance to form a relationship outside the one you despised, perhaps . . ."

Laney flattened her lips. "Too little, too late. Just like your father."

Rose quivered.

With infinite precision, Laney folded the quilt in thirds and draped it over the chair. "Mily isn't delusional. She's smarter than the rest of us combined. She recognized Mrs. K right away as her daughter."

Rose straightened, a vein in her neck throbbing. "You don't forget your child, Laney. Ever."

She gave Rose a cold stare. "Apparently, some of us do, Lokelani. Some of us do."

Kai frowned. "I realize you're upset, Laney. You have every right to be, but you two need to talk and work this out."

Laney glared. "I think we've said about all we need to say to each other."

Shaking his head, he dusted his hands on the thighs of his jeans. "*Pa'akiki wahine*."

Laney snorted. "Stubborn? In this particular roomful of women I hardly qualify for that title."

He moved toward the hallway. "I'm going to check on Mily."

The tense silence between the three women lasted only as long as it took him to barrel into the kitchen moments later, his boots clomping across the koa floor. "She's gone and the front door's wide open."

Rose's lips trembled. "She probably overheard us fighting and didn't understand . . ."

His jaw worked. "Oh, I think she understood all too well the two people she loves most in the world were acting like they hated each other."

She darted a guilty glance Rose's way. "My fault. I shouldn't have . . ."

"Nobody's and everybody's fault," Rose countered. "Doesn't matter now. All that matters is finding her."

Teah shuffled her feet. Kai posited a hand on her shoulder. "You stay here, Mama Teah, in case she returns to the house. Elyse and Daniel will be here any minute and they won't know what's going on unless someone is here to relay the news."

"I'll search the barns," Laney offered. "She and I often go there to give the horses a treat."

"And I'll go down to the cross where we held the luau last night. Maybe she returned to the last happy place she remembers." Rose slipped her hand into her denim capris and extracted a cell phone. "I'll call Scott. He'll want to help with the search."

Teah grabbed hold of Kai's arm. "Should we call the police?"

He bit his lip. "Not yet. I'll drive toward the main road. She can't have gotten far. I'll check out my house and the cove. If I don't spot her there, then I'll call 911 for assistance." He paused on his way out to the lanai. "We need to pray and pray hard for Mily to be found. There's a storm front approaching from the east. Going to be a nasty afternoon with high surf."

"Pule," Rose whispered. "Pray for Mother to be found safe and . . . " her gaze traveled to Laney. "Pray for all of us."

He rested a hand on Laney's arm. The worry in his eyes she knew reflected in her own. But beneath the worry, she recognized the strength and encouragement he attempted to convey in a simple touch.

And as she headed out behind him, she prayed for Mily, the entire 'ohana, herself, and Kai to find their way to each other again.

Laney's stomach rumbled, but food was the last thing on her mind. It'd been hours and still no sign of Mily. Elyse, Ben, Pastor K, and the police had joined the search. Kai had gone to Hilo to borrow the chopper from his boss for an aerial search over the heavily wooded ranch terrain. Dark clouds threatened on the horizon out to sea.

"Where are you, Mily?" she whispered to the sky. She'd wondered if Mily might've remembered her and Kai talking about visiting the Franklin waterfall yesterday and after saddling Mango, she'd headed out there hoping and praying for some sign of her tutu.

Retracing her steps at the base of the waterfall, she detected only the rustling of the insects and the cacophony of birds. Steeling her heart that was pounding like a staccato drumbeat, she forced herself to peer into the pool, praying she wouldn't find her grandmother floating face down in the tranquil waters.

She sighed with relief at the clear, empty depths at her feet. Another thought intruded and Laney shielded her eyes with her hand as she studied the rocky incline at the top of the waterfall. Surely Mily wouldn't have attempted to climb the cliff . . . ? Not at her age? She squeezed her eyes shut, momentarily overcome with dizziness at the sight of the high, steep cliff walls.

But Mily's mind often played tricks on the old woman. Some days convinced she was again the young bride Jared brought home from Maui, other days Mily believed herself to be a new mother, confusing her baby, Rose, with Rose's baby, Alana.

No sign, however, of Mily at the top. Heaving a sigh of relief and feeling the first splatters of rain, she spotted something in the brush beyond the pool along the trail that led to the ocean. Hurrying over, she snatched at the pink shawl Mily wore around her shoulders earlier today in the cool, misty conditions of early morning in the Upcountry.

With a quick prayer of gratitude, she whipped her cell phone out of her jean pocket and positioned it to the circle of light in the middle of the grove. Nothing. Too far out for cell coverage.

Observing flattened leaf-fronds, she noted the trampled forest floor. Forging ahead, she located a muddy flip-flop print and scuffmarks across a bed of moss-covered ground.

"Mily?" she yelled over the raucous noises of the rainforest.

A faint sound replied. A human voice. Surging forward in relief, she burst out of the jungle and into the open onto a trail that skirted the churning, foaming Pacific below.

Perfectly composed with her legs crossed in a lotus position, Mily perched on a jagged promontory boulder overlooking the black rocks beneath. She waved and lifted her face to the sky as the downpour began.

"Mily!" She hugged the rock wall, willing herself not to look down. "What're you doing out here?" She scuttled forward, inching her way to her grandmother.

Her grandmother's face puckered at the concern in Laney's voice. She unwound her legs.

Laney thrust out her hand. "Wait. Don't move. I'll be there in a moment."

She clenched her teeth and dropped to her hands and knees. The sharp edges of the lava rocks bit into her flesh. Almost there. She kept one eye on her grandmother and the other onto her precarious position on the rock ledge.

Mily's eyes widened at something behind Laney and she waved again, her frantic, albeit joyful, motion setting off a tiny avalanche of volcanic cinders.

Laney dared not turn around. She prayed Kai was only a few yards behind her. He'd know what to do. He always did.

He was a born rescuer. Not her. She was usually the one needing rescue.

She groped at the rocky surface. One tiny slip . . . ?

Next stop Atlantis.

"Be still, Mily," she hissed between her gritted teeth, more forcefully than she'd intended.

Mily wagged her finger at her granddaughter. "You no speak to your elders that way, missy." Mily raised her head over Laney's shoulder. "You teach her better." In one graceful motion, Mily rose to her feet.

She prayed she'd live long enough to be that limber at Mily's age. Her ears caught the scrabble of rock as someone else skittered their way out onto the promontory behind her. Her hands fumbled and slid on the rain-slick rocks. Stifling a small scream, she dug the toes of her hiking boots into the unyielding stone, grabbing for traction.

God, are You listening? Are You there?

Mily planted her hands on her skinny hips. "Rose, tell your daughter she not talk to her tutu in that tone of voice."

She dropped her head and groaned. Rose. Not Kai. She was still on her own with this one, then.

"Laney," called Rose. "Be still, honey. I know you don't like heights. I'll be there in a minute. Hang on and wait for me."

Mily nodded, the rain continuing to flatten her white hair against her skull. "Rose climbed these rocks with her little friends." She gestured at her daughter creeping along the rock jettison. "You show Alana the lava tube you played in every summer."

Somehow, Rose remained upright. More power to her, Laney conceded. She'd not inherited the mountain goat gene from her.

Maybe the acrophobia came from her mysterious low-life biological father. "Great," she muttered under her breath. "Of all the things to inherit from him."

Rose bypassed her, taking a more direct and easier route. When Rose reached Mily's position, Laney collapsed against the rocky ground, hugging the life force of gravity beneath her. Allowing a moment for her heart to start beating again, she snake-bellied her orientation to face Rose and Mily.

"I'm going to escort Mama out to the trail." Rose scooped Mily's elbow and negotiated their way toward the safety of the rainforest. "I'll be back for you."

Like when she left me on the Carrigans' doorstep?

Sure she would.

Laney eased to a squat, balancing on the balls of her feet.

First life lesson, courtesy of Rose Franklin?

Never depend on anyone besides yourself.

Did that also include God?

She gulped, an unease niggling at the fringes of her mind that had little to do with the roiling water below.

After escorting Mily a safe distance away, Rose returned. Dropping to her denim-clad knees, Rose reached for her. "Take my hand, Laney. Let me help you."

She shook her head. "I don't need your help." She peered over the edge at the cauldron of water.

Rose frowned. "Don't look down. You'll make yourself dizzy." She jerked her hand in Laney's direction. "Stop being as stubborn as me. Trust me and take my hand—"

"No way I'm ever trusting you. I can take care of myself." Setting her jaw, she jolted to her full height.

Too quickly to regain her equilibrium.

She swayed.

"Not so fas—" Rose lunged as Laney's boot slipped off the edge.

Her arms flailed. Rose grabbed for her shirttail, catching a piece of the hem. Fabric ripped. Mily and Rose cried out, the sounds echoing against the steep canyon wall.

But the earth dropped out from beneath Laney. She raised her arms to cover her head and heard the sound of her voice screaming.

She braced herself for impact, one prayer—*Help me, God*—all she had time to breathe.

17

Rose scrambled agile as Kolohe down toward where Laney lay. "Hang on, honey!" Her wiry, waist-length salt and pepper hair whipped in the strong wind gusts. The waves thundered against the rocks.

Lowering her arms from around her head, Laney groaned.

"Don't try to move," Rose commanded.

Laney caught the thread of terror in her voice.

"Something could be broken. Let me check you out first." The implication, a broken spinal cord. Sometimes, from the panic in Rose's customary unruffled nurse demeanor, when it came to those closest to you there was such a thing as knowing too much.

Like loving too much?

She tried wiggling her toes and felt sensation. She exhaled. No broken back. But she was unable to free one booted foot from a vise where she'd landed in a crevice between two black rocks.

Raising on her elbows and peering at the tumultuous waves below the rocks, she realized certain death had been averted because she'd landed on a rocky shelf jutting three-fourths down the cliff. Her hands saved her face except for whopper-size bruises she'd see in the mirror tomorrow. But she thanked God there'd be a tomorrow for her after the headlong fall she'd taken.

Her elbows poked through the torn patches of her shirt. She drew herself, one knee to her chin, against the face of the cliff and surveyed the rest of the damage to her body. Her bloody knees glimmered through the shredded fabric of her Wranglers.

But hey, minor damage considering she was alive.

Something flew past the rim of the shelf to shatter on the rocks beneath. She propped herself higher as Rose wended her way to Laney's position. Laney glanced over the shelf and watched the twisted wire frames of Rose's glasses disappear, snatched away by a wave of water.

"Laney?" called Mily's thin voice from the top.

Rose jumped the last two feet to land beside Laney. Both of them squinted at Mily's worried face hanging over the cliff. Rose shooed her hand toward the forest. "Not so close to the edge, Mama." She dropped to her knees to examine Laney's foot jammed in the fissure. She worked her way up Laney's gone-stiff form, probing for breaks and cuts until she captured Laney's face between her hands.

Laney's lips trembled at the compassion and love she detected in her birth mother's eyes.

"Mother?" yelled Rose, releasing Laney's face and sinking upon her haunches. "I'm going to need you to go for help. Laney's foot is caught and I'm going to try to free it. But it's not going to be easy. I'm going to need assistance."

"Tide's coming in, Lokelani," scolded the old woman. "You know your father's told you a thousand times to pay attention to the rhythm of the earth."

Rose and Laney exchanged a look. Rose moistened her lips. "I know, Mother. That's why I need you to go quickly through the forest, past the waterfall and home to the ranch. Find Kai. Tell him where we are," she shouted above the crashing of the surf.

"Maybe you'd better go, Rose." Laney swallowed. "I'm not sure she can make it."

Rose shook her head. "I'm not sure you didn't hit your head on the way down." She brushed a lock of Laney's hair out of her face. "Possibility of a head injury. You could go into shock. I'm trained to deal with those kinds of complications." She craned her neck upward. "Go, Mother. I need you to go fast. Laney needs you to go find Kai. He'll know what to do."

Above them, Mily smiled and smoothed the tangled strands of her rain-flattened locks. "I'll get Jared. He's so sorry, Rose, for how he treated you and your baby. I'll be right back with your father. He'll make sure Alana is safe."

"Moth—"

Mily's head disappeared from their sight. Rose sighed.

"I'm not sure that was the right thing to do," Laney murmured.

Rose settled beside her, their backs against the rocky wall. "It's the only thing we could do."

Laney inspected the pounding water. "She's right. The tide's coming in."

Rose straightened her shoulders. "We'll be fine. Mama will find Kai. God will take care of us. He always has."

She threw Rose a skeptical look.

Rose's eyes narrowed. "Well, hasn't He? Where's your trust? You're still alive, aren't you?"

She sneaked another glance at the rising water. "For now." An uneasy silence settled between them, broken only by the shrieking of the wind.

"His name was Rob McCullen."

Laney darted a look at Rose. "Who?" But her heart already knew the answer.

Rose stared at the darkening horizon. "He was raised in the foothills of the Blue Ridge Mountains, a small town in North Carolina, by his grandmother. When she died, he joined the army."

Laney huddled into the ledge, her teeth chattering as the storm picked up in intensity. The fury of the driving rain stung her eyes and the rising waves crept ever closer.

"My father, Jared, was a controlling man. When I escaped his watchful eye at college on Oahu, I went a little wild. Rob and I met at a party in Pearl City. He came with his base buddies. I came with my sorority sisters. It wasn't the kind of scene, I learned later, Rob usually frequented. Sadly, for me all too typical of those early college years." Rose eased herself between Laney and the cold rock surface. "Here, let me warm you." She opened her arms.

Pulling back, Laney stiffened.

A frisson of hurt pockmarked Rose's face. She took a breath. "He was the sweetest, kindest soul I'd ever met, till I met Scott nearly a decade later. Lonely for the mountains of his birth, I told him about the mountains of my home. We struck up an unlikely friendship that night."

Her mouth pulled downward. "We were young, impetuous. Got things all out of God's order. We believed we'd have the rest of our lives to take things slower. But for those magical six months before he transferred to the mainland . . ." She sighed. "I was beyond devastated when I arrived and found he'd died a week earlier in a training mission."

The spray stung the cuts on Laney's hands and knees.

Rose swiveled, placing a hand on Laney's arm. "Did you have a good life, Laney?"

She found herself unable to break away from the pained intensity of Rose's eyes.

"That question haunted me in the dark hours of the night when I'd awaken drenched in sweat, second-guessing my decision to leave you with the Carrigans." Rose plucked at the fringes of Laney's frayed red plaid shirt. "Had I done the right thing by you? I didn't know Tom Carrigan, only Gisela." Her eyes welled with unshed tears. "I worried if he'd accepted you as his own child. If he'd found it in his heart to love you. If they'd both loved you enough for the three of us."

Something akin to compassion seared Laney's heart. A semblance of understanding passed between them. "Yes," she whispered. "They did. He does." She took hold of Rose's cold hand and rubbed it between her palms.

Rose's lips quivered. "Even after Scott and God loved me through withdrawal and rehab with a love that wouldn't let me go, I agonized over whether you were hurting, sick with another ear infection, coughing the croupy cough you'd begun to exhibit in the tenement slum I could afford. Once," Rose gave a mocking laugh. "Once when you would've been about ten, I dreamed you broke your arm falling out of a tree and when I awoke," she glanced away, a sheepish look on her face, "my arm ached for a good hour."

"My right arm," Laney whispered in the wind. "We lived in Phoenix at the time. I'd just started fifth grade."

Rose didn't bother to wipe away the tears that trailed down her cheeks. "When I walked away from you, I left you all I had to give you, a quilt sewn with love, infused with the mana—spirit—of my being. I gave you the only thing of me that could stay with you. But I loved you too much, Laney, not to walk away and give you the chance of a better life."

Laney studied the blue-green sea around them, acknowledged the power of its anger, and felt some of her own seep away.

"You told me that first day we talked you had two children . . ."

"One on the mainland." She gave Laney a tremulous smile. "And you were the other."

Her breath hitched.

"You have a sister who's longed to meet you since she was old enough to understand she had an older sister. She's a junior at the university in Santa Barbara. Her name's Olina. It means 'joy,' for God in His grace when I'd reached the end of myself gave me Himself, then Scott, and finally, another daughter to love."

Laney nodded. "I'm glad for you, Rose. I'm glad you were able to forget—"

"I never forgot you." Rose gripped Laney's hand. "I have a stack of letters each of us—Scott, Olina, and myself—wrote to you every year on your birthday."

Laney gaped at Rose, her brow furrowed. "Why did you never mail them?"

Rose jutted her jaw at the rising current of water, slapping at their feet. "You didn't belong to me. You belonged with the Carrigans, and I had no right to interfere in their relationship with you."

"Then why, Rose, did you write them?"

Rose's shoulders slumped. "Because I couldn't be there to celebrate your life with you, but on that one day, I could celebrate—we celebrated—God's gift of life in Alana Rose Carrigan. My little aloha rose."

It always came back to aloha. Always the good-byes.

The first rush of water surged over her ankle. "You'd better go, Rose. It's getting dark. I don't think Mily made it to the ranch. If help is going to come, it'll have to be summoned by you."

Rose shook her head. "I'm not going anywhere."

She grabbed hold of Rose's steadying hand and pushed herself upright, standing on one leg as far as her trapped foot allowed. "The tide's almost here. You need to leave."

"I'm not leaving you again."

The unspoken "again" hung in the air.

"Olina will need her mother, Rose."

Rose planted herself, arms crossed, at Laney's side. "Olina has a father, too. I think today my beloved—pilialoha—firstborn, stubborn daughter needs me more."

"Please, Rose . . ."

Rose ignored her and bent, her fingers digging at the rocks that encapsulated Laney's boot. "Pule, my sweet Laney. Never forget we live our lives in the power of prayer."

Too soon, the water rose to Laney's knee and Rose, most of her body underwater except for her head, pried and jabbed at the rocks with bloody hands.

"Don't do this to your family, Rose." She grasped Rose's shoulder. "You and I have made our peace with each other. I understand the sacrifice like Jochebed you made for me, and I thank you for the gift of life you gave me when you could've so easily followed the path of least resistance to Jared's urging. I thank you for the love that loved me enough to let me go to good people." A wave frothed at Laney's chest.

Rose dove headfirst under the water. The water swirled against Laney's legs as Rose kicked and clawed at the vise . . .

Until all underwater motion stilled.

She strained her eyes to track Rose's movement beneath the churlish surf. But nothing. No longer any hands upon the shoelaces of her boot. Panic bubbled in her chest.

Nobody could hold their breath that long.

"Rose! Answer me—"

Saltwater flooded her mouth and she choked. Spitting out the water, she bobbed, her leg still caught.

"God!" she screamed in a primal cry. "Don't let me lose her again."

A tug on her ankle, wrenching pain and she floated upward. Free at last.

In the pouring torrent, her hands scrabbled for a handhold to leverage herself higher. She dug in the toes of the one remaining steel-plated hiking boot. Her other socked foot she flattened against the slick rock surface like a gecko seeking a toehold.

Her hand found a crevice and hung on, her fingers locked in a death grip. With her other hand, she beat the empty water within her reach. "Rose!" she sobbed. "Mama, don't l-l-leave me."

Rose sprang from the depths of the water, throwing herself at Laney's outstretched arm. She jerked Rose closer, her shoulder distending as she hung on for dear life—Rose's life—to a long length of Rose's beautiful hair as the moana tide fought and grappled to pluck Rose from the land of the living.

Her lungs bursting and her chest heaving, Rose flung herself face first into the rock beside Laney. She encircled her mother with the protection of her body and inserting her hands underneath Rose's arms, crawled inch by exhausting inch higher.

Several feet ahead for now of the jealous waves, she paused to regain her breath. Rose choked and sputtered. She and Rose clung to the warmth of the other.

Rose tilted her head toward the water, her eyebrows raised into a question mark. "You hear, Alana?"

Laney blinked to clear her stinging eyes of the saltwater. "Hear what?"

Rose pointed to the sky. A slow grin broke out across her face.

She cocked her head, straining to hear above the roar of the ocean and the ferocity of the wind. But Rose was right, a wonderful, life-saving sound.

The sound of helicopter rotors.

"A nursing mother might forget her own baby," Rose shouted above the din. "And I promise I never forgot you, Laney. Ever." Rose gestured at the sky. "But God has promised never to forget you. Or me. Or any of His dear, pilialoha children."

Her eyes drank in the sight of the red, white and blue Aloha Tour helicopter speeding their way. "Kai?"

Rose nodded. "They're certified to be first responders in cases of emergency. The month before you came, he and the EMS-trained crew airlifted a movie director and his leading lady to safety out of the Valley during a flash flood."

"He's a handy guy to have around, isn't he?"

Rose laughed out loud. "Truer words . . ."

She watched as the chopper hovered and shuddered in the wind shears off the sea. "It's too dangerous." Her eyes widened as she witnessed the epic struggle Kai fought inside the cockpit to keep the aircraft stable. "Go back!" She waved her arm.

Rose's grip tightened. She leaned her mouth closer to Laney's ear. "He won't go back. Kai never gives up on anything or anyone he loves. I know he loves you, Laney, even if he can't admit it to himself yet."

With the copter about 150 feet above their heads, Rose covered Laney's body with her own as the rotors whipped the spray from the waves. Foot by precious foot, Kai lowered the aircraft alongside their position, careful to keep the rotating blades free and clear of the cliff surface.

Reaching their precarious location, a man emerged from the open side of the chopper, hanging on with one arm, his feet clenched on the perch. He held out his hand for Rose. "Climb on the skids," he yelled. "I'll stabilize you."

She jabbed her finger at Laney to go first. Laney shook her head.

"Come on," the man shouted at the top of his lungs. "Can't maintain this bucking bronco in this wind forever."

Under duress, Laney kept one hand on Rose's shoulder and extricated her socked foot from the cliff face, her toes searching for the skid perch. The man leaned, grabbing hold of her extended arm. "Let go of her," he yelled. "I've got you. Trust me."

Did it always come back to that in the end?

Her eyes riveted one last time onto Rose. With a smile, Rose nudged her to be off. Biting the inside of her cheek, Laney retracted her booted foot from the safety of her toehold, released Rose, and leaped for the skids. Her foot missed and dangled in mid-air.

Yanking her closer, the man wrapped his arm around her torso as she crawled the last few feet into the chopper. Gasping for breath, she hugged the seat. Her heart pounding, she swiveled to ascertain Rose's situation.

With a tiny salute, the man turned his attention to Rose. Within minutes, Rose was enfolded into the protective covering of the helicopter. She and Laney held fast to each other.

She fixed her eyes on the back of Kai's head in the cockpit. Hunched over and opening a first aid kit, the EMT reported the mission complete and successful. Kai jerked around as if to make sure for himself.

Laney mouthed a thank-you. The tense lines around his eyes softened until a sudden squall forced his attention to the controls.

As she answered the EMT's routine questions, and allowed him to treat and bandage her minor scrapes and cuts, she continued a silent stream of prayer for Kai as he wrestled in a life and death struggle to maintain altitude and momentum against the fury of a storm that threatened to pluck them from the sky and ram the chopper into the side of the cliff.

His worst fear coming to life in front of his eyes, a replay of Afghanistan. But her God and Kai's was a God about the do-overs, and she prayed for Kai to be given a second chance to make things right, a chance to save and not lose lives this time.

And in answer to her earnest prayers, a lull in the wind allowed Kai to move the chopper away from the cliff, up and over the rain forest and toward Hilo. With the best training in the world—courtesy of Uncle Sam, her dad's army and God's divine ability intervening in the midst of their human frailty—Kai landed the copter safely at the airstrip.

Removing the headphones, Kai launched from the cockpit to the ground, ducking his head under the still rotating blades and had the door to the back flung open before the EMT could react. Leaning in, he scooped her into his arms and—his head bowed over hers—made a dash between raindrops to the protection of the hangar.

Clutched in his arms, she wished he'd never let her go, but too soon for her comfort, he lowered her body upon a couch in the pilot's lounge. "The paramedics are on the way." His lips blue, his face shone with the strain of fear.

"I'm okay, Kai." Though he'd released her, he hadn't let go of her hand, his thumb brushing her skin. "What about Tutu? Did she find her way to the ranch?" She gulped. "Is she okay?"

Kai's lips tightened. "She made it through the forest to where you'd left Mango. She released him knowing he'd return to the ranch faster than she ever could. After securing Mango, Ben spotted her halfway across the meadow and later radioed me your situation and approximate location on the search grid we were conducting."

She heaved a sigh of relief. The EMT escorted Rose into the lounge. "Mily's safe and okay," she called to her mother. "She came through for us."

Rose collapsed in relief against the stalwart form of the EMT.

The sound of a siren rose over the gusting wind outside. Kai touched her cheek with his finger. He straightened and pivoted to go.

"Can't you take us home, Kai?" Laney begged.

"You need to be examined by medical professionals. Just to be sure . . ." He ran a hand, a shaking hand, through his rain-plastered hair. "I'll be around." He strode out the door.

The creak of gurney wheels clattered down the hall. With the medics probing and prodding at her black and blue body, she agreed to be taken to the local hospital for an X-ray of her head and ankle at Rose's insistence.

As she was being loaded into the ambulance, Laney noted the storm passed as quickly as it arose. Streaks of blue marbled through the barrage of gray. She kept her eyes peeled for a rainbow but had no joy.

Nor in another longed-for sighting of her beloved—pilialoha—rescuer cowboy, either.

18

After the rescue, she'd had several days to recover from her slight injuries. Several days to get to know her mother better. To know her husband, Scott—her new stepfather?—who as stepfathers went would be a terrific one. She'd spoken over Skype with her new sister, Olina.

Her dad emailed photos from her childhood—pictures of dance recitals, soccer tournaments, graduations, and proms. Mily, Rose, and Teah pored over all of them, surrounding Laney with the love of her 'ohana.

All of them, except for Kai.

Giving her a lot of time to think, to talk with her mother, Rose, and her dad, and most of all, to pray. Something she should've spent more time doing from the start.

She longed to free Kai from the protective shell he'd wrapped around himself and his heart. She yearned to free him from the gaping pit, the hole that scarred his life since the time he was a boy. To be the great man she believed lay trapped inside a wound that had never healed since his mother died.

After rethinking her motivation for pursuing the Jakarta story, she placed a call to her editor. Her motivations and desires had changed. She canceled her flight and decided to pass on the Jakarta trip as she sensed God telling her to take a breath and wait.

For a future with Kai?

To stay or to go? Hawai'i or D.C?

She prayed for the courage and faith to be the Laney that God wanted her to be. She didn't know what the next step was that God had for her, but wherever it was, He'd go with her. As would the spirit of her new 'ohana.

That afternoon, the family gathered on the lanai after a sumptuous feast put on by Rose, to whom Teah had surrendered kitchen duties. The front door and the door to the lanai stood wide open to allow the house to catch any ocean breezes. With Mily stretched out in a chaise lounge, Elyse, Scott, and Rose sipped fruity drinks.

With umbrellas, Laney observed with a smile. Because like her, Rose adored little pink parasols.

Teah stuffed Laney's breadfruit quilt cushion with fiberfill. She'd stitched the three sides inside out on her sewing machine. "I'll leave a small space after I stuff it for you to slip-stitch shut. Yeah?" Teah crammed another wad of fiberfill into the rectangular pillow.

Laney raised her eyebrows at Rose.

No worries. I'll show you how, mouthed Rose when Teah's back turned.

Teah's head snapped around. "What?" Teah made a palms-up motion. "Easy as lava flowing off a volcano. I teach you everything you ever need to know, yeah?"

Swallowing her grin, Laney lowered her lashes, taking another sip of her drink. The smile on her face crumbled at the sound of Kai's truck pulling into the circular driveway at the front of the house. Her heart stutter-stepped.

He'd been significantly absent from their luncheon. Hiding in his turtle shell, Teah explained with a sniff earlier.

She tensed, expecting any moment to hear the sound of his feet slapping down the hallway. Instead, he charged around the side of the house and tromped over to them. Her mouth went dry.

Was this the moment God had been telling her to wait for? Was this the sign? Two days had been two days too long without the sight of those clear blue eyes of his.

Which at the moment looked a little bloodshot. As if he hadn't slept well. In several days.

He scowled at the sight of her in the wicker chair. "You're still here?"

Teah sucked in a breath. "Kai . . ."

A sign, all right. Crystal clear as the waters off the cove.

Laney hunched her shoulders. "Apparently much to your sorrow. Like a bad penny that just keeps turning up."

His face flushed. "I didn't mean it that way. The time got away from me. I thought maybe I'd missed you before your flight left."

She darted a guilty look at Rose and Teah. She hadn't meant to keep it a secret. Everybody but Kai knew she'd canceled her flight for today.

A fact he would've been privy to as well—if he'd bothered to pick up a phone since the rescue.

"Laney has—"

She cut off Elyse's response with a shake of her head. And rising to her feet, absurdly glad—at the top of the steps with him at ground level—for once she managed to look him straight in the eye. "If you've got anything to say to me," her lips tightened. "Then I suggest you say it, Barnes." She leaned against the railing. "I think I've made my feelings pretty clear."

He swallowed. "I-I need . . ." He moistened his lips and tried again. "We need to talk." He gestured toward the lawn.

She folded her arms. "You can say anything you need to say to me right here."

He let out an exasperated sigh, jamming his hands into his front pockets. "You've got issues, Laney Carrigan. Always got to make everything so difficult."

She rolled her eyes. "Did you just call *me* a drama queen?" She poked him in the chest. "News flash, Kai Barnes. We've both got issues. Issues like trust versus fear."

Teah huffed to her feet. "For heaven's sake, talk to each other. Here? There?" she jeered. "Anywhere, but talk. Put the rest of us out of our misery." She clucked her tongue, gathering discarded cups onto a wooden tray. "Two of the brattiest children I've ever had the misfortune to know."

Scott exchanged an amused look with Rose. Mily straightened in her chair. "What did I miss?"

Rose patted her hand. "Nothing, Mama. The fireworks are about to begin."

"Stubborn, muleheaded . . ." Teah jabbed her finger in the air. "Please, do the rest of the world a favor and work out your insecurities with each other. Spare two other perfectly innocent human beings who might lack the good sense to avoid matrimony with either of you."

Teah heaved the tray, balancing it across her hip. "You two deserve each other for sheer pigheadedness." She sashayed into the darkened interior. Scott put a hand over his mouth.

Laney and Kai gaped after her and then at each other.

"Be sure and tell us how you really feel, Ma," Kai called after her.

Laney moved past him down the steps, leaving him to follow.

Or not.

Underneath the shade of the banyan tree, she swiveled, barreling into the iron rock of his chest. She bounced off. Her lips parted.

She'd not heard him behind her. Sometimes she forgot about his army stealth training. Her pulse quickened. She sharpened her tone to hide her anxiety. "What do you want from me?"

"I-I want . . ." He dropped his gaze and took a breath. "I want to talk you out of going to Jakarta." He pointed at the group on the lanai. "You've not told them, have you, what you plan to do when you go there?"

This was about Jakarta?

She sighed. "Old news, Kai. If you'd bothered to talk to me—"

"Not old news." His jaw worked. "You getting yourself killed is not old news to me."

She crossed her arms. "I've decided not to go to Jakarta, if that makes you any happier." She snorted to show him what she thought of the likelihood of that—him being happier.

A gust of air whooshed out of his mouth. "I'm glad you've come to your senses and realized what's good for you."

Her eyes narrowed into slits. She drew herself up. All five foot three of her.

Cocking her head, her voice dropped to a dangerous whisper. "What's good for me?"

He nodded. "Good for Mily and your mother, too."

"And you, Kai?" She painted a smile on her face. A smile she'd seen Kolohe wear when he'd sighted his prey. "Good for you, too? You'd get to see me every day on your terms, at your convenience."

He frowned, his brow molded into a V. "I think no good will come from you leaving the 'ohana."

"The 'ohana? Not you?"

He clamped his lips together. "That's what I said, wasn't it?"

"And what about what I said to you at the waterfall, Kai?"

He shook his head. "You can't love me." He clasped his hands behind his back and stood, his feet shoulder-width apart, as if at attention. "I'm not going down that road with you, Laney. Not now. Not ever. I-I can't be the man you deserve."

His words and the silence that followed hung in the air between them.

She peered into his face. "Did you ever stop to think about the man God wants you to be? The plans He has for you? Plans that go nowhere in your feeble strength, but if you'd let go of your fear and trust His strength, plans that could take you places you've never dreamed of. He wants to free you from the guilt and shame. True freedom. Real wings to fly."

He raked his hand over his head. "It's not that easy."

"Nothing worth having ever is." She clutched his arm. "When are you finally going to come out from underneath that bed, Kai?"

His mouth hanging open, he threw her a sharp look.

"Do you know what your problem is, Kai Barnes?"

"No," his jaw jutted. "Do tell what *my* problem is, Laney Carrigan."

"Your problem is you think you're God."

He flinched.

"And you're not." Laney refused to let go of his arm. "Not. God. Kai. Barnes. God's spent your entire lifetime performing one SAR over you after another. You are not your father. But God rescued you from that. You couldn't rescue that soldier or your crew, but God could and did bring you out alive. Why not the others? Why not Hank?"

She shrugged. "I don't know, but then I'm not God. And neither are you."

The muscles beneath his shirtsleeve quivered underneath the palm of her hand. His fist clenched and opened. Laboring for each breath, his nostrils flared. He jerked his arm out of her grasp.

"Come into the sunlight and take the gift of not just family Uncle Pete offered or the salvation Scott showed you, but the gift God offers His children each and every day. Can you not see His hand of love? How He longs—?"

"Stop turning this into something about me. It's about you. What's good for you and the 'ohana." Wheeling, he stalked toward the house.

She dogged his steps, laying a restraining hand on his elbow. "You don't get to decide what's good for me." She waved her hand in the direction of the lanai. "Not you. Not my dad. Not Rose." She planted her hands on her hips. "Only God gets to do that from now on. If He tells me to go to D.C., I'll go to D.C. If He tells me to go to Jakarta next month, then that's what I'll do."

Kai glared at her. He'd spent a sleepless night—two sleepless nights—trying to figure out a way to make her stay. A way other than promising something he couldn't deliver.

But this—the outrage shimmered in heat waves off her petite form—this wasn't going the way he'd planned.

"If you think I'm going to wait around here?" Her arm swept the expanse of the ranch. "Wait for you to get over yourself—and I don't doubt eventually you will because you've got a good pastor. And despite your hardheaded, self-inflicted idiocy, I believe you do love God. One day you're going to wake up and accept it's Him in you and not the other way around that makes all things possible."

She dropped her arms to her side, but her eyes bored into his soul. He winced at the sadness and regret that peeked out at him. Something tore inside his chest.

"I'm not going to stand in line with the other fluffy kittens queued up on this island to get your attention. Not my idea of a good time, much less a good life."

He growled. "Enough with the fluffy kittens."

She turned her back on him.

Panic grabbed hold of his throat. "So you're going to run away? Like you always do?" he choked out.

She kept her face toward the lanai. "No. Not running. Not anymore. I'm walking away. Walking toward the roots God meant for me all along." She glanced over her shoulder at him. "Maybe not this rainbow. But I know," she laid a hand over her chest. "I know He has one just for me. One that brings me to a man who longs to know and love me. A man I can know and love back. And children . . ." She sighed. "My pot at the end of the rainbow."

Mounting the steps, she planted a kiss on Mily's cheek and angled toward his sister. "If we hurry, Elyse, I can still catch the red eye to LAX."

The loss of her rushed over him like a tsunami wave.

Elyse darted a glance at him, frozen where Laney deserted him on the lawn. "If you're sure that's what you want."

She gave Rose a small hug. "Not what I want, but what I need to do for now."

Elyse nodded. "I'll drive you there as soon as you're ready."

He forced his feet to move closer to his family.

"Won't take me long." She didn't look back. "I've learned to always travel light."

19

As Laney disappeared inside the house, she took with her the last of every fond hope Kai ever dared to dream. The knot in his belly constricted. Kai couldn't seem to replenish his lungs with enough oxygen.

"She'll never come back," whispered Rose. Scott stroked her hand.

Elyse scowled at Kai. "Or not until she brings a husband with her."

Her words sucker-punched him. Flashbacks of fire, reverberating booms, and the metallic smell of blood—his mother's blood—overwhelmed his senses. He had to get away from here. Away from Laney. Away from his 'ohana.

Time. He needed time. Time to sort out this mess he'd made of his life. The mess Laney had made of his heart.

Breathing room. Space. The makings of a headache pulsed at his temples. It'd been so long since he'd had an episode, the blinding migraines that dogged him night after night.

Not today. Why now? Not here.

He shoved away from the lanai, careening toward the barn. His breath ragged, he grabbed the saddle pad off the door of Muffin's stall. He'd not had one of those episodes since . . . ?

Since Laney came.

Kai brushed his hand over the rippling strength of horseflesh. Muffin stamped and blew out a whuffling breath, as if sensing his favorite human's restlessness. He needed to find a place to think. A place to pray.

His conscience pricked. Probably something he should've done two nights ago instead of thinking he'd come up with a perfect solution. He'd only worked himself into a lather. Muffin's tail swished across his face as he tightened the saddle's girth.

Panic clawed at his chest as he adjusted the bridle. Got to get away. Before he lost it and did something . . .

Something that gnawed at his insides. Before the words he whispered in his dreams made it all the way out of his lips.

Because if Laney knew—what he could no longer deny to himself—she'd never leave. Though wasn't that exactly what he'd been trying to get her to do all along? To stay? But at what cost to his carefully gathered shards of control?

He swung his leg over Muffin's back. To let her in—he shuddered—he couldn't face it. The contempt or worse, pity, he'd see in her eyes when she saw him for what he was, how he saw himself.

Maybe she was right to go. He'd been wrong to try to keep her here. He'd ruin her life if she stayed, like he'd already ruined his.

He pointed Muffin's nose toward the meadow. He'd feel better, he assured himself, with the soothing, rhythm of horseflesh under his saddle. As so many of his former colleagues in the armed services would, too, once the Equine Therapy Center opened. His dream come true.

A dream Laney made happen.

Digging in his heels, he spurred Muffin into a gallop. Sprinting across the grass, he jolted at the memory of another madcap dash across this pasture. "Whoa!" He tugged at the reins.

Muffin reared and Kai fought to maintain his seat. But one look at the shadowy interior of the rain forest and he knew he'd find no peace at the waterfall.

Not today. Maybe not ever.

He wheeled Muffin in the other direction, leaning forward in the saddle as they trotted over a series of hills that separated his property from the ranch. He emerged onto the beach, not far from the black rocks where he and Laney . . .

"God!" he railed at the cloudless blue sky.

Was there no place safe from memories of her? Memories like a consuming conflagration. Muffin whinnied, a nervous pawing at the sand. Kai's head throbbed. He clutched his stomach.

He clicked his tongue under his bottom teeth and urged Muffin up the path toward home. He'd get a quick bite to eat, return Muffin to his stall and retrieve his truck parked at the ranch house. She'd be gone by then.

Entering through the dense jungle cover, he approached the lanai and dropped heavy to the ground. He looped the reins over the porch railing. His nose tickled at the familiar sweet scent of the jasmine that covered the pergola.

Gritting his teeth, he stomped inside the kitchen, filled a spare basin with water, and left it under Muffin's nose. Returning to the kitchen, he grabbed an energy bar. He ripped open the packaging and yanked off a chunk with his teeth. He chewed, willing himself to swallow. His throat tightened.

Kolohe materialized from the hallway with a low purr and rubbed against his ankles.

He choked, spitting out bits of granola. Kolohe planted himself on the toe of his boot and proceeded to self-groom.

Kai wiggled his boot. Kolohe didn't budge. Ignored him, in fact.

"Blasted cat." He shook his foot. "Stupid stray."

With great dignity, Kolohe stirred himself and with one last flick of his tail against Kai's denim leg, drifted down the hallway.

A stupid stray?

Like him. He sighed. And right now, Kolohe was probably his only friend.

If you don't count God, a voice in his head chided.

Laney was right. Far too often, he forgot to count God into the equation of his life and his fears. He ran a weary hand over the beard stubble he'd not taken the time to shave this morning. Leaving his boots on, he hurried after Kolohe, eager to make amends.

Calling for the cat, he detected a rustle near his bed. Getting on his knees, he lifted the bedspread and spotted a pair of glowing eyes in the far reaches underneath the bed.

"Kolohe?" He extended a hand. "Come out. It's okay, I promise."

Whispers of those same words . . . so long ago.

He froze, his hand in midair. The chopper spiraling out of control against a blazing desert sunset. Visions of himself as that frightened seven-year-old boy.

Too afraid then and now to move forward into the life Christ had for him. Recognizing the illusion of his so-called control, tears sprang to his eyes.

How foolish he would've been to refuse the offer of help and love from Daddy Pete. How stupid to have refused Pastor K's life-changing message when he'd come home. Why did he still cling to the past with its fear and guilt?

Why so afraid to embrace God's latest gift of love for him?

Laney—another good gift from His Father. God didn't play games with hearts and He'd put a love for Laney in his heart for a reason.

A love he didn't have to deny. A love God yearned for him to embrace.

His hand dropped to his thigh. He leaned his forehead against the mattress. His choice to surrender the guilt and fear to God, to focus on what God had for him now. Focus on the plans God wanted him to do with the love and strength He'd provided.

Or, he moaned, he could linger in the fear. Wallow in the pseudo guilt. But if he chose that path, he chose to deny not only God's love for him, but to deny as well the power of the cross to save.

Laney had been right about him. Story of his life? He'd spent his whole life not flying so much as trying to beat the air and his world into submission.

His mind flashed to those days when he'd worked with the old man, Jared, carving and coaxing the wooden beams to life. A symbol of death and shame. He recalled how oftentimes Jared's tears dripped upon the chisel in his clenched hand, the tears soaking into the grain of the wood.

Understanding only reached, for him and for Jared, at a place of utter brokenness. The cross not a symbol of death and defeat. But, a symbol of life and hope.

For to stay cocooned in the fear denied God's hand outstretched to him as Pete's had been so long ago. To remain in the guilt declared the cross insufficient. Insufficient for the fear, insufficient to make him the husband, father, and son he could and should be.

"Jesus," he whispered, his lips brushing against the soft cotton coverlet. Christ had already done these things for him and in him. He'd been rooted in fear, the fear like chains anchoring his chopper to the earth.

Chains loosed by Christ. The guilt and fear nailed to the cross. No condemnation, he recalled a Bible passage, no condemnation in Christ.

He murmured the words into the silence. He repeated the verse, shouting the words at his fears.

All he had to do was to look at the cross and choose—he gasped at the enormity of it—choose to trust, to never be afraid again. Easy to say.

And the hardest thing in the world to do.

Then, he'd truly fly on the wings of God's unsearchable forgiveness and strength, finding real peace. Real freedom for his soul.

He poured out his fears before God, burying his face into his hands and between his knees. Hot tears leaked between his fingers. A lifetime of anxieties ebbed away—along with the migraine—out of his head and heart, replaced by the incoming wave of a sweet, gentle peace.

A wet, rough tongue rasped over his knuckles. His eyes flew open. Kolohe, the stray.

Like him, once lost but now found. He nestled his face against Kolohe's fur and pondered the one fear that yet remained.

Not his father. Not Afghanistan. Nor the PTSD.

Ever since Laney arrived, his dreams had been haunted by his fear to love her, unable in his sleep to accept the lies he told himself during the day. He loved her. Plain and simple.

What he felt for her? There was nothing remotely simple about it.

Fragments, wisps, of recent dreams floated through his mind. This is what kept him awake at night, afraid to fall asleep again and dream . . .

Of her.

His greatest fear come true, the thread of panic that unraveled when she'd marched into the house. Away from the 'ohana.

Who was he kidding?

Away from him.

He couldn't fathom life without Laney. He'd spent his whole life holding his breath, waiting for her . . . And as sure as he knew the sun would rise, he believed God put them together.

As for his fears?

His newfound peace resurfaced, calming and quieting his turmoil. God would work it out.

Kolohe's head butted against his shoulder. With a flick of his tail, Kolohe sauntered over to the door and scratched to be let out. As if done with mollycoddling his human and ready to resume his independent persona.

Resembling someone else Kai knew?

His eyes darted to the clock on his bedside table. How long had he . . . ? Was it too late? Had he missed his chance with her?

Kai scrambled to his feet and swayed against the bed as the blood rushed slowly—too slowly—into his too long immobile limbs. He didn't have time for this. Not if he wanted to catch her before she left the ranch.

Because he had a bad feeling in the pit of his stomach that once she left the ranch . . .

Yanking open the door, he barreled out of the house and untied Muffin from the porch. He swung into the saddle and plucked his hat from the saddle horn. "Waha!" he yelled, clapping his Stetson into Muffin's side.

Bamboo leaves slapped at him as he and Muffin dashed through the hill country toward the ranch house. He and Laney had both been on a journey, seeking a connection.

Journeys whose paths intersected with each other. That kind of huaka'i required truth and heart and extraordinary courage.

The same kind of courage she'd displayed in traveling halfway across the world to find her family. The kind of courage required of those who sought God. The courage intrinsic to any who sought a place to belong and someone to love.

As he and Muffin darted out from the jungle undergrowth and plowed to a stop in front of the ranch house, he prayed he wasn't already too late.

"Laney!" he called, one leg in the process of swinging off.

"She's gone." Rose stood in the door.

He dropped into the saddle. His hands trembled, entwined in the leather reins.

Rose stepped out from the shadows. "But she's only been gone a few minutes. I delayed her as long as I could. I knew you'd return." She gestured across the pastures. "If you hurry . . ."

He gripped the reins. "Thank you, Rose."

She tossed her wiry hair over her shoulder. "Thank you for loving my daughter." She smiled, her eyes turning into half-moons. "Now go and love her well, Kai Barnes."

He clucked his tongue and swung Muffin past the corral. No time to take the truck. He'd never catch her if he stuck to the road.

But if he took the shortcut across the pastures, he stood a chance of stopping her before she reached the highway. He dug his heels into Muffin's side, urging him beyond the trot, past the canter and into a gallop.

Time to run. Run toward his dreams.

Racing across the windswept plain, he lost his hat and Muffin's sides heaved. Froth escaped from between Muffin's teeth and the bit. Lifting out of the saddle, Kai leaned forward as far as he could balance, sinking his boots into the stirrups.

He let Muffin have his head, shoving his hands into Muffin's raven mane to save Muffin's mouth. He positioned his weight through his shoulders, keeping his eyes fixed straight ahead, encouraging Muffin to greater bursts of speed.

The wind whooshed past his bare head. Ahead to the left, just shy of the Franklin Ranch arch, he spotted Elyse's little blue sedan.

"Help me, God," he prayed. "Help me to catch up with her." He prayed for the right words, the courage to say the words Laney needed in order to stay.

Laney fingered the plastic frames of her pink eyeglasses in her navy skirt pocket. She leaned against the leather seat, ordering her shoulders to relax, to uncoil. Anger churned in her belly. She'd never imagined—considering her past baggage with her dad and Rose—herself capable of feeling this much anger. A burning that rivaled Pele herself.

And, a mind-numbing hurt.

Elyse, her hands gripping the wheel, flicked a glance in the rearview mirror. She frowned, easing her foot on the accelerator.

Laney jerked her head. "Why are you slowing?"

Elyse remained mute, her eyes trained ahead.

Laney checked her wristwatch. "If we hurry, we'll have time to stop by your apartment and say good-bye to Ben and Daniel."

Elyse responded by removing her foot from the pedal.

She watched the needle on the speedometer fall. "What're you doing? What's—?"

Out of the corner of her eye, she caught a blur of movement on the right. Something black and fast, flashing past the car on the other side of the fence.

Her eyes widened as Kai and Muffin whizzed by, parallel to the car. Her head shot over to Elyse who stretched her foot in the direction of the brake. "Don't you dare stop!"

She jabbed a finger at her cousin. "Put your foot on the accelerator and give it the gas."

"I think my brother wants to talk to you."

"Well, I don't want to talk to him. I'm talked out with him."

"Stubborn wahine . . ." Elyse muttered under her breath.

"Elyse . . ." she warned, her voice rising.

If they could make it to the highway, the fence would stop Kai as effectively as anything she could say.

He hunched forward, in one fluid motion turning Muffin's nose in the direction facing the passenger side of the car. Muffin didn't lose an ounce of speed. The distance between them narrowed.

She studied his head bent close to Muffin's, Kai's short black hair mixing and mingling with Muffin's longer mane. The look in his eyes . . . His eyes dark as a blue typhoon over the Pacific. She gasped.

He wouldn't. He couldn't. Could he?

And then—if she lived to be a hundred—a sight she'd never forget.

Kai and Muffin leaped straight into the air. All four of the horse's hooves half folded underneath his body. In the air, rider and mount with one purpose.

Her heart thudded. She wanted to close her eyes, but she couldn't take her eyes off them. She groaned out loud, praying they'd clear the wire fence.

Muffin and Kai sailed over, resembling something from *The Man from Snowy River.* Kai leaned way back in the saddle, gripping the saddle horn and the other arm flung over his head. Muffin's hooves touched the surface of the earth and landed with a decisive thump two car lengths in the road ahead of them.

She grabbed the dashboard with one hand and the strap of her seat belt with the other. Both of them screaming, Elyse throttled the steering wheel, slamming her foot and the brake against the floorboards. The car fishtailed. Gravel flew beneath the spinning tires.

Elyse regained control, the car shuddering to a stop a mere five feet from where Kai sat atop the horse. Underneath the ranch's arch, Elyse closed her eyes and laid her forehead against the wheel. "Stupid brudda. Always got to make big body . . ." She glared at Laney. "You two are going to be the death of all of us."

He vaulted off the horse as his legs ate up the distance. "Laney," he shouted. "I want to talk to you."

She gave him a nice view of her shoulder.

Kai banged on the door.

"Hey," Elyse yelled. "Watch the paint job, brudda."

"Would you get out of the car, Laney?" He rattled the door handle.

Panicked, Laney jabbed the locking mechanism on her door. "I've got nothing to say to you."

Elyse cut the engine. Laney's eyes bored a hole in Elyse's forehead.

"Would you turn around and look at me?" he pleaded.

Laney—she knew it was childish—put her hands over her ears. "I can't hear you."

"I know you can hear me. Please, Laney," he begged. "Get out of the car and let me talk to you. You don't have to talk to me. Just let me talk to you."

"No."

He kicked a tire and grunted in pain. Muffin strolled over to a patch of dandelions lining the ditch bank. "If you don't open this door, right this minute, I'm going to—"

"You're going to what?" Pivoting, she quirked an eyebrow at him. "You and whose army?"

He poked out his lips and took a deep breath. "I'm going to crawl through the sunroof." He planted his hands flat against the roof of the car.

Laney's head snapped skyward. She made a grab for the keys in the ignition.

Elyse was faster.

"Give me those keys, Elyse Ching," she growled.

Elyse shook her head. "Not happening."

She held out her hand. "The keys. Don't make me get rough with you. My dad trained me to deal with hostiles."

Elyse dropped the keys down her shirt and gave Laney an I-dare-you smile.

Laney lunged for Elyse. The car rocked as Kai clambered up the side.

She grabbed for the armrest, her nostrils flaring. "Stop shaking the car. Get off, Barnes."

Kai's head popped over the sunroof. "Please, Laney. Kala mai, forgive me for my stupidity and for hurting you." He released a jagged breath.

Her brow puckering, she examined her knuckles, turning white in her death grip on the edge of the seat, unable to meet his gaze.

"God and you finally got my attention. I've given him my fears, my past." His voice wobbled. "And my future. A future I pray includes a home and family of my own." He swallowed. "With you."

Her eyes lifted to meet his. What she perceived there took her breath. An openness, a humility, a light that reminded her of what she'd seen in Scott's eyes for Rose and in her dad's for her mom and now Wendy.

"Aloha, my nani lokelani rose."

Doubt ate away at her stomach. Not the words she longed to hear. She reached into her pocket and positioned the glasses on her face. "Hello or good-bye, Kai? Story of my life."

He exchanged a puzzled look with his sister. Elyse shook her head. "I thought you understood, Laney." At Laney's blank look, she nodded. "On the quilt label, Rose wrote aloha for you. Surely you knew what she meant?"

Laney's chin quivered. "The label reads Aloha, Rose."

"Not just hello or good-bye, honey." Kai gave her a one-sided smile.

Elyse touched her hand. "Aloha also means 'I love you.'"

Her breath hitched.

Not Good-bye, Rose—as in her mother abandoning her?

But I love you—as in I love you enough to give you a better life.

I love you . . .

The most beautiful words in any language.

She craned her neck, assessing Kai's earnest face. Did he mean what she'd hoped and prayed for?

As in I love you—enough to give up my fears and offer my heart? Her bottom lip quavered.

Kai slid off the roof and down the side of the car. "Aloha, Laney. *Aloha wau iā 'oe*, I really love you."

Relief and joy washed over her.

"*E ho'i mai,* come home." He held out his hand. "Come home to me."

His eyes, oh those eyes, caressed her face.

She sprung the lock. Amidst much door dinging, she swiveled her feet to the ground. He caught her hand in his and gently pulled her from the car.

He removed the glasses from her face. "You don't need these."

"No," she whispered, leaning into him on her tiptoes. "Not anymore." His arms encircled her.

Safe, cherished, claimed. Not forgotten.

The engine roared to life behind them. He shoved the door shut with the heel of his boot.

"I think you got this now, brudda," Elyse called, reversing. The car rattled across the cattle guard. Finding a turnaround, she performed a one-eighty and sped off toward home.

"Aloha, I love you, my *ku'upio*." He brought his mouth to hers, a kiss that burned away the confusion of the past weeks. "My sweetheart."

She melted into his arms. Luxuriated in the feel of his lips against hers, reveled in the hard muscle of his shoulders beneath the palms of her hands. The aroma that was Kai filled her nostrils—sunshine, hay, horse, and a touch of cocoa butter.

"I love you, Kai." She smiled into his eyes. "Maybe from the first time you walked into the airport all tall, dark, and cowboy."

His eyes welled. "Maholo, Laney." His fingers lingered in the folds of her hair. "Thank you for loving me. Used by God to rescue me from myself." He twined into her. "Roots and wings, a great combination. Who'd have thought?"

Muffin snorted, nudging them apart with his head. She laughed. With an exaggerated grimace, he wiped the horse drool off his shoulder onto his jeans.

"And, Laney?" The corners of his mouth lifted. "How would you feel about spending the next sixty or so years surrounded by Kona coffee trees and horse poop? Stray cats and stray cowboys?"

She arched a teasing look at him. "But only certain cats and cowboys need apply."

He grinned, broadening his chest. "How about a cowboy pilot who's found all the sky he'll ever need in a certain crazy, stubborn . . ."

She cocked her head in the direction of Muffin and the fence. "I'd be careful, haole, who you call crazy."

He sent a look her way that tingled deep down to her toes. "A certain crazy, stubborn, beautiful, exciting sky called Alana."

"Well, when you put it that way, I can't think of anything else I'd like better." She wrapped her arms around his neck and dangled her feet off the ground. "And is it true there's a rainbow spotted over a certain green-shuttered bungalow sometimes twice a day?"

Corralled in the circle of his arms, Kai's lips against hers were her answer.

Epilogue

Six Months Later

Laney peeked through the lace curtains. Neighbors, friends, and family gathered on the lawn in white folding chairs beneath the shadow of the cross, bedecked on this special day with a rainbow of flowering leis.

She spotted Wendy and her not-as-annoying-as-she'd-thought stepbrother, Connor, on the bride's side of the grassy aisle. Scott—in his rarely worn reverend vestments—waited at the base of the cross, surrounded by the lokelani roses. A small table draped with the Lokelani baby quilt held multiple strands of the sweet-scented pīkake resembling pearls, accented with carefully placed lokelani buds. Next to it, the lei she'd drape over Kai's head, the masculine ti lei.

Laney and her quilt had come full circle.

An old Fort Rucker buddy of Kai's had flown in for the ceremony, the first of many weddings to come. Her dad provided the financial go-ahead for the tropical wedding fantasy of Laney's dreams to kick-start Elyse's fledgling business. Kai's PTSD-recovering soldier-friend would stay to inaugurate the Equine Therapy Center, which didn't officially open until the coming summer.

To the slack key sounds of "Island Style," she watched the lieutenant escort the diminutive Mily, beautiful in orchid purple and matching lei, to a seat next to Wendy.

Mily still here—Laney breathed a prayer of thanksgiving—at home on the ranch and still recognizing them all and enjoying both of her new granddaughters. Her mental deterioration slowed, thanks also to Rose's diligent web searches for drug trials and alternative treatments to combat the disease.

Teah ambled forward on the arm of a widowed neighbor, who'd not hesitated over the last few months to invite himself to nightly portions of Teah's best Spam recipes. Her coral hibiscus muumuu swayed to the rhythm of the rolling surf on the shore beneath the cross.

At the sound of a gentle, ukulele version of the Hawai'ian Wedding Song, Kai appeared from the corner of the house accompanied by his best man, Ben, who'd also provided the wedding luau to follow. At Ben's side, Daniel held fast to the pillow entrusted to his care. Her breath caught at the sight of Kai, dapper and so elegant—who knew she'd be such a sucker for a man in a uniform?—in his army dress blues. Daniel and Ben wore white slacks and royal blue aloha shirts. Greeting the guests, the trio strolled toward Scott at the foot of the cross.

Wearing a dark pink that matched the roses, Elyse, her arms full of bright tropical flowers, did a graceful saunter down the aisle, her eyes smiling and fixed on her favorite men in the world. Laney's eyes watered at the sight of her newly found sister, Olina, who followed on Elyse's heels. Olina, the sister Laney always dreamed of, right down to the copper tints in the roots of the college coed's hair. On the lanai, Laney's father, trim and efficient in his uniform, waited for her to emerge from her soon-to-be vacated bedroom at the Franklin ranch house.

"God is good," her mother, Rose, whispered, smoothing a curl under the haku lei encircling Laney's head. The rest of her hair waved against the spaghetti straps of her almost bare shoulders. She allowed the curtain to fall into place.

"All the time." Smiling at her mother, she brushed her hand across the simple lace shift, embossed white on white with a pua, flower, pattern. The front hem of her dress gathered to just above her knee. The back of the dress flowed to a small train, easy for trailing over the grass or to dance a wedding hula later in the evening.

She fingered a strand of her hair. Long and silky, the way Kai liked it. A soft blush rose in her cheeks at the thought of a few other things he'd expressed a preference for in regards to herself over the last few months. Like after morning chores and helping the church ladies piece and stitch a wedding quilt for her new home, leisurely horseback rides to every corner of the ranch and lots of alfresco picnics at "their" waterfall. With A. Hoffmann in permanent retirement, her travel editor had found a new project for Laney Carrigan, a project close to her new home and to her heart.

The new assignment? An in-depth travel guide on the Big Island, written by—here's a novel concept—a Native Hawai'ian like herself. The project would take several years and if successful, he'd promised her a subsequent series on each of the major islands in the Hawai'ian chain. She and Rose glided into the kitchen.

Her dad popped his head around the door frame. "Ready to go?" His eyes widened and teared. "Laney, my darlin' girl."

Rose shook her finger at him. "Don't you start, Tom Carrigan. I'm only holding it together by the most fragile of threads."

Her dad held out his arm. She inserted hers in the crook of his elbow and placed her other arm through Rose's. Together, they set a gentle pace across the lanai to the wedding party beyond.

Gisela, Rose, and her dad. The three of them each playing an essential role in who Laney had become and, on this special day, who Laney was still becoming.

Kai's eyes glistened as she paused for a moment at the first row of chairs. The happy smile he gave her, his strong white teeth flashing in the afternoon sun, revealed the changes God had wrought in his life over the last few months. The man she'd known from the beginning he could be.

At a signal from Elyse, she stepped forward, her heart locked onto Kai's face. Reaching the makeshift altar, Scott opened his Bible. "Who gives this bride to this man today?"

Rose and Tom exchanged a sweet look. "Both her mothers and I do," the brigadier thundered and sniffed. He kissed Laney's cheek and waited while Rose gave her a swift, strong hug.

Kai moved to her side and together they faced Scott, the cross, and the Pacific blue. She strained to take in Scott's words of wisdom, glad Elyse had the foresight to tape the ceremony so she and Kai could revisit this day in the years to come.

Solemnly, they took turns repeating the vows as Scott instructed. They exchanged rings. Kai's hand shook as he struggled to place it upon the right finger. He closed his eyes and let out a whew of relief when he succeeded. The crowd and Laney laughed at the expression on his face.

Nice to know she wasn't the only nervous one.

She handed Olina her bouquet and took the ti leaf open-ended lei from Scott. She angled toward Kai and curled it around his neck. "Aloha, Kai," she whispered for his ears alone.

Kai, his heart in his eyes, lifted the pīkake over her head and placed it with tender care around her neck. "Aloha back to you, Laney bird."

Her lips twitched. “It’s going to be interesting . . .”

Kai smirked. “Never a dull moment with you . . .”

He leaned forward. Her lips parted.

Scott cleared his throat. “If you two don’t mind, I’d like to finish the rest of the ceremony?”

The crowd tittered. She and Kai clasped hands. Scott wound the *maile* lei around both of their wrists. “Symbolizing the sacred union God has brought together,” he intoned. “Let no one put asunder.”

Scott grinned. “Okay,” he nudged Kai. “Now you may kiss your bride.”

“Don’t have to tell me twice.” Kai’s hands covered Laney’s. “You’re stuck with me now.” His lips found hers.

The crowd roared with applause.

Laney released a small sigh of pleasure above the classic sounds of Brudda Iz’s “Rainbow” that they’d chosen for their recessional. The wedding guests pelted them with flower petals as they sped down the aisle.

Not to their journey’s end, but to its beginning.

Upon reaching the lanai, she whispered, “Spam anyone?”

Just so she could watch him laugh out loud.

Stuck, all right. If by stuck, you meant deliriously happy.

Because she’d found her forever home at last with her wonderful, tall, dark, and Hawai‘ian cowboy.

Laney's Hawai'ian Dictionary

'Aina—homeland

Brudda—brother

E ho'i mai—come home

'Elepaio—Hawai'ian rainforest bird

Haku—head lei

Hale—traditional thatched dwelling

Haole—Caucasian

Haupia—creamy coconut pudding

Honu—green sea turtle

Ho'oku'kahi—reconciliation

Ho'oponopono—to set things right, forgiveness, reconciliation

Huaka'i—a journey

Huliau—turning point

Imu—underground pit oven

Kahuna—expert

Kala mai—forgive me

Kapa moe—traditional Hawai'ian bedcovering made from beaten and felted tree bark

Kapu—forbidden

Keiki—child

Kolea—bird that legend says drew ancient Polynesian mariners to the Hawai'ian island chain

Kona—leeward, may also refer to a brand of coffee

Ku'upio—sweetheart

Lauhala—leaves used in traditional hula skirts

Laulau—pork, chicken or fish wrapped and steamed in ti leaves, luau food

Maholo—thank you

Maile—lei used in a wedding ceremony to bind bride and groom's hands in symbol of unity

Mana—spirit
Mele—songs
Moana—ocean
Na'au—heart
Nani—pretty
'Oha—taro stems
'Ohana—family
Pa'akiki—stubborn
Paniolo—Hawai'ian cowboy
Pilialoha—beloved
Poi—purple pastelike food from mashed taro
Po'o—head lei
Pua—flower
Pule—prayer
Shaka—Hawai'ian greeting hand gesture
'Ulu—breadfruit
Tutu—grandmother
Wahine—woman

Discussion Questions

1. What was the significance of Laney's pink spectacles in the beginning? How had her need for the spectacles changed by the end?
2. Which character in *Aloha Rose* did you identify with the most? Why?
3. How do Gisela and Tom, and all adoptive parents, reflect a picture of God's heart for His *pilialoha*, beloved, children?
4. What did the city of refuge, Pu'uhonua, mean to Kai? What does sanctuary, a second chance, and forgiveness, *ho'oponopono*, mean to you?
5. If you were to create a book of remembrance for your own life's journey, what would you include?
6. Even though Kai became a Christian, he continued to struggle with guilt for past failures. Have you ever had a problem letting go of the past? Which is harder for you, to embrace God's forgiveness or to forgive yourself?
7. How did God bring good out of Kai's experiences as a boy, in Afghanistan, and with his friend Hank? How did God bring good out of Laney's abandonment and adoption? How do you see God's hand of grace in Rose's life? In your life?
8. Laney's biological mother made many mistakes yet how did God bring good out of her failures? How has God brought good out of your failures in the past?
9. What held Kai back from "catching up" to Laney's understanding of God's love for him? What, if anything, holds you back from fully embracing God's love? Is there anything in your life that denies the power of the cross, its sufficiency to save?

10. What was the turning point, the *huliau*, in Kai's relationship with God? With Laney? What was the turning point in Laney's relationship with God, her dad Tom, and her birth mother, Rose? Has there been a *huliau* in your own life with God? Within particular relationships?
11. What rainbow was Laney really chasing? Why that rainbow? What kind of rainbows do you find yourself chasing?
12. What was Kai's initial feeling regarding fences and boundaries? How did what he did in chapter 19 reflect his change of heart?
13. Roots versus wings. Sea versus sky. How do these metaphors illustrate what Laney and Kai in God's grace bring to each other?
14. Kai came to the conclusion that they were all on a journey, a *huaka'i*, and that truth, heart, and courage were required to seek God, love, and a place to belong. What kind of courage have you been called upon to exhibit in the midst of your own *huaka'i*?
15. Teah stitched the song of her life with her needles, Mily danced the music of her heart, and Laney stitched her life with her words. What is the song your life sings?

Want to learn more about author
Lisa Carter and check out other great
fiction from Abingdon Press?

Sign up for our fiction newsletter at
www.AbingdonPress.com
to read interviews with your favorite authors, find tips for starting a reading group, and stay posted on what new titles are on the horizon. It's a place to connect with other fiction readers or post a comment about this book.

Be sure to visit Lisa online!

www.LisaCarterAuthor.com

We hope you enjoyed *Aloha Rose* and that you will continue to read the Quilts of Love series of books from Abingdon Press. Here's an excerpt from the next book in the series, Lynette Sowell's *Tempest's Course*.

Tempest's Course

Lynette Sowell

Prologue

April 1853
New Bedford, Massachusetts

They say a madwoman cannot make sense of the world around her, let alone write about it, but I can. My empty arms are full, but my heart tells me that it will never be full again. The one light of my life is gone from me, and I have no embers from which to coax a new spark.

My atonement is futile. I have no other choice other than the one before me. If Almighty God is listening from Heaven, surely He will accept this sacrifice. Perhaps the generations to follow will as well.

1

Present Day

Kelly Frost tried not to shiver as she stood on the sidewalk in front of Gray House, but she did anyway. The breeze drifting from New Bedford's waterfront had some bite in it, even for May. Kelly squinted against the sun's glare reflecting off a car door, now slammed shut.

An efficient-looking woman made her way with precise steps to the gate that protected the front lawn of Gray House from nosy passersby and visitors. "Sorry I'm late. I would have told you to meet me at the real estate office, but the house is closer." She unlocked the gate and swung it open. The iron-work complained at the disturbance.

"Not a problem," Kelly said as she followed the woman—Mrs. Acres, was it?—up the cobbled sidewalk, then the wooden steps.

"I've been instructed to open the house for you while you complete your assessment of the piece, then lock up when you're ready to go." Mrs. Acres now worked the front door lock with an ancient key. "How long do you think you'll need?"

"An hour, most likely." She'd made assessments of antique and ancient textiles before, and this current request should be little different than other times in the past.

"I'll be back in two. Mincie's at the groomers, and she'll be done before you will be." Mrs. Acres leaned on the front door, then bumped it with her shoulder. "Stubborn door. I can't tell you the last time we opened the place up."

The heavy wooden door swung inward and the scent of closed-up house—stale air and dust—struck them. Something tickled the inside of Kelly's nose, but it was Mrs. Acres who sneezed.

"Oh, my, the dust." Mrs. Acres shook her head. "Do you know where the quilt is?"

Kelly nodded. "I was told the quilt should be in the master bedroom on the second floor. The one with the Italian marble fireplace." She hoped the lady wouldn't start a long conversation. Small talk made her itch, like freshly mown grass. She shifted her tote bag on her shoulder.

"Two hours, and I'll be back." Mrs. Acres turned on her heel, then paused before she exited the house. "Don't steal the silver. We count it." With that, she gave a little giggle and shut the front door behind her.

The entryway alone made Kelly stare. What woodwork. The curved banister of the great main staircase snaked upward to the second floor. As she stood in the entryway, she could see down a long hallway with rooms off each side. Immediately to her right stood a set of wooden pocket doors. Her curious bent made her want to start walking, room by room, to see what treasures lay inside. Or dust magnets, rather. Now it was her turn to sneeze.

Instead, thoughts of her skinny bank account spurred her to take the creaking stairs to the second floor and find the master bedroom. Depending on the work required to restore the quilt, she hoped to at least pay the bills for the rest of the year. Beyond that, well, she'd figure something out. She always did, because she'd always had to.

The wood of the banister was cool and smooth under her fingertips. Again, the history hanging in the air made her pause at the top of the steps. The house supposedly hadn't had a resident in at least fifty years, perhaps longer. Or so Mrs. Acres had guessed. Kelly stepped from room to room, to see which one had the marble fireplace. Furniture draped in heavy cloth would probably resemble ghosts at night, with moonbeams streaming through the window glass. Even in the daytime, her overactive imagination caused another shiver, this one not from a cool breeze. Which room? She'd counted no less than four chimneys sprouting from the rooftop when she stood outside. That meant at least eight fireplaces, possibly more.

Master bedroom. There were two bedrooms that could have qualified. She found the right room, with its dark mahogany furniture uncovered, a folded-up piece of cream-colored cloth on the bed. The quilt.

Kelly set her tote bag on the bed and took out some gloves. As if the oil from her fingertips would cause any more damage to this poor, tattered, sewn mass of patches. Dirt, the age of years, and what looked to be singes from a fire all qualified this work for the rag bag. Yet someone, namely the head of Firstborn Holdings, LLC, had sent her a request for a bid to restore the neglected and abused fabric.

"All you need is a little love and careful handling," she said aloud, her voice echoing in the room. The folded-up layers of fabric needed to be inspected, inch by inch, which meant Kelly needed to find a place to spread out the quilt. Somewhere with better lighting than the bedroom. One of the inner shutters that covered the windowpanes effectively blocked out the sunlight, but even with both shutters open, the light wouldn't nearly be enough.

She should have ventured enough small talk to ask Mrs. Acres if the electricity was connected in the vacant whaling captain's mansion. She tried a light switch. Nothing. Downstairs there was likely a dining room and a table, with better natural light. Kelly refolded the quilt, then grabbed her tote bag and headed downstairs.

Time to see what was behind those double pocket doors. Holding the quilt tucked under one elbow, Kelly tugged on the right door. It groaned and complained as it slid on its track, but disappeared as it entered the pocket in the wall. A living room, with more furniture draped with sheets, covering a room-size wool carpet, Persian if she was correct on the pattern. Now that was something worth restoring. But then she'd need a studio to do that, and staff willing to help her. The woven pattern was the height of interior decoration at its time, its oriental influences apparent. Had the owner of the house purchased it on one of his expeditions, or traded for it in some exotic port of call?

Diagonally across the room lay another set of pocket doors, so Kelly headed for those, and slide one of them open. Pay dirt.

A mahogany dining room table ran the length of the space and could comfortably sit sixteen diners. Its flat surface would be ideal to inspect the quilt, and a quartet of windows would give plenty of light. Kelly arranged the quilt on the table before she opened the shutters to let some sunlight into the room, taking care not to let the light fall directly onto the old fabric waiting for her on the table.

She removed her notebook and pen from her tote bag, along with a measuring tape. Yes, this was the first real nibble of work she'd had since the disaster with the Boston Fine Arts Museum. Maybe if she got this bid, the owner might want the other textiles in the home seen to as well. Maybe she could scrounge up a few interns to help her for free, if they'd be brave enough to put her name on their résumé.

The frayed binding told her that the quilt was mere stitches away from disintegrating. When she stepped back and looked at the whole design, she saw the classic mariner's compass pattern. The design made her smile. How appropriate for New Bedford. Gray House was situated on County Street, close to the historic district of the former whaling capital of the world. The rays of five compasses spread out from five points on the quilt's field. The muted hues of the diamond-shaped blocks that made the compass patterns told her that someone had used this quilt quite a lot in its day.

She took out her telephone and dialed the phone number for the contact she had at Firstborn Holdings, a Mr. William Chandler. A voice mail message answered.

"Mr. Chandler, this is Kelly Frost of Frost Textile Services. I'm at Gray House in New Bedford and I'm looking at the quilt. I need to know more information about it, if you could find out for me. Where was it stored? Has anyone else ever worked on it? Please call me back when you have a few moments and I'll give you all my questions."

She set down her phone and continued inspecting the piece. One edge of the quilt, the one frayed and pulling away from the binding, had an uneven edge. Burn marks. Had someone tried to burn it once? The batting had all but disintegrated.

Maybe she didn't need to know the entire history of the quilt, but if some "helpful" person had tried gluing it or using the wrong thread to keep it together, she needed to know that. She continued assessing the quilt and making notes, plus taking digital photographs that she could refer to later. From there she'd tally the sum of her restoration services and give William Chandler and his cohorts an estimate of services.

She pulled out her camera and photographed the quilt section by section, zooming in on some particularly troubled areas. If someone saw this rumpled up in a pile, it would appear ready for the ragbag.

A shadow passed by one of the windows. Kelly jumped. No one could enter the yard except through the iron gate, or unless they hopped the wall-like fence of bricks, almost five feet tall that surrounded the property. Or could they indeed hop the fence? She set down her pen.

Then a man's face appeared in the next window. Dark eyes with furrowed dark brows, topped by unruly hair. Kelly bit back a scream. The face disappeared. Another one entered her mind's eye.

Kelly Frost, you good-for-nothing piece of trash. Get your hind end out of the house and into the garage.

She clutched at her throat as she struggled to breathe. She hated being jumpy. Her former staff of workers knew better than to sneak up behind her as she worked. No one ever dared to hide behind doors or jumped out and said "boo." That resulted in spilled coffee.

Kelly snatched up her phone. Should she dial 911? Or was that too drastic? Mrs. Acres? She would know if someone had access to the grounds. The front door banged open. The phone slipped from Kelly's fingers and hit the woven rug with a thump.

Tom Pereira winced as the front door struck the chair rail in the entryway. He hadn't intended the large bang that followed. Well, maybe he had. If there was some punk in this house, squatting, Tom could deal with them. Unless they were armed. He hadn't thought about that before charging into Gray House. His responsibility was the grounds and exterior, not the interior.

The place smelled like old people and dust, and Tom tried not to cough.

"Whatever you're doing in here, I can have the boys of New Bedford on the doorstep this side of three minutes," he called out. Okay, so that was probably an overstatement on his part. "So get out here and tell me what's going on."

One of the pocket doors to the front parlor was open. The sound of rustling fabric came from beyond. "Did you hear me? In case you didn't know, I push one button and the cops are here."

He strode across a fancy, ancient rug and through another set of pocket doors, and stopped in the doorway separating the parlor from the dining room.

A figure with hair the color of pale sunlight with golden undertones stood beside the immense dining room table. "Same here, whoever you are." She held a cell phone in one hand, her thumb at the ready. Her glare could freeze the harbor water.

"How'd you get in here?"

"Just like you. Through the front door." The young woman stuck her chin out. "I have business here. Mrs. Acres at the property management office let me in."

Tom backed off. No one had told him someone was going to access the house today. But then, they didn't have to. He was only maintenance and grounds keeping, exterior of the building issues only. "All right then. What kind of business?"

"Why is it your business to find out mine?" Her gaze didn't flinch from meeting his eyes.

He stepped forward, extending his hand. "We're starting off all wrong here. I'm Tom Pereira. I work for the owner of the house. Lawn work, landscaping, the greenhouses, outdoor maintenance. I saw someone inside, didn't know you were coming. Mrs. Acres didn't mention it."

She set her phone down on the dining table. "Kelly Frost." They shook hands. Her fingertips had calluses. Tom glanced down at her slim hands. "Frost Textile Services. I've been invited to make a bid on restoring this quilt, sewn by Captain Gray's wife. Mrs. Acres brought me here so I can inspect the quilt on site and then write up my recommendations."

"I'm sorry I scared you."

"You didn't scare me." But her posture when he entered the room told him she was lying. She blinked at him, her icy expression thawing a few degrees.

"Anyway, I'll let you get back to your work. I'll be outside if you need anything." He retreated toward the open pocket doors, trying not to clomp his work boots on the parquet floor.

"Thanks." She turned her attention back to the fabric spread across the dining room table. Tom watched her long enough to see her right hand tremble as she reached for the old fabric. She clenched her hand into a fist.

Back outside in the sunshine, Tom took a deep breath. The longer he worked at Gray House, the more questions he had about its absent owner. When a guy needed work and the perfect job opening came up, he didn't ask questions. Snow plowing the driveway and clearing the sidewalks and roof of snow during the winter had turned into repairing holes in the stone walls surrounding the historic property, then fixing the leak in the koi pond in the backyard. All this attention, for a house no one lived in or used, that he knew of.

But then, Tom didn't care, really, as long as his money was deposited the first of each month into his account. The job was an answer to prayers that he'd bombarded heaven with ever since his discharge from the military. No crowds, no office politics. Just a chance to get his hands dirty and get paid for it.

Nonetheless, he punched the number on speed dial for Mrs. Acres' office. "Yes, uh, this is Tom Pereira. I'm at Gray House.

There's a lady here looking at a quilt. I'm wondering what that's all about."

"I'm sorry, Mrs. Acres is out at the moment," said the female voice on the other end of the phone. "I really don't know anything about the Gray House account. It's restricted."

"Restricted?"

"Mrs. Acres said only she handles this account, so I leave it to her."

"I see. Well, if you could please have her call me when she returns to the office."

"I'll do that, Mr. Pereira."

He was left staring at his phone. Tom shook his head, then clipped his phone onto his belt. There was plenty enough to do outside, like trimming the rose bushes and pruning back the hedges. He ought to mention to Mrs. Acres that the side porch would likely need painting, and possibly a few of the planks replaced. One of three porches, this one faced the side closest to the driveway. It wrapped around the side of the house and ended at the old carriage house at the rear of the property.

Funny, after not quite six months, he'd developed an attachment to the grand old house, almost like a fondness for a great-aunt. An elegant lady, but a little rough around the edges. With love and attention, she'd be back to her prime.

Maybe that's why the pretty stranger had come. Someone had taken an interest in the interior of the building—at long last. He didn't envy them the tasks that awaited. Textiles were the least of the issues inside.

Tom paused at the dining room window where he'd first glimpsed Kelly. She sat hunched over the quilt, her nose inches from the fabric. She scribbled some notes, then sat up. Tom continued along before she caught him. That's all he'd need, getting branded a stalker by someone he barely knew. Maybe he was a stalker, preferring to watch from a distance.

Most days, he didn't feel disabled. Thirty-one was too young to be medically discharged from the Army. But when your coping skills weren't the best and your back had more metal in it than a hardware store, thirty-one was plenty old enough.

Tom hopped off the porch and headed for the greenhouse. He'd known next to nothing about planting, but figured getting fresh blooms started wasn't that hard. His phone warbled. Mom.

"Hey, Ma."

"Tommy, you going to be home for supper tonight? Nick and Angela are coming with the kids. Plus Bella's arriving soon, toting all her junk home from the university."

"Sure, why not?" He regretted his tone immediately.

"It's been three weeks. A mother wants to see her son sometimes, especially living in the same town."

He felt the sensation of a noose around his neck. "I know, I'm sorry." There'd be three hours of seeing yet again how far he'd fallen short in his father's eyes. Comparisons with Nick, and now even his baby sister, Isabella, finishing her freshman year at UMass.

"See you at six, then?"

"I'll be there." He paused. "Love you, Ma."

"I love you too, son."

Tom ended the call. Family reminded you of what you'd done right, and didn't let you forget where you'd gone wrong. He let out a pent-up breath. *Lord, give me strength.*

Abingdon fiction™

Every Quilt Has A Story

Enjoy the Quilts of Love novels from Abingdon Fiction

Visit us Online
www.AbingdonFiction.com

Find us on Facebook
Abingdon Press | Fiction

Follow us on Twitter
@AbingdonFiction